Freedom Child

Freedom Child

Book One
The Ajadi Series

by Chandra Ingram

Ingram Press 2016 California

www.freedomchild.net

ISBN-13: 978-0692751558 (Ingram Press)
ISBN-10: 0692751556
Copyright @ 2016 Ingram Press
All Rights Reserved.

SUMMARY: Entangled in the corruption, avarice and cruelty of a repressive society, two girls risk everything to escape the chains of slavery, as they begin a dangerous journey and personal discovery of basic human dignity and self-identity.

For further information, email *chandra@freedomchild.net*

Printed in the United States of America.
August 2016
Ingram Press

Dedication

This book is dedicated to the millions of voiceless women, men and children still enslaved around the world today.

About the Author

Born on July 4, 1998, America's independence day, it is no coincidence that the desire for freedom runs through my veins.

When I was eight years old, my family embarked on an expatriate assignment taking us to Bangalore, India, my new home for the next three and a half years. While living in India we traveled to other impoverished nations such as Thailand, Cambodia, Vietnam, South Africa, Indonesia, Egypt and Nepal, where I witnessed extreme poverty firsthand. These experiences impacted me most upon my return home to California. Here, surrounded by affluence, education and resources, I was struck by the gross disparity between the quality of my life and that of the children in these countries. What shocked me most was that a vast majority of my friends and family were ignorant of the prevalence of slavery in the modern world.

I distinctly remember my first time in India, as a fairly ignorant eight-year old. When I locked eyes with a poor Indian girl who approached us begging for money. She seemed to be the same age as me and I didn't understand why she wasn't in school; it was the first time I realized that not every child had the life that I had. It was also not the last. For three and a half years, my brother and I drove through the streets, watching children our own age and younger begging on the streets, performing, and tapping on our windows for spare change.

My dedication to this cause began in the 6th grade after a guest speaker visited my school in Bangalore. It was this speaker's inspirational presentation and introduction to the topic of modern slavery that derived my passion for helping to end the injustice. Although I do not remember his name, I created my character John in his likeness.

I found an opportunity to increase awareness when my seventh-grade English teacher, Mrs. Halla, gave our class an assignment to start the first few pages of a book. Beginning as a three-page story, *Freedom Child* soon grew into a novel.

However, it took a challenging, exciting and invigorating six-year journey to get here.

In the eighth grade, after visiting the Holocaust Museum in Washington D.C, I remember breaking down and crying in my hotel room. The millions of innocent people murdered in the Holocaust had no way to scream for help or share their stories. I felt helpless about how to help the millions oppressed by the Holocaust of today: modern-day slavery. How was I, a 13-year-old girl, supposed to help put an end to such a colossal evil?

My English teacher, Mrs. Senner, helped me realize I *could* do something. As long as I had my freedom, I could give a voice to the voiceless. Great books shake our complacency, reminding us that society is flawed and sparking the passion to ensure social justice will prevail. Powerful stories, with inspirational and horrific characters, have the power to touch our hearts and turn our minds. This was my goal when I began writing my book. My intentions were not simply to educate readers about the injustice, but to instill in them a call to action, encouraging them to join the efforts to eradicate modern-day slavery.

My three-page short story evolved into a novel exposing the widespread corruption in India. Over the summer of my sophomore year in high school, I returned to India to further my research. Although I had witnessed child labor and extreme poverty in India, I sought a thorough understanding. My trip allowed me to discover the many root causes of slavery such as lack of education, poverty, corruption and caste. With the help of a generous organization, Jeevika, I was able to interview more than 65 current and former slaves. We visited silk factories, agriculture farms and granite quarries. Furious slave masters chased us out of a brick factory. We lived with the Dalit and Muslim communities and heard their heartbreaking stories about unfathomably cruel discrimination.

I have done endless hours of research, on the field and off, through an independent study and by reading countless books, journals, research papers, articles and websites.

Throughout my book, I weaved in the true stories that I heard or saw. Even though Freedom Child is a fictional novel, it is based on realities faced by millions of men, women and children every day. In my junior year I was able to share my story and experiences with my school, which can be viewed on YouTube at:

https://www.youtube.com/watch?v=E3RwRDZHriQ

Two summers later my high school, Sacred Heart Preparatory, granted me the Legacy Scholarship allowing me to return to India to work with Anita Reddy to research what I saw as two of many possible solutions: education and awareness of individual rights. In my senior year of high school, I continued my research in greater depth through a Senior Honors Independent Study: *"The Influence of Corruption, Poverty, and the Caste System on Modern Day Slave Labor in India, and the Power of Self-Identity and India's Public Policy as Solutions."* My research, stories, and some of my interviews can be found on my website:

freedomchild.net

Mahatma Gandhi said it best: *"Be* the change you want to see in the world." I look up to my grandfather and the many other leaders in my life who have influenced me, remembering it takes only one person to change the world. I hope I can make a difference.

Acknowledgements

As a girl at the age of twelve, eighteen, and every age in between, I never could have accomplished writing *Freedom Child* without the help and generosity of countless people in my life. *Freedom Child* is indebted to the immense support, encouragement, and constructive criticism from my friends, family, teachers, school administrators, coaches, classmates, and editors.

First, I would like to acknowledge my mother who has been my number one supporter and has stuck by my side through all of my outlandish adventures. She was by my side escaping a brick factory from angry landowners and she was by my side editing my mercurial plot ideas and style of writing. I would also like to thank my father for his meticulous attention to detail and vigilant eye when checking my novel for authenticity and credibility. Without my parents, I would be neither the person nor the author I am today.

I want to thank those who shared the details of their hardships with me, as I know the courage it took to tell their stories aloud.

As a fourteen-year-old girl yearning to do hands on research in the field I was passionate about, I found it quite challenging to find organizations willing to risk the liability of working with a young girl.

I am beyond grateful for Jeevika and Kiranbhai for allowing me to come visit them in Karnataka, India and witness their organization in action. I traveled with Jeevika all over Karnataka, visiting the areas where slave labor was occurring and heard incredible stories of hardship and courage. Through Jeevika, I acquired a new appreciation for those who have selflessly dedicated their lives to helping others. Anita Reddy also took me in as her own and believed in my research and me, enabling myself to further understand the root causes of modern slavery and find solutions to eradicate the issue at its core. I would also like to give a special thanks to Balaji, a dear friend, who made this trip and research possible with his exquisite translations and dedication to our cause.

I would also like to thank Stonehill International School in Bangalore, as well as my English teachers, Mrs. Halla and Mrs. Senner at St. Andrews Episcopal School in Saratoga for emboldening my aberrant endeavor and encouraging me to continue this wild journey.

Thank you to Jillian Manus for taking the time to read my entire book on one plane ride and provide feedback that inspired a whole new twist to my novel. It was her advice that helped me divide Freedom Child, originally a novel consisting of three characters' stories, into the creation of a series. Between the two books I incorporate a vast majority of my research and collected stories.

For their additional help with editing my work, I would also like to thank Roopa (Mangalmurti) McNealis as well as Prathibha Sudhir and Archana Handa for supporting my research in India.

Last but not least, I would like to thank Mukti and Ruchita. Although fictional characters, these two girls inspire me everyday and continually shape me into the individual I aspire to be.

TABLE OF CONTENTS

MEMORIES

(Mukti)

I was caged.

They were free.

The children ran around in half-clothed bodies with no worries. Women wrapped in majestic maroons and lavenders, with malati flowers strung in their hair, jingled with each step. Their wrists and ankles glittered with bangles and anklets, as the sewage-filled lake echoed with their harmonious hum.

Over the horizon, a mist crept over countless rice farms. Far below, hunchbacked dots harvested ample quantities of rice. The mist mocked the irony of the tragic scene as it passed through, touching the faces of the starved workers surrounded by copious food. Fingers deep in the other direction, past the thin forests of eucalyptus trees, the mist chased the wild dogs as they wandered the never-silent streets of Bangalore.

People rushed through the uneven cement sidewalks and past the open-sided shops that bustled with business and friendly banter. Piles of forgotten plastic bags, scattered along alleyways, danced in the listless wind. Cows roamed through the streets, unafraid of the stop-and-go traffic and screaming horns. Rickshaws and vans stepped on their accelerators and slammed on their brakes, squeezing through any tight spaces.

Beautiful kingfishers darted in and out of the darkened layer of smog, fluttering their wings freely in an unintentional ridicule of the predictable drudgery that was the day ahead of me.

I woke up on the hard, rocky, wet ground, wearing my

best kurta shalwar. The colors had faded from its tiring age, and the cotton had shrunk over the years. But it was still the better choice over my only other dress, which had a large tear at the knee. Like any other thirteen-year-old girl enslaved on a quarry, my scaly skin resembled a shedding snake's. But unlike the snake, I was trapped in my flaking body. I pulled at my knotted and tangled black hair, a hornet's nest suffocated by dust, and remembered where I was.

"Mukti, look at us!" the peas laughed, tumbling over the rocks.

I leaned over to my right to see my younger brothers, Raj and Arjun. Their skinny legs struggled to balance on a pile of rocks, and I felt a crooked smile try to break through my locked lips.

My older sister Priya was already working out in the grounds with Sanat. I spotted her carrying a stack of cut stone on her head in the distance. Her braided hair cascaded down to her waist, painted in dust. The creases on her forehead were darker today, and darkened each day, as she pushed herself to her limit. Every day when I saw the ferocity in her muddy eyes, I felt motivated to keep fighting. Yet they twinkled with a soft sadness. At fifteen, Priya carried herself like the elderly, wise women of our old village. And since she was endowed at 13 years old to Sanat, she walked with elegance and docility. She behaved like she was taught to behave and never talked back. At times I thought her obedience was cowardly. She never stood up for herself. She never put up a fight. But with time, I came to understand that her silence was her way of fighting. It was her way of surviving.

I saw Sanat lift a basket of stones and place them on Priya's head in the distance. She blushed timidly and scurried off. Next to her scrawny, frail companion, my sister looked strong, as her thin biceps bulged and flexed. Late at night, I would sometimes ask my sister what it was like to be endowed to another man. But Priya usually brushed off the topic like dust on her shoulder. I lay there tracing my wrists, as though they were already chained. I felt my rib cage closing, suffocating me like bars I couldn't retract.

To my luck, my name was never mentioned in any proposals.

"Mukti! If you don't start acting more like your sister I'll be stuck with you forever! No one wants to marry a spoiled girl!"

My mother's scolding usually ranted along this direction.

My eyes drifted back to my two rambunctious brothers. Each morning I woke up to their boisterous laughs filling the quarry. Arjun and Raj were two peas in a pod, hence their nickname. And they may as well have been connected by string, because they never left each other's sight. Through the thick debris, I made out their skeletons and sun-roasted skin. I could identify Arjun by his spikey hair and Raj by his thick hair, draping over his eyes like curtains.

Raj, meaning King, was bossing Arjun around by the pickup truck. Suddenly he started flapping his arms like a bird and circled his brother. He did this because Arjun's name meant peacock. Arjun stomped his feet and screamed that he was named after the powerful son of Lord Indra who fought alongside Lord Krishna. I always told him that he should be proud to be a peacock. It represented his colorful personality.

One afternoon I argued, "You'd be lucky to be a peacock, Arjun. If you were a bird, you'd be free."

The peas never had a chance to go to school before

3

they were taken here. Yet, they were exceptionally bright and had a natural curiosity. After watching their bodies chase each other in circles, I grew tired.

Watching the peas, I came to understand the freedom in ignorance. I always wanted to grow up, so I could be like Priya. But I realized it was easier to be naive than to be trapped in reality. I missed the freedom of being myself. I missed its sweet escape.

On the quarry, we mined for granite, the most abundant element in our area, along with marble and sandstone. The mountains used to be giant. The elderly would tell us fables, claiming the three peaks used to be brave warriors exploring the lands of India. *Ondhu dinaa Devaru[1] avarannu pareekshisidaa.* One day God tested them. And when they failed to obey Him, they were turned to stone. I liked pretending they were warriors watching over me. Now I was forced to hack at them like they were worthless rubble.

"Wake up *gandu*[2]! It's already 5:30. You're loading SIG's order of granite today," screamed a jamadar[3]. He was one of the men who ordered us around the quarry.

I groaned and rolled over onto my sore back. The rising sun showed no mercy to my newly born eyes, opening as if for the first time. Realizing that I had fallen back asleep after the wake up call, I jolted up. I was an hour and a half late to the grounds. And depending on the weather that night, I would have roughly sixteen hours left in my day.

My dream slipped through my grasp like mist through my slim fingers. I stretched my arms, yawned, and filled my

---

[1] *Devaru-* irrespective to religion Devaru is referenced to God in all communities who speak Kannada
[2] *Gandu-* dirty, filthy
[3] Jamadar- one who monitors the workers or slaves

4

lungs with dry, hot air. Sitting up, I looked outside the filthy shed. Through the hole of bricks in the wall I could see all the other children working. Three had arrived just this year. I watched them throw white pebbles into a pile that looked like a mountain of sugar. Sandhya hunched her back, scooped a pile into a metal bowl, then carried it to those who were bagging it.

Sandhya had become my closest friend. I distinctly remember my first day on the quarry. I was weak. Vulnerable. My eyes wandered the infinite space and my legs struggled to catch up to my actions. I couldn't figure out my left from my right, and suddenly when I placed my hand out before me, I could see only the outline of my fingers. My throat started coughing up debris. Then an empathetic hand fell on my shoulder. I had fallen to the ground, but Sandhya was at my side in seconds to lift me up.

The first few weeks became bearable with Sandhya. One day we even found humor in our work. It was a long Sunday, and the quarry continued to fill with the dreadful thuds of slamming hammers. Our minds rambled through the solitary hours, as they usually do. But Priya caught our forlorn faces and decided we needed a distraction. So she braided Sandhya's and my head together to connect us from sunrise until sunset. We learned to emulate each other's rhythms for an entire day, while the knocking of our heads created a lingering numb. Yet I never really noticed the pain. Sandhya's contagious laugh distracted me.

That night, Priya attempted to untangle our heads. Somehow Sandhya's hair, smooth like glass, fell back perfectly in place. She turned to me and snorted obnoxiously.

"Mukti! Your hair!" she pointed and laughed.

"You look like a bird's nest that was attacked by a monkey," Arjun added to the mocking of me.

"Muuchchu Baayi!" Shut your mouth! I mouthed back, picking at my knotted hair.

Sometimes when I looked at Sandhya I saw Priya in her. Other times all I saw were the distant tears in her eyes. The two of us saw the world from two completely different perspectives. As a baby, her first steps scorched the tenderness beneath her feet. An interminable fear planted in her heart the day she was born, and I could never save her from it.

Her key to survival was *invisibility*. She avoided anything that made her a potential target for Shubar or the jamadars.

She tried to pull me back with her, but I struggled.

I remembered my first beatings. It was my first week, and I was yet to be disciplined. Sandhya and I had finished carrying the latest piles of granite stones across the south end of the quarry and stopped to take a rest. We barely spoke a word. Our pounding breaths said enough.

Suddenly an unexpected pain stung my ankles from behind. And again. I screamed in agony. A sharp whip continued to fall on my back legs, and the hastening leather burned my skin until it began to bleed. I couldn't turn around. Then the jamadar began to scream at me. I was never to stop working again. I had a debt to pay.

Finally the stinging stopped. I fell to my knees and bawled. My hands rummaged the ground until they found what I was looking for. The small rock fumbled around in my fingers. I turned to find the jamadar's slender back escaping into the distance and raised my arm.

"No!" Sandhya screamed, tackling my arm and freeing the rock from it.

She held me in her arms and whispered to me.

"I've been here my whole life, Mukti. I know what these men are capable of."

And every time since, she pointed to her left cheek. She traced the distinctive scar, shaped like a boomerang. She reminded me why she had to be obedient. She reminded me what Shubar's whip had left behind.

"Mukti, I need you. I can't lose you."

Her eyes, with thick lashes covered in dust and battered together, were pleading. My eyes stung from the clouded air, unprotected.

Although Sandhya learned to contain her emotions at an early age, her curiosity ran free. With time I helped paint her imagination with the colors it lacked. Never having passed the barbed wire, Sandhya asked questions that only I could answer.

"What's the city like, Mukti?" she asked one night as we dangled our feet off the branches of the banyan tree. "Is it as crowded as they say it is?"

"Oh, yes! It's crazy. It's scary sometimes too."

"Why?"

"It's so busy that you can get lost in the crowd if you don't pay attention. Ro and I would go into the city with my mother a lot." I paused. "But if I could be anywhere right now...it wouldn't be the city."

"Where would you be?"

"Back in my village," I murmured. My fingers rubbed

the flimsy bark.

She nodded, trying to imagine life outside the wires. Another time she asked me about my old school. Sandhya, like my brothers, had never been to school before.

"What's school like? Is it like those nights with Namita-masi?"

"No, it's very different," I responded, imagining myself in my old classroom. "We all wore the same tidy uniforms. The girls always had their hair tied in braided pigtails, so we weren't distracted from our schoolwork. We had *real* teachers who taught us new things every day. You'd love it, Sandhya. You'd get to meet a bunch of new friends too."

She tackled me with a new question. "Is shopping in the city like when the people buy rock from our quarry?"

"Not exactly. You go with friends and family. You look through flashy items that grab your attention, but you usually can't get them. My mom always had to tell me no. Sometimes she would buy me a sweet, though."

"What are sweets like?"

"They're nothing special," I lied.

"Okay," she said, looking at me with wide, budding eyes, "Would you take me shopping, Mukti?"

"If we ever get out of here, it will be the first thing we do."

"You promise? You won't forget?"

"I promise."

She smiled at me and tried to fathom a life outside the quarry.

"Sometimes I feel like there *is* no other world outside of here, Mukti. I try and picture it when you describe it, but maybe this is all there is. It's just you, me and the burning rock under our feet."

I hated when she said things like that.

"Sandhya, that's not true. I'll make sure we see it again one day," I said, putting my arm around her slumped shoulder.

"You do Mukti. You're my escape to the outside world every day."

But then she would look back out into the distance, narrowing her eyes at the distant mountains as if she could see past them, and sigh. My heart cried. I needed someone to dream of a future with me. But more than anything, I wanted to dream of my past.

Eventually the jamadar stopped yelling at me for sleeping in and left the sleeping quarter. I leaned against the cement wall. My mind took me back eight years ago, to my village.

*   *   *

It was the crack of dawn. The sun was crawling up the horizon, and I had just climbed to the roof of my hut like I did every other morning. I crawled over to the side and let my feet dangle over the edge.

"Psst!" a little voice whispered from below.

I looked over the edge and saw her smiling up at me.

"Is there any room for me up there?"

"No. It's all taken up. Sorry," I responded in a cold tone with obvious hints of sarcasm.

"Scoot over!" She laughed pushing me to the left.

I looked around her, confused. "Where's your journal?"

"Right here!" She pulled the tiny booklet out from her scarf and rolled her eyes. Why did I even ask?

I lay back down and stared at the sky—now a hazy purple. My ears listened to the scribbling of her pen. Each morning found us like this. Ruchita would write in her journal, and I would let my thoughts run aimlessly, free from any pen's constraint. Soon the entire village would be awake, and the quiet chirps of the birds would fade into the background. The fields would grow busy with friendly chatter, and the day's bustle would become white noise to my ears.

For now, though, it was just Ruchita, the floating lamp, and me.

The sky flickered with new bursts of light. The floating lamp rose over the fields, allowing the tiny green specks to poke through the dimness. The crops stretched their arms high, slowly waking up from their peaceful night's rest. In a few hours, they would greet Ruchita and me as we worked knee-deep in the fields, because we didn't have school on Sundays.

I sighed deeply.

Ruchita rolled over. "What is it?" she asked.

"We just live in such a beautiful world."

I tore my eyes away from the sky and let them admire

something just as beautiful: Ruchita.

My best friend was flawless. Her face was clean of imperfections. Her golden skin glimmered in the morning light as her silky black hair blew gently in the wind. She was prettier than any goddess, and she didn't even know it.

A grin formed on her face, "Do you think your mom would let you go to the city today?" She asked as if she already had an adventure planned.

"She took us last week! No way she takes us again."

"She'll call us spoiled," Ruchita laughed.

"True! Plus, they need as much help as they can get in the fields this month. And I'm excited to go with Father. He said he'd help me today."

"You're not going to stay with me?"

"Of course I am! You'll be with Father and me!"

"What about Priya?" she asked seriously.

I laughed. "You're funny."

"Imagine Priya muddy, working in the fields!" she joked back.

"I can't picture her getting one finger dirty, let alone both hands."

Before the sun could climb higher than the rooftops, my father had led Ruchita and me out into the fields. Our skinny legs sank all the way into the wet mud, so we had to take big steps to climb our way out. We pretended to be big monsters climbing through the slumps of mud. Ruchita, however, didn't sink as far into the water, as her legs were much longer than mine. Eventually, my father grabbed my wrist and pulled me over his shoulders.

"Yay!" I exclaimed. "Papa, spin me around!"

"You're so tall, Mukti!" Ro screamed up at me.

My high-pitched laughs pierced the air. My father pretended to tip over and spun me around in circles until I was too dizzy to see.

"Ahhh! Papa, stop! You'll drop me." I giggled.

"I'd never drop you, silly!" he assured me. And I was glad because I didn't actually want the dizziness to fade.

Finally, we found ourselves staring at the abundant patch of rice. My mouth dropped in awe.

"We're supposed to harvest this *entire* patch today?"

My father gently placed me back on the ground.

"We have until the sun sets."

"But it's so big! We'll never finish, Papa."

"Don't be so negative. We can do it."

I nodded my head confidently and climbed into the middle of the patch. Mud already covered my body from head to toe.

"Where do we start?"

Ever since I could stand without falling into the water, I

had been helping my family in the fields. Our family's income and meals depended on the rice we grew.

Everything I knew about harvesting rice my father taught me. First, we ploughed the fields and applied cow dung as fertilizer. Then the men smoothened the ground so we could transplant the seeds into the soil by hand. Nakshita-kaki, Omisha-kaki, Suruchi-masi and I gathered in a square with water up to our ankles and a bundle of seeds in our hands. Each seed looked like a tall blade of grass that we would plunge into the soil beneath the water in a million rows and columns, perfectly spaced out.

On our land we had clay loam soil, and after the crops were level with water and there was proper irrigation, the rice crops would cultivate. In some places where there are hills, it was known as dry or upland rice, where farmers had to make terraces to plant their rice. Down in the plains with heavy rainfall where I lived, it was much easier to keep the rice watered. Once the crops grew, I was given a tool to dig up the rice plant. Although I never really understood how Mama and all the other women transformed the ripened crops into edible rice, besides by banging it against a basket, I was sure I'd learn when I was older.

The glowing lamp had already travelled across the sky and was falling towards the horizon again. I stood up and examined my fingernails. They were filled with grime and mud. To my left, Ruchita was still pulling out crops in the ground. Somehow, her skin glowed with perfection, untouched by a speck of mud. I picked up a fist of mud and, with a grin on my face, threw it. The brown sludge plummeted through the air and splattered across her chin.

I burst into laughter. Before I had time to duck, she had already thrown a fistful back at me. She missed miserably and ended up hitting my father instead. My stomach erupted in hysterical laughter. Both of our eyes bulged out of our sockets as we watched my father turn around. He suddenly charged at us, and before we could move his big arms had swooped us off our feet.

"Ahhhhh!"

"What am I going to do with you two mischievous little ones, huh?"

"It wasn't us! We swear!"

"How am I going to explain to your mother how I got mud all over myself?"

We giggled, unsure. "I don't know!"

"Come on, my little rebels. Let's get back before it gets too dark."

I looked behind me at the golden huts in the distance.

The village seemed to run in perfect chaos.

Viewed from the fields, the villagers were only black dots. A small group of women trailed behind the village. They balanced the last pots of water on their heads while other dots rushed around, dragging their young ones home for dinner. These were the elder mothers. The last dots to join the village—like Ruchita, my father and I—were those working in the fields.

The sun dipped its head beneath the horizon, telling me my day had come to a rest. The workday was over, and now it was time to pray, eat and be with my family.

I smiled as the sun rested over the golden homes. I

loved my village.

Ruchita and I walked our separate ways. We kept our goodbyes short and sweet out of fear that her parents might see my father and me.

"Night, Mukti!"

"Night, Ro-ro!"

"I'll see you tomorrow."

"On the roof?"

"Where else?" She winked.

Her dim figure disappeared behind her door, and my father and I were alone again. His eyes squinted in discomfort. I reached for his hand and squeezed it.

"Don't think of him, Father. You have a bigger heart, and that's what matters."

Instead of squeezing my hand in return, his face darkened. "I worry about your friendship with Ruchita, Mukti."

My heart fell like a coconut high from the palms.

"But you love Ruchita, Papa! She's like another daughter to you."

"She is, beta. But I fear your friendship will only end in pain," he sighed. "I don't expect you to understand it right now. I just know these things, and I only want to protect you."

My hands tightened into fists. "Ruchita would never hurt me!"

My father knelt down so he could look at me face to face.

"It's not Ruchita who will hurt you. Her father will make her turn her back. You know how he is. He already disapproves of Ruchita playing with you, and when she gets older, he will only want to protect her more. Ruchita is beautiful and her family is wealthy. You might not be envious now, but as you grow up, it is something you will naturally feel. I'm not saying you have to say goodbye now, Mukti, but your love for her is dangerous. Your love for her is almost bigger than for your own sister. Maybe you should start spending some more time with Priya."

I scowled. "Priya doesn't want to spend time with me. She's too busy being grown up. Ruchita is the one who's there for me, Papa. You'll see. It'll be Ruchita who loves me forever."

His face creased in distress, but he let the conversation pass.

I could see my little home now. The walls were tattered from old age, and rain had taken its toll on the paint and roof. Our henchu[4] roof prevented the rain from flooding our home during the monsoon season, and the piles of dead palm leaves kept in the warmth. Some of our neighbors' homes used cow dung for additional protection.

I sprinted to the doorway, where my mother was already waiting for us. She stopped us and pointed to our feet covered in dried mud and dust. No words were necessary. Before we could enter we had to wash our feet.

My father had me sit down on the cement. A path went around all the houses in our village. Our drainage system, smelling of sewage, kept our village from flooding. My father

---

[4] Henchu- the tiles that make up the roofs of villages

filled a plastic cup with water and, pouring it over my feet, scrubbed the grime from in between my toes.

I wriggled and squealed, "Haha, stop! It tickles."

Then I remembered I wasn't happy with my father, so I puffed out my cheeks. He rolled his eyes and told me to help my mother inside. Before I rushed in I lifted my feet and admired their cleanness.

I giggled. "Hello, feet! It's been awhile since I've seen you."

When I entered the room, the mats had already been placed in a circle around the two pots of dhal. I almost slipped on the cement floor as I ran through the front room into the back kitchen. The walls were stacked so high with tin pots and pans that they almost touched the roof. In the corner, our small aged stove crackled as it slowly cooled down.

"Mukti! Get your hands away from the stove," yelled Priya, yanking my hands away. "You're so careless. Get out of the kitchen!"

I could still hear her muttering angrily when I left the room. Obediently, I walked over to the mats and sat patiently, waiting for my family. I breathed in the sweet smell of the spicy dhal and suddenly I couldn't wait any longer. Checking for any witnesses, I scanned the room. I plunged my fingers into the bowl of rice and snuck a handful into my mouth.

"Mukti!" a sweet voice accused from the doorway.

My eyes widened and I put on my innocent face. But my masi[5] wasn't Priya. She didn't expect me to be perfect.

---

[5] Masi-Aunt on mother's side

17

"There are always eyes that can see you, beta. Don't think you can fool me," she said with a wink.

My masi walked with boldness and made sure the whole world knew who she was. Everyone adored her and envied her obvious fortune, already having had three children. They were my younger cousins, all under the age of four. Sometimes I forgot I was only six when I considered myself too mature to play with them. I always assumed I was as old as Ruchita and Priya.

The whole family squeezed into our hut and was chattering with cheerful conversation. Once Priya finished serving our relatives, my parents and then me, she sat beside me on our shared matt.

"How were the fields with papa today?" Priya asked between mouthfuls.

"It was so much fun! Me and Ruchita—"

"You were with Ruchita?" she asked surprised.

"Of course!"

Priya's voice quivered, "Why do you always do everything with her?"

I paused for a brief moment, not sure what to say—but I knew exactly what I wanted to say.

"It's not like you're around to play with."

Her face distorted with anger, "Well maybe that's because I actually have to help out around here! Mother's pregnant, and suddenly I have to pick up all the slack while you run around and play all day! Did you ever think of that?"

"I didn't mean to upset you, Priya," I mumbled.

"Well, how did you expect me to feel?"

She got up and began serving seconds even though there was barely any rice left. Then again, there never was.

My eyes began to tear, but my masi took my hand before I could start bawling in front of everyone. She carried me outside and rocked me in her lap.

"What's wrong, darling?"

"It's Priya," I choked.

"What did she say?"

"She's always yelling at me! I'm never good enough for her."

"Oh, Mukti, you just have to realize she has a lot on her shoulders right now. She's taken on a lot of responsibility now that your mother is pregnant, and she has a lot of stress she's managing on her own. You should be easier on her."

I wiggled out of her grip.

"I just want my sister back."

I broke free, and before I seemed to know it, was climbing up the side of the hut, balancing on the bamboo as I pulled myself over the roof. I collapsed on the unstable straw, tears running down my cheeks.

My body ached for one of Ruchita's comforting hugs. Yet I knew I could never break through her family's barrier.

She was at her Kathak[6] class in the city tonight for a special recital. It was in these hours that I missed her most, when I felt the slight separation between us. I don't mean the geographic distance between my village and the city, but the gap between our families. She would always have access to a world my family could never enter.

She tried to teach me one of her dances once. It only highlighted our differences more. My attempts to emulate her ever-moving heels made my head dizzy. I stumbled over and confused Ro too. We laughed and both agreed right then and there that I would never be a dancer. It was then that I also realized I would never be Ro.

My father's words began to ring in my head, slowly making sense to me.

Ruchita's mother was the sweetest woman, with rosy cheeks full of joy. She cherished my friendship with Ruchita, too. It was Ro's father who never accepted me. He distanced himself from the entire village. It was frustrating that Ruchita's family was always welcome in my home but we were never welcome in theirs. I didn't understand why our caste made us different. Ro and her mother were Dalits too. But Ro's father was from an upper caste, and he had risked everything by marrying Ro's mother.

Ironically, I respected Ro's father less because of his status. I didn't love Ruchita because she looked like a goddess. She was the kindest girl I knew. It was her tendency to exceed expectations that made me admire her most. She was strong and confident—qualities I could only dream of.

I wiped the tears from my face, knowing what Ruchita would tell me.

---

[6] Kathak-form of dance

"Find your confidence, Mukti, and then, place that faith and trust in us."

I was right.

"Mukti! How can you even think such things!" Ruchita said in shock the next day. "Our friendship will last forever. Your family is being paranoid. You need to have more faith. If you let others tear you down, you will be nothing more than the dirt. If you let others bring you up, you will be as tall as me one day!" She winked, knowing exactly how to cheer me up.

We sat there in silence for a few minutes and watched the clouds shift. I hesitated to ask the questions that still troubled me.

"Ro?"

She rolled back on her side, "Yes, Mukti?"

"Why does your father think he's so much—"

"Better than the rest of you?" she finished.

"Yeah…"

"I don't know, Mukti. It's complicated."

"How so?"

"I think it's the part of him that remembers his old life. He grew up in Bangalore with his family and came to the village when he fell in love with my mother. Their marriage wasn't arranged. He was forbidden to marry a Dalit. He stayed here with her side of the family, but he acts like he gave up another love—his city—to be with her. I think he feels like he's sacrificed a part of himself. He thinks he deserves more than a small village life. So he believes his caste and education make him better than everyone here."

"He's never thought much of your being educated, though."

"Well, I'm a girl. I won't be reading books my whole life," she answered sharply. I knew those words tasted bitter in her mouth. "He still thinks it's important for me to know Hindi, because he grew up speaking Hindi and Kannada. I think that's because he wants me to experience that part of his life...not because knowing how to read and write would help me in the future."

"I guess that makes sense."

I lay back down and stared at the fading sky.

Then I rolled back over again. "You don't think he'll ever move you back there do you?"

"No. My mother's family is here. He wouldn't take her away from them."

"Okay. Good," I said with a smile.

The clouds moved over our heads, the fields turned inside out, and seemingly in the blink of an eye, a year had passed by. My twin brothers were born and the heavy burden on Priya's shoulders had been lifted.

A few weeks ago my sister and I came home to the most wonderful surprise.

"Papa! Mama! We're home!"

My mom rushed out of the back room. She wiped her

hands, dirty with oils and spices, before reaching out to us.

"How was school, my lovelies?"

I rambled on about all the things I had learned, while Priya took off her shawl and began cleaning off our muddy shoes.

"That's wonderful! You and Priya have been doing so well in school. In fact, your father and I even—"

My father popped in through the door, "Wait, don't tell them! It's my surprise after all!"

Priya politely greeted my father at the doorway.

I bounced up and down "What is it? What is it, Papa!"

My father lifted something from beneath Priya's sleeping mat.

Priya's face beamed in excitement as he handed the smooth, black plate to her. Excitedly I ran up and snatched the stencil for myself.

"Mukti! Don't break it!"

"How cool! Our own stencil! How can we write on it?" I asked.

My father took a pack of chalk from beneath the mat. "Don't lose them! They're all you have."

"Thank you so much, Papa." Priya thanked my father humbly, touching his feet in respect.

"Thanks, Papa!" I shouted.

My fingers traced over the rough board. I imagined all the math problems and drawings and games I would scribble.

"Let's show Ruchita!" I told Priya, as we admired the stencil.

She rolled her eyes. "Must we share everything with her?"

"Yes."

"What if she gets jealous?"

"She has her journal! She doesn't need anything else to write on. She'll be happy for us!"

"You know how her father is with these things." Priya sighed. "I think it's best we keep it between you and me."

I didn't like keeping secrets from Ro, but I didn't want to upset Priya either, so I kept my mouth shut for now.

The next day on the way to school my head buzzed. I held the secret in for at least four minutes before I blurted it out to Ro. Priya glared at me, but I didn't care. I knew Ro better than she did. She would be happy for us.

Ever since we had gotten the stencil, Priya and I had been practicing our schoolwork at home each evening. Within three weeks my teachers viewed me as "advanced." My math had already improved with Priya's help.

Ruchita came over to study with us a few times, but she quickly regretted it. Her father found out and scolded her. He had no tolerance for Ro wasting her time on studies. During his lecture, he said Priya and I were bad influences on her. When Ro told me this I rolled my eyes. His perception of Ruchita's beauty was distorted. Her flawless skin and bright smile formed only the surface to her beauty. If her father had spent a little more time trying to see the real Ro, he would realize she had even more beauty on the inside.

UNDERWATER
(Mukti)

Each morning we woke up in darkness. Priya, Ro and I trekked to school in the dim morning light, excited by all the possibilities of the coming day before us. I struggled to keep up with my companions whose legs were twice as long as mine. Although the ten-kilometer walk was lengthy, our conversations always ended abruptly. The three of us had grown extremely close over the past year, and I cherished our shared time together. It was in these moments—away from our guardians and rules—that our light-hearted spirits danced the freest.

About halfway through our walk a ball of fire lit up the sky and a pale blue canvas enveloped the sky. We had reached the city and could see the streets drenched from last night's rain. The three of us ran through the crowds, dodging puddles and laughing as our boots splashed one another with rainwater. By the time we reached school, my white sneakers were brown. My little pink princess backpack with the stunning Cinderella on it was splattered with mud, too.

"Oh, no! Priya!" I cried, clutching my mud-spotted bag.

"Don't worry, Mukti. Let me wipe it off." She took the bag and cleaned it with her shawlwar.

I hugged it as though it were my most precious possession.

"Thanks, Priya."

Ro's face suddenly dropped. I looked up to see what was wrong.

"Priya! Mukti! The gates are closing!"

My eyes watched the big red gates slowly sliding together in the distance. We were late!

The three of us sprinted to the edge of school, shouting, "Wait! Don't close the gates! Please!"

But the guards, dressed in light-blue uniforms, knew they weren't allowed to. If we were late, we were late, and we would miss school.

My heart thudded in my chest. Our parents would be furious if we missed school.

Luckily, we squeezed through the entrance in time. The gates locked behind us with an echoing clang.

"That was a close one!" I said panting. Priya's face was red and spotty. She wasn't used to getting into trouble.

Then I realized something. "Where's Ro?"

Behind us, Ruchita's fists clenched the rusty reddened bars. She was on the outside.

Priya sighed, "Ruchita, what are you going to do?"

Ro's high spirits never diminished.

"Don't worry about me! You two go ahead."

I hesitated anyway.

"Come on, Mukti. Let's go!" Priya whined. "We're going to be late for class."

"We can't just leave her!"

But then Ruchita did what she did best. She winked, and we knew she would be in class with Priya in no time.

At break the school doors opened and a stream of children burst out, quickly filling the golden dirt field. Boys instantly tackled each other for a deflated soccer ball, while the girls gathered in small groups, eating biscuits and gossiping. I scurried out with a different intention. My eyes searched the redundant plaid uniforms until I spotted her silky hair glistening in the sun.

"How'd you do it? How'd you get in?" I exclaimed, running over to Ro.

"The less you know, the better," she said with a grin.

She never ceased to amaze me.

"Oh, please!" Priya said, bursting my bubble. "She climbed over the back of the school wall."

I rolled my eyes. "Didn't the guards see you?"

"Yup!"

"And they let you go?"

"All I had to do was flip my hair, and they didn't say a word," she chortled.

I laughed, half wishing my looks could help me get away with things too.

The next day I woke up and looked at the night sky, searching for any remaining stars sparkling through the haze. This morning they were all hiding.

Eagerly I put on my skirt and shoes. I heard giggling behind me. Priya was mocking me.

"What are you doing, Mukti?" My sister laughed. "It's Sunday."

I blushed.

"*Aiyyoooo.*" Oops.

I scrambled onto the roof and waited impatiently for my devilish companion to join me. My eyes scanned the fields, level with rising rice heads. We were in the waiting season. All Ro and I had to do was watch the crops grow and hope they wouldn't fail.

"Mukti? Mukti!" I heard a voice scream from below. It was my mother's.

"Yes?"

"Why don't you help Priya and me in the kitchen today?"

"No, Mama! I have plans with Ro today! She'll be waiting for me. It would be rude to abandon her."

"I'm sure her father would want her doing the same thing, Mukti! You aren't children anymore. You're becoming young ladies. You get to play all week!"

"School isn't playing, Mama! It's work. This is the only day we have to rest," I argued.

"I hardly think you and Ruchita will be resting."

I didn't respond but lay back down, hoping she would

go away.

"Mukti!!!"

I squeezed my eyes shut and pretended to fly away. She couldn't make me.

Eventually she gave up and went back inside. I could hear her cursing me under her breath, probably for not being more like Priya. My feet swung back and forth off the edge of the roof, faster and faster. Where was she?

I decided to meet Ro at her house so my mother couldn't drag me off the roof.

The village was slowly waking. The morning was like a long yawn. It made me antsy. Ruchita's home was by far the biggest in the village and at the edge, away from the rest of us. I could see the windows were dark and the door shut tight. I listened at a safe distance for any signs of life. All I heard was my heart beating.

Then the sound of rushing water broke the silence, reminding me that I was supposed to meet Ro by the river. As I sprinted towards the water, I heard my father's words warning me to stay away from the edge.

"Careful, Mukti! The water is dangerous this time of year when the water is so high. You will get swept up and taken by the tide. Stay on the other side of me."

I wandered along the edge. It seemed I would never find Ro. Maybe she had forgotten too and was waiting for me on the roof.

My knees buckled and my feet ached. If I kept walking, Ruchita might never find me.

So I waited. I ran my fingers through the tall brush and listened to the ambient sounds. Massive dragonflies buzzed above the tips of grass, zapping their wings in the air. The sharp whistling of the wind vibrated in my ears. My hair fluttered yet remained tame in the gentle wind. I heard men shout in the distance. Like the dragonflies' wings, my mind fluttered.

I thought of Ro and her double life. She glided like a princess but acted like a warrior, laughed like a queen and talked like a king, looked like a butterfly but was a tiger on the inside. She was everything society wanted her to be, and everything they never expected her to be. Everything her father demanded and everything I admired.

A tiny flame lit up inside me. It was the first time I felt it. It flickered brighter the more I thought of Ro. My fingers rummaged through the dirt until I found a pebble. I tossed it into the water, releasing anger.

The smooth current tempted me, but I knew just a little farther up the water quickened and splashed, eddying around rocks and becoming whirlpools. I wasn't strong enough to swim against that current.

Ruchita was, though.

But of course she was.

I dipped my toes into the cool water. I walked in a little further, but the sand kept slipping underneath my feet. I looked around and found a rock to hold onto. The water crept up to my knees. I smiled with accomplishment. I had defied my parents' rule to stay away from the river.

That brief moment of triumph slipped away as the rock began to wiggle beneath my weight. I struggled to keep my balance. The rock tumbled over, pulling me down with it, face-first into the river.

I panicked as my body dipped beneath the surface of the cold water. My feet searched for ground but found only more water. Instinct told me to fling my arms and legs violently and scream. I spat out water that tasted like sewage. My cries were weak against the river's drift. I reached up but failed to touch the surface, the line separating me from life and death.

I thought of my family—my boisterous father, tender mother, prudent sister and precious peas. I loved them so much and I didn't get a chance to say goodbye. I didn't want to say goodbye.

I blinked hard. I'm sure there were tears, but they washed away in the murky water.

I was in the fields again, spinning in my father's strong arms. The world around me blurred. Clouds turned the sky white. Distant huts became a golden smudge. The never-ending fields were a green haze. My heart felt light and pure. The world seemed so distant and harmless.

I opened my eyes. Panic shook me like lightning. The black water pushed me down further. Muddy debris swarmed by in a whirlpool. The water was black—empty—endless. The river grew heavy as if the water were thickening. I choked in a breath, but the water flooded down my throat and into my lungs, drowning me. Panicking, I gasped again but the water was relentless. It kept flooding my insides. My eyes blinked away invisible tears.

My mother's voice vibrated over the water as if shouting from above.

"Mukti! No! Mukti!"

I saw her in a field of brown grass near the river. She and Priya were on the other side of the muddy water, whispering. My eyes watched as if they were in a movie.

"Mama? Mama?" I called out.

"She's gone now. It's just you and me now. You won't disappoint me like she did will you? You won't leave me like she did? Abandoning her family responsibility."

"I'm here! I'm right here!" I screamed, "Mama! I'm still here! Look at me, Mama! Don't you see me? Don't you hear me?"

My fists fought against the water, trying to break through, but a thick barrier prevented anyone from seeing or hearing me. I was already dead to Mama and Priya.

I reached up again, grabbing, praying I'd latch onto something from the life I once had. I wanted my eight years back. I wanted to relive each moment. I wanted to rebreathe each breath, walk each step, laugh each laugh. The water slipped between my fingers. My fists clenched around nothing.

I opened my eyes again. A flash of light bounced off the surface of the water. Was it the sun? The murky debris seemed to disperse. A blurry figure sank towards me, but I couldn't see. My eyes wouldn't open anymore. I could feel my body losing control. I was losing control. I felt myself stop fighting and quickly lost my fear. The feeling slipped away as I felt my body grew numb. I wasn't anything anymore, just a body sinking deeper and deeper.

A hand encircled my wrist, closing around it like a vise. My body glided through the obscure water as it yanked me out of the depths, bringing me to the surface.

The air tingled my wet skin. The wind kissed my face.

"*Mukti! Mukti!*" The voice kept shouting and the pressure kept pushing. As the river poured out my mouth, I sucked in a mouthful of air.

How precious was that air.

The moment was surreal, like being born again. I knew I was gaining a new life, getting another chance.

My eyes flickered. I could feel my chest heaving, struggling to breathe.

"*Mukti? Mukti, can you hear me?*"

Her sweet voice reassured me. I was safe. I was alive. Those words were like sugar. My eyes fought through the blurriness and focused on the face above me.

It was Ro.

I pulled myself off the ground and clung to her. Her arms wrapped around me.

My chest pulsed up and down. "Ro, I thought I was dead. I thought...I lost you, everything."

"It's okay, Mukti. You're here. You're okay. You're alive. Don't worry anymore. I'll catch you next time. I promise."

She held me close, stroking my wet hair. I sobbed.

The sun dried my skin and soaked up the pain.

"Let's get you back home. Your family must be

worried. You missed lunch."

I didn't want to see them though. I was afraid they'd be mad.

My father was waiting in the doorway. His face was red—but with worry. The sight of him made me start bawling. Before I could blink twice he was beside me, holding me.

"What happened? Are you okay? I was so worried, Mukti!"

My mouth quivered.

Ruchita was the one who answered. "I was walking to the river to meet her, and I saw her fall in. I sprinted to her as fast as I could, but I was still far away. She must have been underwater at least—I don't know. Two minutes. I jumped in and—"

I saw the tears run down her cheeks.

Ro shook. "I thought she was dead—she wasn't breathing—"

My father cut her off and pulled her into the hug.

"It's okay. It's okay. The two of you are safe now. All that matters is you two are okay."

He squeezed us tighter. I smelled the cinnamon on his hot breath. The scraggly hairs on his face tickled my skin.

My father breathed in a deep sigh. "Come on now. Let's find you two some dry clothes."

The wind whispered in my ears, echoing of days past. Back in my reality the shed-like room was empty, with only dust and bugs on the quarry ground. I took a deep breath, remembering the last time my father held me in his arms. I wished I never let go. My eyes started to burn. Maybe it was from the dry, clouded air. Or maybe from the pain of the past, haunting me like an ominous shadow. My stomach squeezed against my ribs as I fought back tears.

I rolled over and tried to distract myself. I examined the slash across the cement wall from Shubar's whip. He had swung it at Shankar and barely missed.

It was nice feeling secluded in the usually cramped cement room. Yet, it reminded me of the days I felt most alone. A numbing grief overcame me.

*   *   *

"Mukti! Will you go to the pump and bring me two pots of water!" my mother screamed from the kitchen.

Priya was in the city with my father today. They were trying to sell Neli, our cow, in hopes of bringing home a bundle of cash. The crops weren't thriving as my family had hoped this year. The sun had scorched the ground and dried the fields, leaving the villagers to scrape the bottoms of their bowls each night for the last grains of rice. Each meal might be their last.

I grumbled and wiped off the chalk-work with my wrist. I still used the stencil every day, appreciating the effort it must have cost my father to afford it. My mother had put two large tin pots in the kitchen doorway for me to fill up.

I trudged on the dirt trail towards the water pump. The

sun glowed in a dull sky, dimmer than usual. It looked exhausted.

"Me to," I mumbled. "Me too."

The farther I walked from the village, the closer I came to a peaceful solitude. By the time I reached the pump, the city was in the near distance. I cranked the metal handle, filling the pots with water until my forehead beaded with sweat.

If I tried hard enough I could convince myself I was in the city. Resting, I sat down and listened for the daily chaotic bustle. There was something peculiar about the city today—a pause amid the usually tumult. It weighed with suspense. Then a sudden panic broke out. The city shook like a stack of metal pots and pans crashing and clanging to the ground.

A knot twisted in my stomach. The city was beyond the thick fields and forest. I couldn't hear anything but my imagination. I looked down at the empty metal pot. It seemed to stare up at me, mocking my laziness after I'd pumped only one pot of water.

"Fine," I muttered.

The metal handle was hot from the sun, but I forced myself to press against it. I didn't want Mama to get mad. In the soundless wind, the rice fields swayed. I peered out towards the city and a black figure appeared. A man. I backed away as he came towards me. I turned to walk back to the village and heard him shouting. His arms waved to get my attention. I waited for him to approach and recognized him as my Masa.

"Mukti-beta!" he shouted, half out of breath. "I need you to find your mother right away. Your father is in trouble. She needs to come to the city right now."

What kind of trouble? I wanted to ask. My quivering lips couldn't form the words.

"Quickly, Mukti!" he yelled.

I dropped the pots and ran. I ran with fear—a fear that knew more than I ever could at that moment. Father was in trouble. There was no better motivation in the world.

The green fields turned into a fuzzy haze and meters turned into kilometers. All I saw was the thin line that led me home.

"Mukti? Where are the pots? *Yaake ninage yenu nenapu iruvudilla, Mukti!* Why can't you remember anything, Mukti! I ask you to do one—"

I collapsed into the kitchen, tugging on my mother's sari. "Mama! Mama! Something's wrong! Masa says you need to go to the city right away. It's father!" I exclaimed.

My mother's face grew serious but showed no signs of panic.

"I will go with your Masa. Stay here. The dhal is on the stove. Don't let it burn." Her monotonous voice neither rose nor fell. I never understood how she managed to control her emotions.

I waited alone inside the hut for hours.

The day flashed before me. My mother's screams. Priya's pale white face. The tears. The chaos. The pain. So much pain. I pictured the accident in my head over and over, as if I were in the city with him. I could envision the loose rope and Neli, our cow, trudging through the street. I saw the bus and the blood. I watched the glass shatter and chaos erupt in the city. Then came the image of my father's body, dear angelic father, stoned and bloody at the hands of the people.

The next few days were emptiness. I felt hollow, as if someone had shoveled out my insides and tossed them in the river. I never experienced such pain. It tore me to pieces over and over. Priya tried to explain how it happened. But she never could get through a full sentence. A riot had started after our cow caused an accident in the city. My father was held responsible, and in fury the people beat him to death.

Every night I woke from the same tormenting nightmare. I was in the river, reaching for the surface and struggling to pull myself to the surface. The second I touched air, my body collapsed backward onto the waves. I woke up in the same sweat every day. The moment I opened my eyes I remembered all over again what I had lost: the one man I could never replace.

The clouds shifted with the seasons and soon I lost my mother too. Or really, she lost herself. My sister and I watched her go mad until we couldn't watch anymore. She tormented herself constantly, scratching her skin and throwing things. She refused to eat and couldn't sleep. I stayed on the roof most days rocking back and forth on my heels, listening to her whimper inside the house. I watched my mother slowly lose grip of her sanity. I felt helpless and unable to save her.

It wasn't long before I remembered waking up and seeing an empty mat—her empty mat—and I knew. I don't know how, but I knew. I ran over to Priya, who was half-asleep with her glassy eyes wide-open, and I shook her limp body.

"Priya! Priya!" I bawled, "Mama's gone. She's gone."

I rolled off of her and collapsed against the hard wall. My body shook as I screamed between sobs.

"No, no, no. *No!*" I muttered, tears streaming down my face.

The peas were awake now, too. They looked at me and began to cry, not sure why they were crying but realizing they should feel the same pain as their big sister.

"Mukti, stop it," Priya said, grabbing my shoulders. "You're going to scare Raj and Arjun."

Her eyes flickered and turned cold. She blinked out the last spark of her youth and looked at me with a new, mature and emotionless stare.

In that moment I lost my sister forever. She abandoned her emotions and innocence. Her new concern for responsibility overpowered any childish secrets she might have whispered in my ear and any desire she might have had to run her fingers gently through my hair at night. Priya was no longer a girl: she was my parent, both parents in fact. She no longer had time for anything but work and prayer. All I wanted from my sister was her love, but she didn't see the importance of that. Love wouldn't feed the peas.

I pushed her hands off of me and climbed onto the roof where I waited for Ro. Tears blurring my vision, I couldn't see the sunrise that morning. But at least I still had Ro. Since the day I lost my father, she had become my rock through everything. She kept me from drowning even when I felt myself head-deep in tears.

The village mourned along with us. When my mother left, the villagers became our key to survival. They brought us their blessings and prayers and kept us alive with leftover food. My masis and masas tried to assume some of the duties of our parents, but Priya refused their help.

"I have everything under control. I can take care of my siblings, Masi. They are my responsibility now."

I missed the trio—Priya, Ro, and I—but I knew Priya had to separate herself from our childishness. Our youthful spirits had already flagged and faded anyway. I didn't laugh as lightheartedly anymore. I didn't jump in puddles. Ro and my walks to school were in silence. Priya no longer attended school and instead stayed home with the peas. I could feel the distance between us like the river. I could scream at her with all my might, but she couldn't hear me anymore.

Suddenly, I heard a crash from the back room. Metal pots and pans clanged together onto the floor.

"Damnit!" Priya cursed.

I followed the noise to the doorway and stopped, afraid to approach the lion's den. I lightly tapped on the kitchen wall, hoping not to startle her. She jumped at everything nowadays.

"Priya? Are you okay?"

She grumbled back, "I'm fine, Mukti. What do you want?"

"Will..." I hesitated, already knowing the answer, "will you come play with us?"

"Mukti, I don't have time to be your friend right now," she said, picking up the pots she had dropped.

"But I just hoped—"

"Mukti! I. Don't. Have. Time!"

The words pierced my heart.

From the roof, Ro had heard everything. I ran into her arms, her kisses as usual comforting me.

"I'll go get us some dried mangos," she said optimistically. They were my favorite. "From Nayana Masi. And we can go for a walk."

She squeezed my hand. Then I watched her scurry off with her brilliant colors fluttering in the wind like a peacock.

Icicles around my heart had been like bars, but now they began to melt, and with the melting some of the pain escaped too. I watched the peacock dance away in the distance until she was a black dot. Even though she was far away, she was closest to my heart.

Above me, the pale blue sky seemed so innocent, so removed. As a gentle wind blew through my hair, I felt whole again. I looked up to the sky and whispered, a tear falling down my cheek, "You see, Papa. It's Ruchita who will love me forever."

It rushed past and left me feeling empty again.

INVISIBLE
(Mukti)

The sky began to wake up. Faded colors yawned and seemed to hesitate in the air. Clouds slowly bumped together and pulled apart, leaving empty spaces in the air. The holes were filled with shadowy blues waiting for the sun to brighten them.

I heard the shuffling of feet below the roof and leaned over the edge to see the tops of two pots of water pitched over the ground. I lay back down and held my breath, bracing myself for the whimpering that I was bound to hear. The house had settled into a routine ever since my mother returned two weeks ago. While the peas spent most of their time away from the house, I retreated to my roof. Priya spent every hour of the day pampering Mama like a newborn infant. And the baby never stopped crying. Even after Priya picked at my mother's knotted hair for three days and spent another one scrubbing off the grime on her skin, she never stopped whining.

Yet, she was Priya's oxygen. She kept Priya's spirit alive. I, on the other hand, had nothing to say to the woman who, in effect, had abandoned us for two months. When she showed up in our doorway, I knew she was no longer my mother. Having her half-empty self back in my life didn't make me feel any more whole.

Instead, I felt invisible in my own home. I found myself on top of the roof with Ro most days. I still missed the trio and our dynamic walks to school, and I knew things would never be the same.

At least I still had Ro.

"What'd you learn in class today?" she asked cheerfully on our walk back home.

"Nothing new."

"I didn't see you at break. Where were you?"

"Classroom."

"Oh." Ro sensed my mood and gave up.

"Sorry, Ro. I just don't feel like talking."

She put her arm around me, "It's okay, Mukti."

My teacher had scolded me again that day for dreaming during her lesson. I wanted to yell back that I wasn't dreaming. I was trying not to think at all, because whenever I let myself think, I would think of *him*.

I lost all motivation to work in school. I sat on the roof with my legs crossed and stared at a problem scribbled in chalk. I huffed. My fist smeared the unfinished chalk work, and I hopped from the roof. Frustrated by my inability to solve anything, I looked for Priya. She was in the corner combing my mother's hair.

Reaching my chalk slate out to her, I pleaded, "Priya, can you help me with my math?"

She refused to meet my gaze. I stood waiting for a response.

"It's just one problem..." I begged, shifting my feet in the dirt. Priya just stood there, brushing my mother's dead hair over and over. It was completely untangled by now, but Priya wouldn't stop. For Priya, her constant touch was the only thing keeping my mother there.

Still no answer.

"I'm falling behind in school again, Priya. The other kids make fun of me. I don't like it. I really need you."

"Mama needs me right now."

Mama had been back for a month.

I returned to the roof and found Ro waiting for me with her legs hanging over the edge. It was as if she knew I was going to need her, but I soon realized she needed me even more right then.

Her face was long and pale. It lacked its usual glow.

"What's wrong?"

Her voice was lifeless, as if someone had taken her soul.

"She's gone."

Suddenly the world seemed hopeless, menacing, barren. I placed my hand on her shoulder, unable to find words. She still looked so put together, as if all emotion were repressed. In place of tears and sadness there was rage. The world had stolen something from her.

"I feel like I've been robbed, Mukti. But I can't—I can't even fight back. I have all this—this anger! But there's..." She paused. "There's no way to get revenge."

She looked puzzled, not comprehending the world.

My eyes started to tear. Hers remained dry.

We sat on the edge of the roof as the sun slowly moved across the sky and stayed there after its fall. As it disappeared beneath the horizon, we leaned our heads together and stared up at the sympathetic stars.

Ruchita's mother had caught malaria two weeks ago and had been in the hospital. I assumed the treatment would drain Ro's family of their money, but never in a million years did I think it would drain them of her life.

After hours of silence I attempted words.

"Is there anything I can do, Ro?"

I watched her stare at the sky and fight against her emotions. She fought them so hard, but finally they broke through. And Ro began to bawl.

"Oh Ro! I'm so sorry," I cried too. "I don't know why these awful things keep happening to us."

I leaned over and hugged her as tightly as I could. I brushed back the hair from her face and sang her a lullaby, the one my father used to sing to me.

Ro had been my rock, saving me from drowning in the river, but in that moment she and I became more than that. We became each other's bridge, a safe path through the turbulent days that threatened to swallow us up.

The next month flew by as Ro and I turned to each other to fill the emptiness we both felt. She was in the city with her father today. Though only twelve kilometers away, I felt incomplete when Ro was away.

The sun flickered between white puffy clouds, forcing me to squint as I looked into the distance. Surrounding my little hut was the bustling village that somehow continued to function. I watched the beams bounce off the henchu and cow-dung roofs and smiled at the bottomless children bumbling around.

My eyes avoided the desolate fields, loathing the feeling of hopelessness and fear they inspired. Behind the cheery activity of the village was the sinking panic over the failure of crops. This wasn't the first year the crops didn't grow. But it was the first time my father wasn't around to scrounge for coins and bags of rice that fed my family. As I watched the crops drooping in the distance, I felt my stomach shrink. Priya was doing the best she could, but her best just wasn't enough.

Two men whom I had never seen before emerged from behind my neighbor's house. I had heard rumors about men coming to villages to recruit for work in the city. I jumped down from the roof and sprinted inside to warn Priya.

"Mukti, slow down. What are you saying?"

My mother groaned in the corner.

"Two men are coming here. I don't know who they are. I've never seen them before. Never."

Priya rolled her eyes. "How do you know they're coming here?"

"They are, Priya. Trust me. I have a bad feeling."

Day after day, my insides churned as I waited for the next bad thing to happen.

I peered outside the door and pointed to the two dark figures in the distance.

"See, Priya. They're coming here. What do you think they want?"

"Maybe they're friends of Papa and are bringing their condolences," she said.

"Maybe," I mumbled, digging my toes into the dirt.

My mother muttered in the corner. She looked unnerved.

"Mother, don't worry. Everything is fine," Priya said soothingly. She shot me a look as if it were my fault Mother was having another panic attack.

The two men stood in the doorway, towering over us. I saw their jaws flex. Their eyes flashed with danger, but their voices lulled us with a calming reassurance. Still, I cowered behind Priya, clinging to her. She handled the situation as my father would have: friendly yet professional. I listened with my lips pressed tightly together.

Their big words made me feel small. I wanted to stand tall against them, but we had no choice but to obey.

"We are very sorry for your loss," one of them said. "Unfortunately, your father has left behind quite a large debt. We know your crops have failed and your village is struggling to bring in money this season. We believe we have a solution for you. To pay off the debt, your family can come work on our property." He looked down as I clutched Priya's legs. "You and your sister will be given a free education at the nearby school as well. You'll be given a place to sleep and food."

The other man spoke: "It should only be temporary, until you work off the debt of course. That is, unless you can pay off the money right now."

"What happens when we finish paying off the money?"

"You can return to your village."

Priya shifted uncomfortably and asked, "2,000 rupees?"

It would take a full season's harvest and excess sales to come up with that kind of money.

The man nodded.

The first one stared down at me again. Our eyes locked. There was a confidence in his eyes that made me tremble, as if he knew something I didn't. They dazzled me with a power I couldn't understand in that moment.

ETERNITY
(Mukti)

I gazed through the openings in the walls that failed to keep out the rain, heat and insects that augured sickness to our sleeping corpses. Walking outside, I noticed the blazing sun had made the air thick and hard to breathe. It was monsoon season, which meant humidity during the day and torrential downpours at night.

Through the thick dust that kicked up from the rocks, I tried to make out the sky and prayed to its infinite reach.

Naanu Devaru[7] *Smaraney*[8] *maadiddheney.* I finished my prayer to God and whispered, "*Devaru avalannu rakshisali.* And I pray you protect Ro, wherever she is, and remind her that I love her very much. Tell her I will be with her soon, as soon as I get out of here. *Jay Shri Raam*[9].

Five years had passed since I last saw Ro. Even though she was unaware of my daily prayers, I never forgot to say them.

Arjun joined me as I hoisted a heavy slab of granite. I placed a cloth ring in between the granite and my head to provide cushion from the hardness.

Today was the same as every other day: sixteen hours of strict routine. Throughout the quarry, hundreds of toiling bodies were split into different groups based on skill set. A huge drill cracked through the granite mountain nearby. I looked to my left and saw workers slamming hammers against the stone. Women dragged lumps of stone from the mounds of

---

[7] *Devaru*- irrespective to religion Devaru is referenced to God in all communities who speak Kannada
[8] *Smaraney*-here Smaraney means chanting a short prayer
[9] *Jay Shri Raam*-way to end prayer

granite to a group who polished them.

My skin cracked under the burning sun. The quarry felt like an oven. Heat permeated the air and refused to dissipate, trapping all of the workers inside. I glanced at the colorful house at the edge of the property. The owners lived there: a reddish pink three-story mansion surrounded by a beautiful garden. We called it the main house.

I often stared at the flat clay rooftop and imagined how it looked inside. The walkways into the home were polished granite that sparkled in the sun. Sandhya told me there was electricity and running water, but none of us believed her. We ourselves had to walk half a kilometer to the nearest water pump.

Jamadars roamed the grounds threatening and watching us work, and often I caught Shubar himself studying us. He stood at his oval window with a big grin, observing the quarry from his mansion. Surrounding his house were jade trees. Their flat leaves shaded the entire garden from the scorching heat. One tree in the middle had delicate white flowers resembling white covered jalebi. I admired it from the ancient banyan tree that provided my only shade.

Sometimes I spotted Darshan watching us from the same window. He never intimidated me. When he was near, a part of me actually relaxed. When his eyes passed over us, they were content. He spotted me and appeared to pause. Without saying a word, he watched me for a moment and continued walking. I pretended not to notice, gripping the small cape chisel in my fingers and hammering it into the granite slab.

As my brother and I walked towards the truck, I wondered where Darshan was today. That thought quickly passed when I noticed the truck was loaded with only one tenth of the required stone. I struggled to balance the heavy rocks that wobbled on my head. Arjun glanced at me and quickly looked away.

We walked past the banyan tree and stopped. I admired the branches draped with roots that resembled waterfalls and stared at the abandoned swing. Years ago Sandhya, Kushala and I had created it by braiding its roots. Sandhya's infectious laugh had bounced off the rocks as the three of us took turns swinging. For a brief moment we'd forget where we were and became children again.

Kushala was a girl we used to know.

Ironically, her name meant safety and happiness, even though her face showed only fear and pain. Her bravery had helped her escape the quarry, but that sweet taste of freedom was short-lived. Regarding her as a fugitive, a policeman in Shubar's good graces returned her to the grounds only a day later.

I remember the day she came back. I stared at her charred cheeks as smoke rose from her face. The burns from Shubar's crushed cigar were still smoldered. A tear dripped between her cuts. Vomit came up my throat. I swallowed it. The burnt girl I saw before me wasn't human.[10]

I hated myself for avoiding Kushala in her last days. Shame and guilt turned everyone away from her. I too couldn't bear the sight of my dying friend. And so Kushala, once so sweet and pure, limped past everyone unacknowledged like a beggar in the streets, as though already dead. My hand wiped a tear from my face.

Soon Nikhil found her lying in the middle of the field with a muted heartbeat, surrounded by a pile of tan-orange

---

[10] True story

rock. The sun's fierce heat had soaked up all of her strength, and I wasn't by her side in her final moments. The jamadars refused to let us cremate her body with the proper religious rituals, and thus not allowing her to move on to the next cycle of life. We buried her by the banyan tree, her favorite spot.

I couldn't get over the tragedy of her passing. All she'd wanted was to leave the quarry, and now she was trapped there for eternity. That word made my blood freeze.

Eternity.

From time to time I saw Sandhya by the banyan tree weeping. The tree towered over her, bigger than anything else in the quarry. She looked so tiny beneath it.

I wanted nothing more than to leave this place, but only a few had ever tried to escape. The ones who did had always been tracked, captured and beaten. It didn't matter how far they travelled. One man made it all the way to Chennai, but like the rest, he was brought back[11].

My dreams were haunted by the boiling water I saw poured over his skin. The man's screams seemed to linger for hours in the quarry until finally the winds picked them up and swept them away.

I wondered if the wind ever carried our screams to the deaf ears of the free. It was as if our lives were submerged beneath deep water and no one bothered to reach their hand into the current. We were voiceless. We drowned over and over again, and those above the water couldn't hear us. We were left to trust no one but ourselves. What was I to them? I fed their luxury. My labor was the foundation of their power. Why would they sacrifice their own happiness for the puppets they

---

[11] True story

53

controlled? Why would they acknowledge our existence when it was easier to ignore us?

One of these days I would get out of here. And unlike those before me, I wouldn't get caught. The city was so close and yet the quarry seemed so far from it. Past the barbed wire it was only a short distance through the exposed granite, mountains and forest of eucalyptus trees. The world was just at the surface of the river. It taunted us with its clear view of the other side, but every day the whirling water pushed us down.

Someday I would break through the surface. But where would I go? I knew I could never return to the warm comfort of my village.

After three years on the quarry, Priya was endowed to Sanat. His family needed a small dowry in advance, and we had no choice but to ask Shubar and Darshan for another loan. This only increased our debt, and the peas then joined us on the quarry to help pay it off. I was forced to watch them lose their innocence and spirited character as they worked by my side with heavy hammers. My heart hurt without them, but it hurt even more watching them live like that—if this was even living.

I looked at the ground so I wouldn't stumble and turned away from the blinding sun. The sound of hatchets slamming into the rocks echoed through the quarry, giving me a headache. My hands were already chalky from the stone. Everyone in the grounds was working assiduously. Altogether, we were about two hundred slaving bodies spread out among the seemingly never-ending property. We were strangers, we were friends, we were families, and we were foreigners to each other. Unable to communicate with half of the bodies who were stolen from numerous states, I felt alone in my cage. Each day seemed to drag on longer than the one before it. I felt the guilt build up for complaining when the man beside me couldn't even speak Kannada.

The emptiness in my stomach was far more gnawing than the hunger I'd felt in my village when the crops failed. My stomach was a bottomless pit, seeming to disappear further and further into my body. The men did keep one of their promises: we were given food. On the quarry, there was a hut that served a small bowl of rice and dhal at the end of each day. After hours of work, we would be given a token to purchase our meal, but the small portions barely fueled our limbs.

With each step I took, the granite grew heavier until I could feel my skull slowly crushing beneath its weight. My shoulders slumped over, and I stumbled with each step. The dust faded the bright colors of my favorite Kurta. I could see concern in Arjun's eyes, but he kept his mouth shut. Suddenly, I lost my balance on the uneven ground. My body slammed into the ground. I crushed my chin against the unforgivingly solid rock. The huge slab fell on top of my back. Arjun's panicked scream echoed in the air.

It felt like eternity before the granite was lifted from me. My eyes fluttered open to see Darshan wetting a rag and wiping the blood off my face. My mother sobbed above me. My face stung. I could feel pieces of dirt scraping my cuts. I couldn't move my foot. I tried to wiggle my ankle. Why couldn't I move my ankle?

"What happened?" I muttered to Darshan.

"You've been passed out for about 10 minutes. Try not to speak. You're hurt."

Although I couldn't feel my legs, those were the sincerest words I'd ever heard from Darshan. They were the only words. He'd never spoken to me before.

Suddenly my head began to ring louder until all the sounds around me seemed to be coming from far away and the world began to spin.

"What are all of you looking at? You have work to do!" I heard a jamadar scream in the distance.

I tried to move my toes in vain. Pain shot up my back. As I strained to hear Darshan's voice, blackness overcame me.

My eyes moved beneath my lids, then slowly opened.

I admired the light pink sponge-painted ceiling. An intricate chandelier adorned with shiny crystals flickered above me. Four fans spun round and round. Or was it one fan? A breeze washed over me.

Blackness.

Someone was wiping my face with a cold wet rag. It felt good against my skin. My body burned. Was I on fire?

Blackness.

A blurry face hovered above me. It smiled, but my vision wouldn't focus. My eyes felt heavy as stones.

Blackness.

Water rushed down my throat. A mosquito landed on my face. My weak arm refused to swat it. My head ached. I still couldn't see straight. Everything spun in circles.

Blackness.

TAKEN
(Ruchita)

Darkness surrounded me. The air wrapped me up like an icy blanket, whipping around my face and freezing the sweat on my skin. Yet, the street burned my feet as though it were made of burning embers. The mixture of my body heat and the bitter wind felt peculiar.

Thud. Thud. Thud. With each step a burst of excruciating pain shot up my leg. I wished I hadn't tripped over that metal water pipe in the alleyway. More sweat beaded my forehead. I wiped the hair out of my face, but my bangs continued to fall on my wet forehead. Everything that moved around me made my heart jump inside my chest. I swam in paranoia as my mind struggled to escape my head.

A street sign flashed before me. Cement sidewalks turned to a blur. My knees buckled, struggling to find balance after a robust woman rammed into my left shoulder. The adrenaline pulsed through my veins. With each step I fell deeper into the maze and became more determined to leave it.

I knew there was no going back.

A shadow bounced on the wall. It seemed to creep up behind me. My head snapped over my shoulder, but I saw the street was empty. The crooked sidewalk seemed to stare back at me. The lights flickered. The night whispered.

Continuing forward, I maintained my steady stride. As my eyes darted around each corner, the dark night mocked my childish fear. Gasping for air, my lungs begged me to slow down. My legs hadn't run this fast since I was seven and Priya, Mukti and I were racing towards our school's closing gates. Despite the pain, I couldn't stop. My body wouldn't let me. Running made me feel free—like I was untouchable.

My fear drove me to keep running. I had to leave the maze. It had been three years since I had seen my father, and I refused to let another moment stand in the way of his embrace. All I wanted was to be with him again and to smell his peppermint breath and to admire his toasty smile. I missed the overwhelming attention he gave me—his beautiful gem.

I shivered. I didn't like to think about the day that I was taken from him. Even though it was just a memory now, marked permanently like a henna, I hated remembering it. A chill ran down my back as their faces appeared and disappeared. Allowing myself to catch my breath, I sat against the wall of a closed shop. I decided to scribble down my thoughts that were distracting me from my escape. I flipped open to the first page of my journal, a glued-in piece of paper, and started reading.

Thursday, November 14, 2002

Taken

My heart is pounding. I have to write quickly. I found a scrap of paper and a dry pen to write with. I miss having my journal with me, but now this is all I have.

I have so much to say, but I don't have any words...

I still remember it like it was yesterday.

I was dancing in my home—the small half brick, part tarp home—in my pink lehenga choli. I was laughing as I listened to the music stuck in my head after my recent Kathak lesson. We were poor after losing my mother, but Baba made sure I continued my lessons. We were no longer in Nirega because my father wanted to come back to the city where he had grown up. But I know the real reason is that we couldn't afford to live in the village anymore. We could only afford to be in the slums. I didn't know I was lying to Mukti when I told her that my father would never move us back to Bangalore, but I never thought he would...

Anyway, my father came in and picked me up. He lifted me over his shoulders and spun me with his strong shoulders that always made me feel safe. I miss him already. I miss his protecting embrace and comforting words, but I know he is doing everything he can to come save me.

We heard a knock on the sidewall by the open doorway. Suddenly, my father hugged me tight. It felt weird. Different almost. He said he loved me and that I was his bright, shining gem. I told him I loved him too. He peered out the opening of our shack where a broad-shouldered man stood. I remember he looked as if he were waiting for something. His eyes looked me up and down as I hid behind my Baba. I was scared, but I thought Baba would protect me. Then the strong, fearless father I once knew let go. I felt the man shove my father out of the way and grab me by the arms.

"Baba! Baba!" I screamed.

The man squeezed my wrists. I tried to break free. I really did. But what I really remember is watching my father fall to his knees and reading his lips say, "I'm so sorry, Ruchita."

I kicked and screamed, trying to fight my way out of the man's grip, but he was so strong. A dirty cloth, with an awful, acid smell, was shoved over my nose and I felt myself slowly falling asleep. My eyes tried to open, but all I saw was blackness. I think a bag was over my head. I felt so loopy. I tried hard to concentrate, but it was hopeless. My feet dragged across the mud as I kicked and screamed. Only a soft cry came out, though.

I could tell we were out of the slums when I felt them lift and shove me into a small area. My body began to panic, feeling trapped in that small space. Soon, all I could do was listen.

"I'll start the car. You handle the money," a voice said.

Someone yanked my arms behind my back and tied them together with a rope that dug into my skin. They did the same to my feet.

My eyes dripped with fear every time I blinked. I couldn't move. What were they doing with me? My teeth scraped against each other, but I wasn't even cold. My whole body panicked again, and I banged my legs against the top of the trunk, screaming at the top of my lungs. I tried to control my breathing but my chest closed. Calming down for a moment, I untwisted myself. I tried to sit up, but my head hit a hard metal barrier and smacked me back down. When the ringing subsided, I managed to squeeze my arms under my bottom and out above my toes.

The blackness consumed me, and even after I shoved it off, I couldn't escape the darkness. The car sank lower to the ground and then popped back up. I could hear the engine running, and then I was shoved out of my position. The car shot forward, banging me around as I lay there soaked in my own tears.

I wanted for my father. Why hadn't he caught up yet? I thought to myself that he must have been beaten so badly that he couldn't chase after us. I know in my heart that he fought for me. He'll find me soon. I know he will. He'll keep fighting. I'm his beautiful little girl. He won't let them keep me here. Wherever I am.

My heart thudded against my chest as I read the passage. My fingers felt around my wrists that suddenly felt chained. I turned the next page and kept reading.

Friday, November 26, 2004

Walls

Walls surround me. I'm trapped. I'm scared. I've started counting everything in numbers. I don't know why. I guess it gives me a sense of stability. Two weeks. Twelve days. Four walls. Ten toes. One girl. Twelve years.

I can't sleep at night. I lay awake outside shivering in the cold and watch the other children around me lie around half naked, smothered in grime and fear. How long until I look like them? How long until I am nothing more than ribs and rags? Another invisible beggar has joined the streets, but this beggar doesn't want to beg for coins. She wants to beg for her freedom, her home, her father and for her best friend, Mukti.

Even the streets have built up walls. I'm

trapped in an open world that I can't escape from.

They whisper to me, "Run away."

But I can't, because these walls enclose me in. I keep screaming, hoping anyone will hear me, but no matter how many times I scream I know I am the only one who hears it, because the walls lock it in.

So I lie here counting.

Two weeks. Twelve Days. Four walls. Five walls. Six walls. Infinite walls.

I set down my journal and banged my head against the solid wall behind me. I remembered how it felt enclosed within those walls, but this wall, the wall behind me, it wasn't trapping me in. My hand found the pen tucked in my shirt and began scribbling.

Thursday, July 28, 2005

Home Towards Freedom

It has been a few more hours since I escaped into the unknown. My legs need another break already. They feel like the watery jelly that my stomach no longer digests. They served us that wiggly slop once a week. It tasted like sugar mixed with blood. Just thinking of the smell makes me want to vomit, but my stomach would have nothing to give.

My whole body has gone numb. I can't even tell if I'm tired anymore or if it's just the same fatigue I've felt for the past three years. The water never stops dripping down my face. No matter how many times I *wipe them with the sleeve of my jacket, more tears keep coming.*

It must be between midnight and two in the morning, as the streets are empty and quiet. I can see the moon through the smoggy sky. It's shining brighter than it ever has before. I had planned on escaping the night it was full. That way there is the most light to guide me. Tonight, its only job is to take me home to freedom.

Wherever she is, I know Mukti is guiding me too. I miss her so much. The day she left Nirega seems so long ago. But she has never felt so close to my heart.

I flipped through my journal and searched for my old stories and memories of my best friend, but soon remembered they were left behind with my old journal in the slums.

When I thought of *home* I didn't think of the dirty slums. I thought of my village, *Nirega*, where Mukti and I used to be free together. I had no idea where she was or what she was doing, but I could still hope she took my advice: be confident in yourself and in us. Hopefully, one day we would find each other again, and it would be as though we never left each other. Our friendship was forever.

I began writing again.

I do still worry about her, though. Through the hard times I was her rock. I kept her face above water, and when I felt myself drowning, she did the same for me.

I can feel her pain from worlds away and

somehow I know she is suffering too. I knew the day she left there was something wrong. I didn't know what this world could do to girls our age. But now that I do, I am scared for her. This is no world for a girl.

I hope she's safe. I hope she's still holding onto a sliver of hope, because that's what keeps me breathing each night. I hope she has something that keeps her face above the water, and I hope she still knows that she always has me. Even though we are worlds apart, in this moment, she is still my rock. She will always be my rock. And one day we will be together again.

I remembered the day she left. My home was with Mukti, wherever she was, and I wondered if she thought about me as much as I thought of her.

The day she left I was in the city with my father. I remembered that off feeling when I returned to the Nirega. There was a low murmur among the villagers and a distant fear hovering above the fields. I lay on the roof alone, waiting. I could feel the hollow home beneath me.

Anita-masi walked by and saw me.

"Ruchita, darling? Is that you?"

I looked over and greeted her with a smile.

"Hi, Anita-masi! How are you?"

Her usual charm was missing. And I quickly lost mine.

"Come down from there, beta."

Hesitantly, I climbed down.

"Have you heard?"

The wind couldn't travel faster than the gossip of the village, but it still beat me. I was the last one to know and it nearly killed me. Anita-masi had to catch me as my knees buckled and I collapsed to the ground. Her soft words only made me feel numb. My strength crumbled like my insides. The holes that Mukti had once filled now reopened. The wind blew through my weak, porous body and knocked me to the ground.

The next few weeks I struggled to pick myself back up. My biggest escape was my journal that I wrote in to pass the time. I didn't have the physical passages anymore, as I had left it in the slums. But I still remembered those last passages.

Thursday, May 9, 2002

Storm

The wind is swirling outside my house, tearing down every tree, uprooting every root and rocking every home. This little house of mine is shaking. The windows are cracking, bound to shatter at any moment. The door is slamming violently in the wind. It howls like dying, screeching crows. Smack! The door slams shut, locking me in. Outside I can see the sky shivering, covered in smog.

My father enters through the broken door. His shirt is torn, shredded, and I can see the blood seeping through the cotton where his heart beats. His dark face is hidden, so I can't read his emotions. In the corner I hide from his unpredictability, waiting and praying. Like the swinging door, he could slam any moment. His anger vibrates in waves throughout the empty home. Its walls are weak and tired, but I pray they will stand a little longer and protect me from the storm outside. I'm just not ready to face it. I'm not ready to face the wind that screams my name and tells me my world is falling apart.

The windows are shaking again, but this time it's not the wind that's pressing against their fragile skin. The river has overflown. I watch the water rise, flooding my village, and I begin counting, for the walls will only hold so much longer. I find my father's strong hand and squeeze it tight. When the water bursts into my home, at least I know I will have him by my side.

And so I'll be saved.

I missed my old journal. Without it, my past felt distant, like a dream. Now all I had were the passages from my recent past. I sighed, flipping through the journal entries. They reminded me why I so desperately needed to escape.

Sunday, December 8, 2002

Everything here is weird. I'm still not used to it. The abandoned building we sleep in is almost nicer than the slums, but I share it with thirty other kids. Each day they give us a quota for the street money we have to get, and a man named Srinivas makes sure we meet it too or we aren't given food that night. If we keep failing to meet the quota, we get the high hand. The first few nights the men kept coming over to me when I was sleeping to make sure I was okay. They didn't want me to get spooked and run off or get hurt. Now I'm starting to think I'll get hurt either way.

Saturday, December 28, 2002

<u>Mine</u>

The sunrise pulls me out of a restless sleep, into the streets, and soon I feel the sunset pulling me back in. We have to be back before dark or they beat us. In the darkness, we are stripped of our day's work, coin by coin, rupee by rupee, and we are sent to bed.

He handed me a shiny golden coin. I squeezed it. The sensation almost brought me to tears. It was mine. I had earned it and it was mine. Something was mine for once. In a few hours it wouldn't be. In a few hours that coin and me would be no different. We would both be possessions in the hands of someone else, unable to possess anything of our own. We had nothing. We were nothing.

A tear slipped from my face, as the coin slipped from my hand and landed in his. I ran from the room and curled my knees into my chest and started to bawl. Tarun found me and hugged me.

"Just wait. I'll find you something that will be yours. And no one can take it from you. They'll have to go through me first!"

I laughed and let my face fall on his shoulder to fall asleep.

The next page was the first real one in my journal. Up to that point, I had been collecting scraps of paper and hiding them in a safe place. Once I had my journal I felt like I had an old piece of me again. I grinned, remembering that day.

*(I don't know what day of the week it is, but a nice
lady on the street told me the date)*
January 1, 2003

<u>A New Beginning</u>

My insides are about to burst with excitement! I
skipped today for the first time in ages, because
today, finally, I have something that is mine. I know
he stole it, but I don't care.

I forgot how much I love to write. I missed the
feeling of losing myself in my story. Some think
writing is work, but not to me. When my hands write
words and transport me into my thoughts, I forget
any other world exists. I forget my own reality. It's
almost an escape. Almost. I don't know how I get so
entirely sucked into this world that doesn't exist, and
yet I don't know why I ever leave it, either. I could write
and write forever, and never return. But if I never
returned I wouldn't be able to feel this relief. This
breath of freedom. This happiness that my body fills
with as the tip of the pen meets the page. And I would
do anything for that feeling.

Tarun thinks I am crazy to want to write so
much. But he also admires that I can. He can't read or
write. Like most of the kids here, he never went to
school. So I promised I would teach him one day.

Baba always told me to stop wasting my time with
my journal.

"It's such a waste for a girl to spend so much time
with her pretty face hidden in a book," he used to say.
But I hid my face in my book anyway.

I flipped through the pages until I found a passage I knew very well.

January 20, 2004

<u>Fort</u>

Street performing is nothing like dance. We don't move to a beat or finish to applause. We bend and crack for the ungrateful, waiting for their spare coins to bounce our way. When I look up I see turned heads. I see turned backs. I step over, spit on the ground and wish to hide behind my shalwar. But the strings above me keep yanking me, moving me. And before I have time to catch my breath, I bend and crack once more.

I remember when I used to dance for myself. I danced for my Baba too, because he always admired that talent of mine. He told me I learned to dance before I could walk. When I started Bharatnatyam[12], my father also made me learn Kathak, which I hated. But it made my father happy so I never complained. I knew if I kept dancing, he wouldn't take away my journal.

It's weird now looking back on my trips to the city. It's weird that I never paid attention to the beggars before. I know they were still there. They are always there—roaming the streets endlessly. But I guess I never really understood who they were. I never thought about them or their

---

[12] Bharatnatyam- another form of Indian classical dance originated in the temples of Tamil Nadu

suffering. I never thought how I made them feel when I looked the other way. Now I know, because I see the same faces run from me. I feel so exposed and vulnerable being put on display day after day, and yet they make me feel invisible, too.

I was recently moved to a new location. I don't have to dance in half rags anymore, because they gave me a beautiful lehenga choli, stitched with falling mirrors and faded red and blue sashes. The tourists even applause! They give us more money too.

Sometimes I pretend I'm a princess dancing for the common people because it makes me feel better and I hate myself less.

Every day I hear threats. I am polluting "their" country. But it's my country too, so I keep dancing...as if I have a choice. And when they call me "trash," I close my eyes and remember the girl playing in her beloved village. I remember those early morning sunrises on top of the roof with Mukti and for a moment I remember I am human, and they can't tell me otherwise.

I flipped to one of my latest entries, suddenly feeling sad that I was leaving. The streets had been my life for the past three years, and although I wouldn't miss the cold construction site or the hours of begging for worthless coins, I would miss the family I was leaving behind.

Saturday, July 16, 2005

Tonight is two nights before the moon is full again. A part of me wants to forget everything about this place, while another feels as if I am betraying my

70

friends. So I'm torn. I'm torn between forgetting the pain and remembering those who helped me through it. I feel so guilty abandoning them after all they've done for me.

Yet, I know that if I take them with me, I'll end up where I started. I wish I could say goodbye, though. But the risk is too big. For once I have to think of what is best for me, and I know it can't be more painful than the life I'm living.

A soft wind brought shivers to my knees. I couldn't let the guilt weigh me down. I needed to move on before they realized I was gone.

I kept running even though I didn't know where I was going. Rickshaws and mopeds raced by, slapping me in the face with a cold rush of wind. Their bright yellows and greens flashed in the corners of my eyes. Ripped posters on the cement walls cluttered together. They were plastered with famous actors in movies that I would never see. Old, dilapidated street shops yawned as I ran past. They were like the elderly watching the world's excitement from afar, no longer able to keep up with its excitement.

A part of me hoped that if I ran far enough I would end up at my father's doorstep, in the safety of his arms. I kept telling myself the hardest part was over. I escaped, right? And yet a part of me knew the hardest part wouldn't be leaving but coming back.

I sighed. I ran towards the past, but I was running right through it. I could dress up in my old clothes, but they'd fall off my bony shoulders. I could laugh and play, but I'd never play in the fields with Mukti again. I could reach for my past, but it would slip through my grasp.

When I reached my father's doorstep, I would have to accept that this was me now. I couldn't scrape off this plastered skin. I so badly wanted to remember who I had been. But now I needed to focus on who I could be.

If I had stayed…if I hadn't escaped…I knew what my fate was. Every time my brothers were handicapped and my sisters were taken by brothel owners, I saw my imminent future unfold.

As the night went on, I found myself needing more breaks. My legs were jelly and the emotions in my head weighed me down.

I opened my journal to a random entry.

April 2003

Today I went from car to car. The rusty white vans and light grey Toyotas spat out gas at every speed bump. Their tires wailed from the rocky roads, as they tried to weave in and out of traffic. I watched two mopeds with a refrigerator balanced between them, moving in sync. Bicycles carried pots, mangos and coconuts for kilometers. Rickshaws were filled with overflowing passengers.

Today was like any other day in the city. Drivers slammed their horns warning the buses they were coming through. Skimpy boys rode barefoot on their bikes as they could afford only the bike, not shoes too.

Today, I saw something new. A dark navy car with tinted windows rolled past. I tapped the window, wondering what was behind the glass. I watched a small girl with hair like the sun smile back at me. Her pale hand held out a Rs.100 bill. Her driver lectured her for giving it to me, and she rolled up the window.

I heard someone coming and quickly left the wall. The image of the girl stuck with me as I ran through the night. I imagined her life, where she lived, if she went to school. Her life was so different from mine, but what made *us* so different? We were both young girls in the same world. Why did she get to live her life, while I had to suffer through mine? I would do anything to be on the other side of that glass—to be the one handing the bill instead of taking it.

I used to think I was at the bottom of the bottom. My father had always despised the slums. So when we lost everything and had to move there, I knew we were living his biggest fear. In the village he shamed beggars, yelling at them for being greedy and lazy as if this were the reason they were on the streets. I knew differently.

I opened my journal and wrote in anger.

July 18, 2004

A Million Bodies—One Pit

Born out of a phosphorescent light brighter than the
whitest hell
we land in a pair of coarse, caring hands.
Eyes, as loving as every mother's, hold us tightly.
Bare, we lie there innocently, waiting.
Our throats, already dry, choke on endless debris.
Enchanted, we reach towards the baby-blue sky, far
and wondrous.
It's a blinding light that showers us from above.
We're surrounded by millions, all writhing in the
same pit.
High above, we watch others try to climb the high dirt
walls.

Struggling, they lose their grip and fall back to the
bottom.
We don't know why, but we want to climb too.
We want to reach that blue sky and discover the world
outside,
Even if we fall.

But still inside the pit we crawl.
We roam the streets.
The dirt wind whips us in the face.
We follow our older brothers and sisters to the edge of
the city.

Our bare feet stomp on the pile of trash as we rummage
to find something of value.
The hot sun blazes down on our bent backs.
Our stomachs moan, upset, as we breathe in our
malodourous future,
Because we know this is our bottomless pit
And we'll never escape it.

My shadow danced on the walls. I searched for the moon to guide me, but the only light came from the fading streetlights. Where was I? I was so lost, and it was far past three in the morning. No one else dared linger in the streets. Except the dogs. My feet stopped dead in my tracks. At the end of the alley, I spotted a pack of dogs—starving and wild. They sniffed a pile of rubbish like savages. Slowly backing up, I held my breath and ran in the other direction.

I wished Tarun was there with me, because he would know what to do. Flipping through the pages again, I found a passage about him.

Tarun taught me one of his tricks today. He's the best pickpocket. I used to be against stealing, and I even scolded Tarun for it. Now that seems silly. The streets change you. The rules are different here. Nothing is justified. Because there is no justice. All that exists is the physical hunger eating up my insides. I resisted the temptation to steal for only so long.

Today I needed to bring in extra money. I came up short of my quota yesterday.

Entering a café shop, I was immediately taken aside by Tarun.

"Never steal from here. They spot you like vultures."

I grumbled and crossed my arms against my chest. We aren't always thieves.

That memory made me recall another one.

Today I found a coin on the sidewalk! It isn't worth much. I mean, clearly. No one else bent down to pick it up. At first I just walked by. The sun was going down, and I was now a few blocks away. I knew I had to be quick on my feet. I knew if I went to pick it up I probably wouldn't make it back in time, so I almost left it in hopes that it would still be there tomorrow. My growling stomach begged to differ. I sprinted back and picked up the coin, then went to the café I always passed. I stared at all the creamy sweets and breathed in their wonderful aroma. The café doesn't have tables or chairs, just a counter stacked with mounds of delicious cookies and fried sweets beckoning those who walk by. An old radio was playing a pop song I had never heard before.

When I walked up to the counter the baker looked me up and down. I asked for the cheapest thing he had and handed him the coin. At that moment I didn't care what I ate. I just wanted to eat something and fast. He took my coin with a warm smile. The second he looked at it in his palm, his face turned red.

Had I done something wrong?

I stopped to remember. To this day I was still furious. He had no right to take my coin.

"How dare you come into my shop with a stolen coin and beg for food! Get out!"

"But…but…it's my coin. It's my money!" I couldn't comprehend how he could steal my money and then accuse me of being the thief! "I didn't steal it! I found it!"

He scowled. "Leave or I'll call the police and tell them I've found a thief in my shop!"

His fat finger pointed towards the street. I didn't have time to argue. I stormed out of the shop without looking back.

I laughed as I looked at the corner of the page in my journal. I had drawn the shopkeeper with an arrow through his head and a picture of me beside him eating all of his pastries.

I stumbled through the gate and into the building entrance, almost knocking Srinivas over. He held out *his hand. At first I thought he was going to smack me, but I realized he just wanted the money that was due. I gave it to him and pushed past to find a spot on the floor beside Tarun. I ranted to him about everything. He just laughed at me "for being so dumb." Apparently, the same thing happens to him all the time. The only difference was Tarun usually had stolen the money.*

I still hate the shopkeeper. I should be used to people taking things from me by now, but I'm not. This world has taken everything from me. My mother, Mukti, my village, my father, and now a coin! Aiyoo Haaladdu[13] ondhu naanya kooda iralillaa! Aaahh...I can't even keep a stupid coin with me. I am so mad.

Anger made me want to leave, but fear made me go.

It was the fear of my future that made me run. I watched the older girls trapped in the same cycle and cried each night. Their bloody faces haunted my dreams. I saw the managers drag them out by the arms, never to be seen again.

I skidded to a stop. Above me, a street sign in bold black letters read *Dharvi Depot Road*. It was the same sign I walked past every day for almost a year. It was the street leading to a field of hundreds of tin huts. Among those hundreds was mine. I was steps away from freedom.

---

[13] *Aiyyoooo Haaladdhu*- means "oh rotten or spoilt"

TRAITOR
(Mukti)

I woke up to a spinning ceiling. The room focused, and I remembered where I was. Darshan had treated me with such care. It had been a week since my accident. The first two days were a blur, but as my head began to clear, Premela was able to fill in the gaps.

I squirmed as she took a hot rag and wiped the blood from my still-oozing cuts.

"Darshan took you here himself you know. He thinks highly of you. He says you are a hard worker."

I stared back at her, stunned. "Me?"

"Yes, beta, you."

I couldn't help but feel a sense of pride. It had been awhile since someone appreciated me.

"Why did he take me here? The jamadars always make us work through our injuries and sickness."

Premela, who was Darshan and Shubar's housemaid, shrugged. "I don't know." She continued bandaging my wounds.

"Ow!" I yelped. The ointment stung.

"Wait here. I'll bring you some food from the kitchen."

I sat on the counter waiting, unsure of what to do. Premela reappeared carrying a bowl full of rice and dhal. I watched the steam rising from the food, and I felt tears in my eyes.

I filled my hands with the warm rice.

"Would you like a roti too, beta?"

I looked up in disbelief. Her eyebrow arched, waiting for an answer. The rice dropped from my hands and I began to sob.

Later that day Premela led me to an empty room. Blankets and a pillow had been spread out on the floor. When I was half asleep, I regained some of my memory.

I recalled walking with Premela through the house. Richly colored carpets embraced the marble floors. Lavish couches with plump cushions surrounded a wooden table. A bowl of spicy cashews and cup of fried namkeen had been left out. Bronze lamps that only dimly lit the room hung from the salmon painted walls. As we passed the bathroom, I espied a glimmering bowl with silver handles. Fascinated, I turned the handles and gasped as water poured from the silver pipe. I marveled at the idea of water being a mere twist of the hand away. What a life!

I spotted a girl close by. She looked a thousand years old. Her hair was a mess and her peeling skin was covered with scars, new and old. Beneath her eyes, dark bags hung low. I noticed the raw cuts in her arms and legs, still oozing blood. As she struggled to walk, limping like an invalid, I realized she was staring straight at me.

"Premela, who is that girl staring at me?"

Premela laughed. "That's your reflection, beta."

"No?"

I watched the timid girl. Her fearful eyes stared back,

and I wondered when it was that I had lost myself.

A week later I had the chance to see myself again. Premela had been playing with my hair and handed me a mirror. With my hair tightly tied back, I could see my bruises were fading. Premela turned the mirror to show the side of my braid, and I smiled to thank her. My lips immediately closed when I saw my crooked, rotten teeth.

Darshan stopped by to check on me often, but as usual he barely spoke a word. I was glad Shubar was out of town that week. His absence is what permitted me to stay in the house. I took a sip of my warm water. Footsteps echoed from the hall. Anxiously I looked up, hoping to see Darshan. My heart stopped when I saw him: Shubar.

His face was red. The bump in his throat trembled.

"*Bevarsi Tholagu illindaa!* Bevarsi[14] get out of this place!"

But my body couldn't move.

"Did you not hear me? Get out! Get out!"

The hairs on my arms and legs stood up. I watched Darshan standing against the wall in the hallway with his head bowed. He didn't hesitate to let Shubar throw me out. Finally, I managed to stand up and rushed out.

As I left, I imagined the slab of granite causing me to topple over again. I couldn't breathe. I wanted to scream. I hated Darshan for being such a coward, but I was no better than him. I was just as much a coward, wasn't I?

Once I reached the door, the yelling began.

---

[14] *Bevarsi*- means one who is abandoned

"How could you let her stay here? I told you to never let a Dalit enter our home!" Shubar fumed. "I created this business. It's my company and my rules. Did you forget that?"

"She's just a kid. She could have been seriously hurt if I kept her out there in that heat." Darshan replied.

"So what?" Shubar spat.

"I was looking out for *your* business, Bhai! We can't have another death on our hands! What do you think the magistrate would do? You can't run this business like there's no one watching anymore! You lost that privilege in 1996!"

"I told you I have the police back on our side! We're safe from the press. If you were a good brother you would trust me, not stab me in the back! You've been just as much a part of this business as I have. If not more! You're starting to sound like Jayanti!"

"You have no right to say her name!" Darshan's screamed. "I helped you bring this business back. Not because I believed in it! But because I owed you. I've stuck around because of Jayanti and because family is supposed to stick together. But I swear the day will never come when I will be kissing your filthy feet! I may have followed you here with empty pockets and a deal to finish but I've done my part. I don't need you or this business anymore! *Ninna Sahawaasa bedappaa!* I hate being associated with you."

"And what would you do? Jayanti left you, Darshan! You have nowhere to go. You can threaten me and pretend you have the guts to leave, but we both know very well that you aren't a man to keep your word." He paused, then snapped, "I'm your older brother and you will treat me with respect!"

Darshan snarled, "I'll stay when you start giving *me*

some respect, and I won't watch you work these children to death."

"They are *Dalits*[15]! They were born to do this work! Let them work out their own karma, Darshan! Stop trying to humanize them. This is the way it is. You know that. It always has been. We are *helping* them! If it weren't for us they have no food to survive. We feed them. We give them a place to sleep. They need the work! And if they don't do it who will? Not us!" Through the window I watched Shubar press his fingers to his temple. "Where is this coming from, Darshan? You've been in this business for years!"

"Some day this whole business is going to crush you. Karma goes both ways, Bhai, and you're going to get what you deserve."

"How exactly?"

"Maybe in your next life you'll be the Dalit, suffering in the hot sun and breaking rocks all day."

Shubar stepped across the room and I heard a crash. Darshan tumbled to the ground.

I limped from the window and across the fiery rocks. In the distance I saw the workers moving like tired ants in the sand. When I joined them, I was bombarded with questions. I was so exhausted that I had to sit down. My chest ached for air. It was hard to breathe.

"What's it like inside?"

"Is it true that they have running water and electricity?"

---

[15] Dalits refers to the class of people called Untouchables. They have a long history of being highly discriminated against in India and are generally made to work in low-pay "dirty" jobs.

"How come you got to go inside? What makes you so special?"

"Do they have marble floors and brass statues?"

"What food did they give you?"

"Did he hurt you?"

"Did he touch you?"

I realized I had been in the main house for almost a week and no one knew what happened to me. The possibility that Darshan was taking advantage of me had never crossed my mind. I hated them for assuming it.

I overheard Sandhya's mom scolding my best friend. "Don't talk to her! She's not pure anymore. She's tainted. You could be next." She said it half in disgust and half in fear for her own daughter. "If I see you talk to her again…"

I heard another remark: "She's a disgrace."

"She can never be married now."

My eyes blinked back tears. I didn't understand why they were mad at me for something I had no control over. I felt claustrophobic in this crowd of strangers.

Suddenly an arm pushed through the crowd and took my hand.

"Thanks, Priya." I gasped.

"Come, come. Let's get out of here. I can't believe they did that to you! And after all you have been through! I will talk to them tonight."

"Priya, please don't. It's just gossip."

Her eyes narrowed, and I watched them fill with tears.

"He didn't, Priya. I swear."

"You can tell me anything, Mukti."

"He *didn't*."

She hugged me tight. I could feel her fighting back her emotions.

"I was so scared, Mukti. I didn't know what was happening to you."

I squeezed her hand.

"I've never been better, Priya. Really." I smiled.

We strolled through the rocky mounds and tried to hide in the crevasses of the mountain. Yet, wherever I turned, there was someone's eye on me. I hated the attention. The rumors were hideous. I wished I had a shawl to cover my face.

Atop the stacks of newly sliced granite cobbles, I saw Raj and Arjun looking at me. They both chewed on neath plants to clean their teeth. Arjun's navy blue collar sagged low, showing his thin wet chest. Raj's hair was grey from the mound of debris on his head. Wearing a frown, he sat on the cobbles with his feet dangling off the side.

"What's wrong?" I asked.

Priya murmered, "They were really worried about you when you were gone. The jamadars would beat them when they asked about you. We had no idea what was going on. Raj was mad at you. But he just misses you, that's all."

"I'm fine now, guys. Don't worry," I said.

I walked over to the pile of cobbles and put my hands on their knees.

"I missed you guys when I was gone! I wished I could have visited you, so you knew that I was okay." I sighed looking back and forth between them. "I was thinking of you two the entire time."

"You're a liar!" Raj shouted, "When Mama left you promised that you would never leave us. Ever!"

A tear fell down my cheek.

"I'm so sorry."

Arjun spoke up. "Sandhya's mom told us not to trust you. Is it true? Are you one of them now? You wouldn't do that, Mukti, would you?"

Over my shoulder, I saw Priya walking towards us.

"Raj. Arjun. You should be ashamed of yourself for thinking such things. Stop being ridiculous!"

"No! Wait," I pleaded. I didn't want them to leave being mad at me. "Arjun, you saw me fall. I would have come back sooner, but I had to get better. Get better so I could come back to you."

Priya interrupted me, "Mukti, you're not helping. Don't make them more worried."

Sighing, I tried one more time.

"Well if you two won't smile for me I'll have to bring out my magic hands!"

"No! Don't tickle us!" Arjun shouted.

I reached for Raj. He ran away.

"No! Hahaha. I told you, you were evil! They've turned you into the tickle monster!"

"Na-na-na-na-na, you can't get me!" Arjun and Raj taunted me by wiggling their fingers near their ears.

I laughed in relief.

"That's enough," Priya instructed. "Mukti will have to use her evil magic later after we finish our work."

She handed me a wedge and shim for splitting the stone. I groaned, dreading the work.

The laborers in the quarry were given jobs based on their skills, age and gender. My general work was in cobble making, which the majority of the children did. My mother's daily jobs included lifting debris, cleaning, loading, unloading and other unskilled work. Semi-skilled workers made big boulders or holes in the granite beds. Men were used to operate our two rusty cranes and compressors.

I positioned myself on my knees. The large square slab of granite was in between my legs. Placing a wedge nail on the stone, I grabbed the hammer and slammed down on it. I'd pound it until the wedge was deeper into the rock. I did this in five other places so it would be easier to split the granite. Avoiding Priya's worried look, I kept my head down and stayed focused.

My brothers continued stacking the new broken pieces into tall rows.

"Arjun! Careful up there! That pile isn't sturdy. You're going to knock it over if you keep running around on it!" Priya shouted.

Raj laughed at him. Arjun jumped down, causing the pile to shake. He ran off past the towers of granite and disappeared.

Priya sighed. "I didn't mean to get him upset."

The clucks and bangs from the steel hitting the rock echoed louder and louder. Priya's face was soaked in sweat. Her forehead looked glossy as the sun bounced off it. I saw her look up.

"We should take a break soon. Your hands are starting to shake. I don't want you to overdo it."

The sounds of nails chiseling into stone gave me a headache. I didn't protest, but I also didn't want to leave the job unfinished.

"There's only a few more slabs left."

We were paid by the number of slabs cut, and we needed to meet our ratio to get food tokens. The stacks of cobbles and granite had grown tremendously high over the past few hours. Our group of twelve had turned a pile of forty slabs of granite into three hundred and sixty.

I patted my hands against my shalwar pants to get the dust off before following Priya.

She offered to do my hair. I was filled with a bubbling

excitement. I let my sister's gentle fingers separate my hair into five strands, intertwining the plaits from the left front of my head and curving them all the way down the side to my right shoulder. Now that my mother's hair was nothing but thin grey strands, Priya always offered to play with mine. I never said no.

As we rested, we talked about how much the quarry had changed. The landowners had recently expanded it, and now we had twice as much work to do. It seemed as if every time we caught up with our work, we'd find ourselves with an even bigger load. More people came to the quarry every day, making it hard to keep track of everyone, especially the workers who didn't speak Kannada.

When she finished braiding Priya smiled.

"You look beautiful."

A month passed and I stopped noticing the harsh stares. At first all I wanted to do was run up to my roof in Nirega and cuddle with Ro. I daydreamed of Ro often, making up conversations between us. She'd refuse to let me feel bad for myself. She told me that I had to face everyone and stop letting them tear me down.

After weeks of hiding from my problems, I finally listened to Ro's advice when Sandhya came to me sobbing again. Her mother had spent the last thirty minutes scolding her.

"She keeps telling me that you are a bad influence and dangerous, but I won't listen to her! Don't worry, Mukti. I won't let her get to me. It isn't fair what she is doing. She keeps spreading those rumors about you. I know Darshan didn't, but she won't believe me. I'm so sorry. You don't deserve this. I just can't stand her saying these things about you." She sobbed lightly against my chest.

We sat on the banyan tree, swinging our legs. I got lost in thought.

I stormed off, leaving my friend shouting after me. "Mukti! Where are you going?"

I was going to end this. Sandhya's mother knelt by the water pump. Her cup of water went flying into the dirt as my hand smacked it from her hands. Tears swelled in her eyes and she begged me for forgiveness. Everyone in the quarry gathered around as she confessed her lies about me.

I giggled at my wishful imagination.

When I came back to reality, I approached Sandhya's mother tentatively. She was wearing a plain brown sari, one of the gloomiest saris I'd ever seen. Her saggy frown turned into a snarl when she saw me coming towards her.

"What do you want?"

I almost turned around right then and ran away. But in my head Ro screamed at me to stay.

"Auntie, I want you to know the truth that's all. We haven't talked since my accident, and I thought you might want to know what happened."

"You thought wrong. And I don't want you hanging around my daughter anymore, either," she spat.

"He didn't hurt me. His maid Premela took care of me. I was kicked out when Shubar came home."

She shook her head. She heard me but wasn't listening.

"I wasn't raped!" My lips trembled. The thought scared

me out of my skin, and I started to cry.

She looked up but said nothing.

I ran to Priya only to find her in a corner coughing, struggling for breath. It was the first of many symptoms to come.

Several nights later, I woke up to the sound of teeth chattering. I wiped my eyes and glanced around the room. In the corner was the outline of a girl. I crawled over to Priya, who was shivering as if it were zero degrees outside. Confused, I wiped the sweat from her forehead. Rain made pitter-patter sounds on the roof.

"Priya, what's wrong?"

"Nothing. I'm fine. I'm just cold. Don't worry about it. Go back to sleep."

"You didn't sleep last night, either."

"Okay," she said with a sigh. I could see she was worried. "I've been getting these random spurts of chills. But they go away. Honestly, it is nothing to worry about."

I whispered, making sure not to wake the others. "Come back to sleep with me. How long have you been getting these chills?"

"About a week. It's fine. It is probably just a simple cold that will pass."

Suddenly she squinted and pressed her fingers to her temple. Her forehead creased. Just watching her made me cringe.

"Priya! Are you okay? What is it?"

"It hurts, Mukti. It really hurts." She banged her head against the wall.

I placed my palm on her forehead. She was burning up.

"Aie! My head feels like it's splitting open, Mukti."

"Priya you have a major fever! You have to rest. You can't work tomorrow."

"No. I'm fine. It's only at night. I'll be fine. Honestly."

Once her headache subsided she went back to sleep. I lay there with my head against the wall for another hour. I knew she wasn't being honest with me. She never lets other people take care of her. She took pride in her independence, but someday this was going to hurt her.

I closed my eyes and felt a deep longing. I wondered how Ro was doing in Nirega, if she was still going to school. I wished she were there with me to comfort Priya. She would know what to say. She always did. I imagined her warm, lasting hugs. Oh, how I missed them. My hands fell over my heart. Somewhere far in the distance I felt a warm connection.

I knew she was thinking of me, too.

SAFETY
(Ruchita)

I raced through the myriad of tents, underground alleyways and corrugated steel shacks packed together like sardines and let my instincts take over. All the homes were no bigger than two fishermen's boats. The skinny paths were streams of rubbish and barely passable. I remembered my first day in the slums. The stench was so strong, I couldn't breathe. Now it smelt like home.

I tried to think of my journal entry that day.

May 11, 2002

Slum. Slum. Slum.

The word rolls off my tongue weird like my father's commonly overcooked rice. The word is still edible, but it takes awhile to chew, and when it goes down it's lumpy in my throat. I fell back on my old habits, unsure of what else to do. So here I am, sitting on the roof of my new slum home, writing in my journal because I don't know what else to do.

Slum. Slum. Slum.

This tin roof gives me a clear view of the kilometers of slums that reach into the distance, into the horizon where they disappear. I can't really see where it all ends, but I know it must, somewhere. Everything does. That is something I've learned recently. Nothing lasts forever, not even friendships or family.

Everything feels strange, like I'm in a dream, not in my own reality. I'm in someone's shoes, living their life, not mine. I guess I can say the walls have fallen. I'm officially surrounded by vulnerability and the open, unsympathetic world. The air stings my brittle skin. Who knows how the world will treat me.

I never thought I'd be here. I never thought I'd have to say goodbye to my village and my old life, but here I am breathing in the city grime, surrounded by muck and clutter, dirt and trash, gossip and tears, hate and crime.

The slums were nothing like my village, and the shack I slept in for months was nothing like a home. I had only dirt and walls to keep me company while my dad was away gambling our lives away. And yet I learned to love it anyway. Our roof consisted of scraps of tin and bright blue tarps that my father and I dragged from an abandoned construction site. I spent my first monsoon season cringing underneath the roof, praying it would hold. The pots and pans clanged against the brick wall from the wind gusts. Yet, I still missed its shelter.

I slowed my pace and thought about one of the last entries in my old journal.

November 10, 2002

Chipping Coin

I'm worried about him again. He keeps promising things will get better, but each time he says so I see his face grow a little paler and his spirit a little darker. He is falling deeper into a well he can't climb out of. I wish he would stop disappearing into the city, because

93

each time he comes back, he arrives more empty-handed than when he left. Yet, it's his only hopeless hope...because he's a chipping coin. When its metal begins to rust, he will erode with it. He bids on fabricated chance. His coin is chipping and his head is chipping with it. Without a golden reputation to feed his esteem, he's losing his balance. He's caustic and I fear the hastening speed of this corrosion.

My head felt woozy. My father represented everything I hated about the world I lived in.

I didn't want to walk back into the addiction, the loss and the gambling. His life had become a game, and he couldn't stop rolling the dice. When we were robbed of my mother, we spent every last rupee trying to save her. It wasn't being alone that scared my father—it was being poor. So every weekend he travelled to the city in hopes of gaining back his money.

It took only a few months for him to gamble away everything—even our home. Refusing to let the village see us scraping the bottom of the bowl, my father moved us to his old city. Without Mukti, Nirega didn't feel like home anymore anyway.

I thought Bangalore could be a fresh start; however, it only tempted my father more, causing his destructive habit to spiral completely out of control. He grew depressed and nothing else mattered but money. Not even his own daughter: his other shining prize. Then he lost me too. I can't imagine what that did to him.

Nervously, I walked through the slums until I saw a familiar face. His lips whispered something I couldn't make out.

"Ruchita? Is that you?"

I sighed in relief and greeted him with joy. "Gopal Uncle! It's been so long! How are you?"

Oddly, he stepped back as if in fear. I took another step forward and he took another step back.

"Your father," he hesitated, "don't live here anymore...assuming he who you looking for."

"Doesn't live here anymore? When did he leave?" I asked.

Gopal scrunched up his face in irritation. He never liked my father, but then again no one did. I can't blame them for that. My father refused to associate with any of them, walking around with his nose in the air and his chest out as if he were better.

When he talked to people in the city he never admitted living in the slums. Unless you caught him sleeping there, you wouldn't believe he did, either. He always made sure to look good—nothing like the bereft man he truly was. I never understood why he was so ashamed of our life. I loved it there, and looking around made me realize just how much I missed it.

Gopal confessed, "Two years ago he move to a new place...a much bigger place. I no heard from him in awhile."

"Do you know where it is?"

Gopal shifted his feet and made shapes in the dirt with his toes. "It's a couple kilometers from here. You could spot it in pitch darkness, though. It's like the sun, but bigger."

"What do you mean?" I remembered Gopal had always been a little weird. But he wasn't making any sense at all.

"So yellow. He and me went one time, but I no go in." Gopal never looked up from his feet. "He thinks he is better than me now. I no fit in."

"Can you help me find it?"

"Um, I think you go past field. The one my son and you go before. I don't know if you remember. It off of the main road. I remember the street starts with an *N*, but I no remember well. Sorry." He stared at his toes, embarrassed. Before I could say thank you, he went back inside without saying goodbye.

"Thank you!" I tried to make him hear in a whisper. Suddenly the slums didn't feel like home anymore.

I continued my journey half asleep. It took a few more hours. Eventually I found the neighborhood with giant homes. With the help of a few kind neighbors who all seemed to know my father well, I managed to find his new home.

Exhausted, I stumbled over a crushed can and almost dropped my journal. I grabbed its leathery skin as if my life depended on it. I tried to stay calm. As long as I had my journal, I still had my life in my own hands.

As the sun shot out its first rays of light, the sky turned a light purple. Finally I spotted it. I tilted my head and admired the old palm tree leaning on the side of the house, protecting it from the scorching sun. It was more vibrant mango than yellow.

My heart pounded in my chest. Gathering myself, I sat down and wrote in my journal. I needed to write down the feelings I wanted to forget. And I *could* forget them, because I knew they would always be here if I wanted to revisit them.

A New Home

*I think I found it! I don't want to get my hopes up,
though, not after the slums. I was so close and yet I
was still so far from finding my father. I'm nervous
all over again. I want to see him, but what if he doesn't
recognize me? What if he doesn't take me in?*

*The house itself is a dream. I stare at the
sandalwood door, but I don't know if I can open it.*

I stood up too fast. The blood rushed from my head.
Losing my balance, I leaned on the palm tree for support.

There was a little red gate at the front porch, and I
slowly pushed it open. It screeched. The front door looked
larger than before. My hand pressed its smooth wood, and the
next hour of my life flashed by.

*I can't describe my feeling when he opened the
door. We sobbed in each other's arms for an hour, and I
fell asleep on his couch. In my dream my father lived
in a castle. He was the Raaja. The King. And as Raaja
he ordered his soldiers to come rescue me. When they
found me, the entire castle turned into a giant party
and everyone was celebrating.*

*Our reunion wasn't extravagant, but it felt that
way. It was just as in my dream. After I woke up I
couldn't find Baba, so I explored the house. The kitchen
is amazing. A red woven carpet, with patterns like my
mother's hennas, covers the floor. A long dinner table*

*takes up the entire room! The six chairs are scooted in
so tight around it that they're mere centimeters from
the green walls. How weird. Six chairs and a long
table for one person. I don't understand why he needs
so much space. There was a chai coffee on the table. It
was cold, but still smelt sweet like home. I tried to read
the newspaper too but kept looking over my shoulder.
Old habits, I guess. I was afraid my father would
catch me and scold me.*

The hallway has many dangling picture frames, but none of the photos are of my mom or me. I wonder why. Maybe it hurts him too much to be reminded of the past. I know that feeling. Just wanting to forget.

When he came home, we sat around the tight kitchen table and talked all night.

"You've lost so much weight. When was the last time you've eaten?"

I looked at my scrawny wrists and shrugged, feeling humiliated. It was obvious he was ashamed of me. He smiled and added, "Don't worry, beta. You'll be back in no time."

He boiled a pot of water.

"I can do that, Baba," I offered. But he refused.

"And the new house?" I asked. I still didn't understand how he could go from the slums to this.

"Don't worry about it."

He let out a deep breath. "I was hoping to save that for later, Daeva—I mean Ruchita," he stumbled over the wrong name. "It's a long conversation and we have so much more to catch up on."

I nodded. It wasn't long before we were both sobbing again. I was in his arms, hugging him. I didn't think telling him about my life would be so hard. I had written about it a thousand times, but saying it out loud was different.

It must have been almost morning when he finally explained his name mishap.

"Things have...changed since you left." he started, "My life...well, it fell to pieces. I was alone. I had never felt so alone in my life. I had nothing. After your mom passed I still had you. But once you were gone too I grew very depressed. Every day I woke up and saw your pretty face, but you weren't there. And you weren't there to tuck in at night. I stopped getting up in the morning. And well, I never left the slums. Some people started to worry, but no one stopped in to ask questions. It wasn't until your Ba came by and took care of me that I realized I couldn't live the rest of my life alone." He paused. I saw the wrinkles on his forehead. They were new. He looked so much older now. His eyebrows had some grey in them. "I...I've met someone, Ruchita."

"Oh," was all I managed to say.

"She's beautiful and well educated. She reminds me of you in the way she speaks. Her name is Daeva. We've been married two years now."

I didn't say anything.

He looked at me, trying to read my face, then looked down.

"Is that how you paid for the house?" I murmured.

"It's her father's home. He is very ill, so Daeva is with him right now. She's the only child still living in her family."

The next minute of silence felt like an hour.

"It will be good for you to have a woman in your life again. At your age you need someone to model after. And you know, teach you how to act and cook and…"

I nodded but said nothing.

The sunlight beamed through the kitchen window. My father decided to show me where I would be staying. I lifted my chin and in a moment forgot our conversation. I had my own room! I couldn't believe it! There were cubbies where I could put my clothes, too. I had to remind my father that I didn't have anything. I took a shower, washing off the grime and sweat of the past three years. When I finished, I braided my hair. Maybe I really could have a new chance at life.

Instinctively, I wanted to run to the roof and share everything with my best friend. Wherever she was, I knew she could sense my happiness.

I pulled a sheet over me and lay down in my new room.

My father appeared in the doorway, "Ruchita? Are you still awake?"

"Yes, Baba?"

"There is something else that I have been meaning to tell you. Or give you."

He tried to smile but couldn't.

"Remember this?"

He held out an old, battered book.

My entire childhood! How could I forget? My jaw dropped. I wanted to scream for joy. I leapt up and grabbed it from his hands. Softly, my fingers traced the cover. I opened it and saw my first entry, in terrible handwriting.

"I can't believe you kept it," I whispered, choking back tears. "I never thought I would see this again."

"It was the only part of you I had left."

He added, "I confess that I read some of the passages. I missed you so much, and sometimes I felt like you were still with me. You truly are a beautiful writer."

"Thank you," I said, blushing.

"If only you put that much time into your dancing, you would be a Bollywood star by now," he said with a wink. He shut the door and left me to revisit my childhood.

I opened the book again.

My nam is Ruchita. I am sics. I luv wryteng. I am lerning how to writ in skul. I also luv dans. I am a danser. I liv with my mom and dad in Nirega. My home is the wun ad the end. That is how I rimembur which wun is min. My techur gav me this buk. She sad I shud writ down my thots in heer. But I wan tu writ storees an dra in heer tu. I am so esitid! I luk forwurd to wryteng in yu.

Bi,
Ruchita

I laughed at my spelling. Forgetting how exhausted I was, I started writing.

Wednesday, July 20, 2005

Safety

I found my father! I can't believe he is actually here! And he has my old journal too! My life is finally being put back together. Literally. I can combine my two journals! I'm excited to start my new life here. Baba hasn't changed much, but everything else has! I thought I would be coming back to my old life, but there is no part of my old life around here.

I miss my mother. My memories of her are fading, which scares me. I know this new woman will never replace her. He loved my mother so much. When she left us Baba always talked about his never-ending love for her. How could he suddenly love someone else? I know he still loves me, but I feel replaced. He was lonely, and I'm glad he found someone. I just hope he has room for me, too.

All of my old entries are still here! I can't believe it. The part of my old life that I thought was lost forever is still with me. Tomorrow I'm going to try to find a way to glue it to my new life. I'm so excited!

BROKEN
(Mukti)

The following afternoon, when the sun was still high in the horizon, we took a break from the overpowering heat. I finished my work in the field. For the first time in days I had enough time to get a real drink of water at the pump. I still envied Darshan and Shubar for their instant water, but I skipped on the rocky ground anyway, dodging sharp pebbles and my hair fluttering behind me.

The quarry felt awfully lonely. I remembered how it was looking back at my village, Nirega, from the rice fields. I'd see all the sprightly dots in the distance, and I'd never feel alone.

Returning to reality, I saw someone watching me on the outskirts of the quarry. Initially I cowered. The jamadars would beat us if we were caught taking breaks or wandering off. My lips curled up and I tasted the blood from their cracks. I took the risk and made even bigger strides towards the pump.

Then the man started walking towards me. My heart pounded, and I quickened my pace. He came closer and I noticed something different about him. He was no jamadar. The man had not spent much time in the sun; his skin was as pale as rice. Dirt smeared his dark blue jeans and black dress shoes, and I saw sweat through his nice cotton shirt. He waved at me.

I looked around. No one else was in sight. He kept waving to me. Behind him, there was a gap in the barbed wire where two swallows were perched. Their bright orange heads and blue backs stood out from the dull rock. The stranger stepped forward and the birds flew off.

At first I thought he might be an undercover policeman, but his genuine concern proved me wrong. The man didn't speak Kannada either. We had to use hand gestures. It took me awhile, but eventually I figured his name was something like *Jawn*. It sounded flat and plain coming off my tongue. I told him I had to leave or a jamadar would find me. His eyes narrowed as if he were sad. It was a strange look. He wasn't sad for himself. For some reason he was sad for me.

Before I slipped away, he handed me a Rs. 500 note. My jaw dropped. At first I wouldn't accept it. He grabbed my shaking hands and slipped it into them. I stood there motionless until he disappeared behind the mountain.

I stared at the bill. I imagined the house full of food I could buy with it. Then I found a big rock and hid it carefully beneath it. I grinned.

I finally reached the water pump and swiped my hand gently through the bucket of water. The echoing ripples subsided. The water settled and I saw a blurry reflection of myself. The girl looking back at me had changed again since I'd last seen her, in the main house. Her cheeks were lifted. Her eyes had resilience. I liked her.

I hurried back to Sandhya. Her silky hair was neatly tucked behind her ears. Dust covered her face, yet she looked captivating. Sweat beaded my forehead as we hammered away at the stubborn granite slabs and I told her everything. We chatted as the day wore on.

Suddenly, through the dust and smog I heard a distant coughing. It was a bloody sound. My heart sank. I ran towards it in a panic.

I locked my eyes on the limp, frail body on the ground. Her black hair fell across her face, covering beautiful eyes. They winced in pain as she gasped for air. Her body shivered.

Sanat was trying to give her water. I kneeled to the ground and we lifted her, carrying her out of the heat.

Behind us, eyes were watching. Through the oval window of the main house I espied Darshan. He stared at me. I looked away.

Sandhya blinked back the dust in the air, and I wiped Priya's pale face.

I knew what my sister had. I knew how deadly it could be. She had all the symptoms. We slept outside on a cement floor. Hundreds of mosquitoes swarmed over our bodies every night.

She whispered in my ear, "I have a headache again."

I knew she had to get help. But then I remembered that morning on the roof with Ro. I remembered her sobs as she screamed at the world for taking her mother from her, because treatment didn't save everyone.

"I can still work," Priya choked. "I can't put extra work on you or Mama."

"Priya, do yourself a favor and just rest. I can take care of you for once."

Her eyes closed. Deliberately or not, I couldn't tell.

Darshan was coming. My body tightened. My toes dug into the hard rock. My lips moved but no sound came out.

We stood in silence. His face was stern.

My mouth moved again. Still no words came.

He didn't look at anyone else. Just me. And suddenly his face loosened.

Everyone waited for me to speak.

"I…um…I."

I looked down.

Darshan's words were dry. "Get back to work."

I don't know why I'd hoped for a different response.

I walked off without saying a word, supporting Priya's limp body. Shubar watched in the distance with his arms crossed over his chest.

My throat fought back the desire to cry. We had no choice. We continued to work tirelessly. We would never stop. Lift. Carry. Dump. Lift. Carry. Dump.

My mind wandered until the slab I was hammering transformed into Shubar's grimacing face. *Slam. Slam. Slam.*

The rock split. Tiny pebbles fell from the crushed sides. I sniffled back tears.

Slam. I pounded down again. Only this time I missed the rock and almost hit my own foot.

"*Aiyyoooo!*" Shoot!

I let go of the hammer and shook out my cramping hands. I was drawn to the droning of a drill. Sanat was handling it. I asked if we could switch tasks for a while, so he could look after Priya. At first he laughed, because girls never powered the drill. I didn't blink. He swallowed hard and rushed to Priya.

I watched them quarrel from afar. Then Priya grabbed his wrists. She tried to hold him back, but he ran towards Shubar. My heart leaped into my throat. What was he doing? Was he out of his mind?

Within seconds after hearing the boy's desperate words Shubar knocked him to the ground. Sanat spit out a tooth. I turned away. I shoved the drill into the rock. My body began to shake. I didn't know how to stop it. Suddenly the drill didn't feel powerful enough. I wanted to scream. My body had the urge to run and chuck something. I needed to rid the wrath that was boiling inside me. My hands pressed hard against the drill.

Crack!

I pretended it was Shubar's skull.

My emotions gradually subsided, and I handed over the big man's tool so I could carry loads of rock with Sandhya.

An orange glow illumined the horizon as the sun finally set. But the workday was far from over. I carried a basket of cobbles over my head and watched the sunset. Through the vibrant glow I saw a small dark shape fluttering through the air. Landing on the ground a few meters ahead of me, I rushed to its rescue. The black bird whimpered. Its bloody wing twitched. I knelt to the ground at a creature once so strong and beautiful now crushed and defeated. I wanted to mend its broken wing so it could fly again.

A large shadow fell over me.

Shubar said with a snicker, "You can't save every injured bird."

"Maybe you're just afraid that I can," I snapped back.

"Ha! You can't even save your own sister let alone a dying bird. Things happen for a reason. Maybe that bird wasn't meant to fly."

"Maybe it would be far away from here if something else hadn't dragged it down from the sky," I murmured. I didn't want to end up like Sanat.

He raised his voice, "Well, maybe the bird got way in over its head and thought it could fly farther than it was capable of. Maybe it's the bird's fault its wing is broken."

"Maybe you just can't stand the fact that some creatures deserve freedom." A tear slipped down my face, but I wiped it away before Shubar could see it.

Avoiding the probable beating for my remarks, I ran away to Priya. I wanted to prove that I could take care of my sister. I didn't find her until later that night when she was already asleep.

I let my head rest on the hard cement floor. The sweet escape of sleep rescued me each night when our bodies were allowed to collapse. Mosquitoes swarmed all over, swooping down on us at their leisure. I stared at a concrete wall for hours until I finally drifted into an uncomfortable dream that was almost as bad as my reality.

My night was constantly interrupted by a gruesome coughing sound. I looked over at Priya and saw her body soaked in sweat. I cradled her in my arms, unsure of what else to do. My mother was awake on the other side of the room. She stared off into the distance as if she were somewhere else. I rocked my sister in my arms, thinking of Shubar's words. The night filled with Priya's moans and my mother's sobs.

If my mom didn't pull herself together soon, I would be

all alone. And I had an overpowering fear I would be.

The sun came before sleep did.

UNTOUCHABLE
(Ruchita)

I watched the second hand of the clock. *Tick. Tick. Tick.* Faster and faster it spun round until my head was spinning, too. All of my energy went into the simple effort to refocus. My eyes darted back and forth between the hypnotic time glass and the scattered books and papers on the floor. My heart beat wildly. *Tick. Tock. Tick. Tock.*

I wanted to focus. I really did. But all I could think about was the sound of Srinivas' belt beating Tarun in the yard. I saw Shivani's shivering hands holding up her two coins—not enough even for a grain of rice. I stared at the words rambling on pages that seemed to go on for an eternity, and then back at the clock. 4:25. I had let the past three hours slip through my fingers just as I did the five before it. Staring at the colossal work in front of me was clearly a waste of time, and if the small hand of a clock was enough to scare me, how would I find the courage to prove my father wrong?

Yet, time could not move faster, and if it never slowed for me, I would never catch up to it. I felt myself falling further and further behind each time I blinked, losing more valuable seconds. I stared at three years of material in front of me, sighing in disappointment. I had been working so hard to squeeze back into my new life, but I would never be where I was before. I hated the idea of being the girl struggling in school.

I faced my work again. I could do this. I just needed to focus. I just needed to start.

Ready. Get set. Go.

The past few weeks had flown by. I had slept through most of them. My hot showers were the joy of my day as I let the warm water from the bucket wash away my past piece by piece. Although I was still skin and bone, I felt as though I had gained some of myself back. Surrounding myself with new knowledge made me feel at peace again. Although at times overwhelming, my work made me feel human again. I was Ruchita again. I devoured the words in front of me and spat them back out in my journal, digesting the new material and absorbing my new open freedom.

At first, returning to my bubble made me feel as empty as my stomach used to be. It only reminded me of how for the past three years my mind, body and heart all had been missing. But as I ate everything I set my eyes on, I started to fill myself back up again. Every day my father placed me on a scale. As I gained more weight, his face gradually lost its look of disapproval.

Initially I threw up everything I ate because my body didn't know what to do with it. After a week, I had eaten all of my father's food. When the pantries were empty, I was tempted to chew on the wooden table. I still felt I was skinny enough to be a beggar. My father suggested I start working in his garden to rebuild muscle. So I left the bookshelf in the evenings to escape into the garden or kitchen, where I let my creativity come to life in the meals I cooked for my father and me.

I shut the book. The crunch of rubble outside disturbed the peaceful quiet. The sound of my father's footsteps raised a sudden panic in me. I tossed the book under the shelf as his words rang in my ear.

Stop wasting your beauty on books, Ruchita! You'll grow grey hairs and wrinkles if you keep stressing so much. And then how will I find you a husband? Your youth won't last forever. Don't waste it on a man's mission.

I pulled myself up in time and started swaying to an

imaginary beat. He peered in the door and smiled when he saw me moving rhythmically.

"Look at my beautiful daughter, working hard as always. I couldn't be more proud."

I blushed.

"Did you finish sweeping the kitchen like I asked?"

I nodded.

"Come take a break and sit down with me. I have to discuss something with you."

I followed him into the kitchen. He touched my still-scraggly hair and stared at it with discontent. I hid it behind my head.

"Don't worry. I'll have Daeva help you fix that."

"What is it you wanted to talk to me about, Baba?"

"Daeva is coming back today, and before you meet her I need you to understand a few things."

"Okay."

"When I met Daeva, she knew me for me: a man of status and education. I was never meant to be in the slums. If Daeva had known about your mother and you she may have never married me."

I kept nodding. I felt like hiding under the table.

"And that is why you can never tell her."

"Tell her what?"

"Tell her about my past. About our past. She doesn't know you are Dalit, either. If she knew, well, it doesn't matter because she never has to know. That's the point, Ruchita. You can't tell her. Do you understand?"

"Yes," I replied. I hated saying yes. But I'd never tell him no. "What do I tell her?"

"Nothing."

"What if she asks? I mean, what lies did you tell?"

"I didn't *lie*. Some things are better left unsaid. Do you understand, Ruchita?"

"Yes, Baba."

"Good."

We turned towards the sound of crunching rubble. Out the window I saw a rickshaw dropping off a woman.

"Stay here. I'll tell you when to come out." He looked me up and down, then added, "Go brush your hair and put on that nice Punjabi dress I bought you. I want Daeva to see how beautiful you are."

He gently closed the door.

I folded my arms and felt my lungs push against my rib cage. How could he ask me to hide the past that I had risked my life to find again? Why was he so ashamed of it? Was I a constant reminder of the past that he hated so much?

I went to my room to change and brush my limp hair.

Before I picked up the brush, I heard a commotion. I pressed my ear to the door but couldn't make out the conversation. Hesitantly, I stepped into the hall.

An intense heat had suffused the house. Daeva's screams flew through the room like flames.

"She just *appeared* out of nowhere? This is ridiculous, Hakesh! You can't be serious! This isn't fair to me! This isn't fair to you!"

My father mumbled something, but I couldn't make it out. Daeva's voice continued to rise.

"I cannot *believe* you would do this to me! Did you really expect me to be okay with this? Am I suddenly supposed to be a mother to her? And to a girl I don't even know! What if we wanted to have kids of our own? Would she just tag along with our family?"

My father's voice came loud and clear this time, "She *is* family, Daeva! Don't use an imaginary family as an argument when that is completely irrelevant! You said you never wanted kids!"

"Exactly! So why would I suddenly want one in my life?"

"Daeva, this is not your decision!"

A crash exploded from the kitchen as glass shattered on the floor.

"Aaaaahhhhh! She is *stealing* my husband!"

I recoiled in fear. This woman was crazy. How could my father possibly love someone like her?

"You listen and you listen good, Daeva. Ruchita is my daughter. *My* daughter! And if you ever try to make her feel otherwise, *you* will be the one thrown out on the street!"

I heard someone stomp out of the room, furious.

She shouted, "This is *my* house! This is *my* money!"

The door slammed, rattling the house. I crawled back into my bubble and closed the door. I curled up in a ball, terrified. When my father returned, he looked like a different person. His eyes were downcast and he was slumped over.

"Daeva is...she's really fragile right now with everything that has happened with her father, and I think this change is overwhelming her. Just give her some time to warm up to you. I know she'll grow to love you. She will. She has to," he said, trying to convince himself more than me.

I tried to muster the courage to meet her.

You are only as good as your first impression.

I went to the bathroom and cleaned up. In the mirror I took a long glance at myself. Then I thought of Mukti and wondered what she would have told me.

She can't ruin your life, Ro. Besides, who doesn't love you? You're so lovable! You don't have to pretend to be someone else. She'll love you for you. And if she doesn't, I'll still love you just as much.

I wiped the tear from my face and held a hand to my heart.

"I miss you, Mukti."

I faced the mirror, this time with more confidence. I

didn't care what I looked like or what she thought of me. I worked this hard to get here, and I was going to stay here. I was free to be myself for once, and this may have been her house, but he was my father. I was here to stay.

I went in the kitchen and saw Daeva standing on the other side of the room with her arms crossed. I looked her up and down. Her long, slender body curved over the table as she glared at me with dark eyes, as if I were a rat entering her trap. Her scaly green sari wrapped around her body, hiding her parched skin. Her teeth bit her lower lip.

She was bad luck to have in the house.

We stared at each other, but neither of us spoke. The silence was awkward. I wouldn't be the first to talk. My father came in and sat between us, banging his hand on the table, frustrated. Daeva slithered out of the room, leaving my father and me alone.

"May I leave now, Baba?" I asked softly.

My father, his eyes glued to the table, nodded. I scurried back to my room and locked the door, fearful the snake might slide in.

I tried to distract myself with a book, but my eyes scanned over the words without reading. I couldn't focus on one thought long enough before bouncing on to another.

I looked out my window, noticing the sky had turned a dark blue. The crescent moon was a dull shade tonight. It looked lonely in the sky, separate from the countless stars that twinkled through the city smog. Watching the sky grow darker and darker, I fell into a restless sleep.

I woke up to the smell of spicy potatoes. I ran to the

kitchen, wrapped in the blanket my father had laid over me the night before. Potatoes in red hot sauce were frying on the stove. Eagerly, I found a seat beside my father, who was reading the newspaper intently.

"How'd you sleep?"

I replied sarcastically, "Best sleep I've had in years."

"Well, maybe next time you should sleep on your mattress. You'll hurt your back if you keep sleeping on the floor." He spoke without lifting his head from the newspaper. "After all, you may want to dance again."

"Sorry, I'm just not used to it," I replied. "I've slept on a floor my entire life."

"Thank you, Daeva," my father said as she put a plate of fresh bread cutlet at his table setting. Hungrily, I watched the steam rising from the potatoes. Without giving me a plate of food, Daeva seated herself. Confused, I turned to see the stove. Empty.

"Did you leave any for me?" I asked.

"Oh, Ruchita," Daeva answered sweetly. "I'm so sorry! I totally forgot about you! I guess I'm not used to cooking for three. Next time, beta."

Furious, I looked at my father.

"Seems like an honest mistake, Ruchita," he said with a shrug, returning to his steaming plate of food. "Why don't you make yourself something?"

"Yes, it will be good for her to learn how to cook. It's very important for a young woman to learn her duties," Daeva agreed.

I sneered behind her back. I had been cooking for my father since I was eight years old! I held my tongue and smiled bitterly.

Sunday, July 31, 2005

Something's Scaly

What's slimy, scaly and has fangs?

Daeva.

I miss my mother so much. My real mother. I wonder what she would be like now. I wish my father would still talk about her. In the slums when he used to tell me stories about her, I could see her in him. I could sense her delicacy in his words and picture her beauty. He said she had as much compassion as an entire village, and I could see my father trying to be like her. I wish she were here with me right now. She would see past that woman's scales. But I know they'll peel back sooner or later, and when they do my father will see the real her. My mother never would have let that snake in the house. She would have protected me, and I just know she would understand me better than anyone else. She would understand why I can't dance anymore and why school isn't a waste of time. She would understand that I will never be that beautiful, flawless girl I once was. She would understand the things that my father can't seem to right now.

The snake tried apologizing to me today. I was reading in front of the bookshelf when she slithered up beside me. Before I could get away, she started to

speak. Her words dripped with venom. She wasn't
sorry. She even had the nerve to say she was excited to
have me here, that she couldn't wait to take me
shopping and doll me up.

Sorry, Daeva. You'll have to find someone else to
doll up, because I refuse to be someone else's doll
again. I won't be your puppet. I know my father was
listening in the hallway. She's scaly. I don't trust
her.

I went back to my room. There was a note on my desk.

Ruchita,

*Here is some money for shopping today. Go buy yourself some
clothes and anything else you need. Daeva will go with you when
you are ready. It will be good for you two to spend some time
together. Hopefully the 500 will be enough, but if not, don't be
shy to ask Daeva for more.*

With all my love,
Baba

I picked up the Rs. 500 bill and sneaked out of the
house. Shopping with Daeva was the last thing I wanted to do,
and I knew she didn't want to go with me, either.

The warm sun kissed my skin. The roar of the city filled
my ears. I wandered through the streets and realized this was
my first time in the city since I had walked it as a beggar. They
felt so unfamiliar. They no longer merely marked the distance I
had to run between the adobe and my work. They no longer
were a decrepit stage where I was forced to dance in
humiliation. They no longer embodied the hatred that degraded
me.

Now the city was a reflection of my freedom. It was every possibility. The shops beckoned me with opportunities to dazzle myself with a new look.

You are only as good as your appearance.

Maybe I would buy myself new bangles, or a new sari. I'd never owned my own before! I passed a convenience store and knew I had to be rational about where I spent my money. To my surprise, the shopkeeper didn't kick me out or ask if I was with a parent. I hated to admit it, but my father was right. Everything was based on how I looked. Although I appeared wealthy on the outside, I still felt like a beggar.

I purchased more toiletries and still had Rs. 270 left to spend on clothes.

Stepping back outside, I observed the people bustling back and forth.

I saw a girl on cement steps frowning at everyone passing by. She rocked her naked baby brother in her lap, making him giggle. Her hair was a nest of dirt. Her dust-encrusted skin hung from her bones. I thought she was stunning.

I approached the steps where the girl was. Before I reached her, a chubby woman stormed out the shop door with a broom in hand. She whacked the kids with the hard reed bristles. The girl screamed in pain, trying to shield her baby brother, and quickly ran away[16]. I stood stunned.

I saw my reflection in the convenience-store glass. I had clear skin, clean hair and a pair of shoes, but I didn't want to be associated with *that* class of people, the kind who beat girls in

---

[16] True story

120

the street.

I felt the money between my fingers. It was mine to spend and no one could take it from me. But that didn't mean I had to spend it.

Before I knew what I was doing, I headed in the direction of the fleeing girl. She sat down in a pile of trash checking her baby brother's head for signs of injury. As I approached, she shifted her brother away from me to her other hip. Her face was hard, as if trying to scare me off. I handed her the bills with a soft smile. A harsh wind blew her hair back and almost knocked the products out of my bag—things she clearly needed more than I did. I set down the bag beside her. I opened my mouth to say something, but instead I walked away, feeling on edge.

I skipped dinner that night. I couldn't stop thinking about the girl. I tried writing about her in my journal but found myself at a loss for words.

I tossed and turned in my sleep. I moved from the mattress to the floor, hoping I might be more at ease there, but was just as uncomfortable. Hours passed and I lay wide awake. I realized it wasn't the bed or the floor that was making me uncomfortable. I was uncomfortable in my own skin.

The next morning my room was lit up by sunlight. I heard rustling in the kitchen and decided to skip breakfast, knowing Daeva was in there. I sneaked into her room to borrow her shampoo and soap that smelled of sugar and flowers. Searching through her dresser, I found a red jewelry box engraved with shiny silver. I opened it to see what was inside: a stack of cash rolled up with a rubber band. I looked out into the hall to make sure no one was coming and unraveled it. I was holding almost 60,000 rupees!

I had never held more than Rs. 500 in my hand. I couldn't believe Daeva had stashed so much away.

I heard Tarun laughing inside my head, mocking me. He knew I didn't have the nerve to take even one bill. I wanted to prove him wrong. Looking around the room decorated with lavish curtains and statues, I realized Daeva had more than enough. The temptation was too powerful. I put three bills into my pocket.

I left the house for the streets and was soon pushed into the swarming crowd.

The city smelled of the rotting trash that tumbled through it. From the slum rooftops, it had always looked like a mythical maze. I wanted to explore it. But down here at ground level, harsh reality hit me in the face.

A half-naked little boy stared up at me. His puffy face tilted sideways in curiosity. I winked at him, and his chubby face lit up with excitement. It was as if I had set off the sparklers on Diwali. When I waved, he giggled an adorable laugh.

"What's your name?" I asked.

He smiled and giggled again. His big brown eyes sparkled.

"I'm Ruchita. You have a beautiful smile."

Timidly, he hid his face in his hands, but I could still see his wonderful smile through the gaps of his fingers.

"Do you like sweets?" I asked with a wink.

With his hands still covering his face, he nodded.

I handed him a coin and said, "Good. Every good boy deserves a sweet every once in a while."

He gasped in disbelief. With his mouth forming a big 'O' his chubby fingers felt the coin. He ran down the alleyway, his bare butt in full view.

I had been wandering the streets for hours. The sky had turned grey. People abandoned the sidewalks. Shops closed their doors. When the streets seemed to whisper, I started running. I sprinted through the alleyways, trying to escape the eeriness. I hummed to distract myself as my heart pounded. A powerful wind bounced me off the brick walls. I saw a dark figure on the other side pass by. I kept running.

"Hey, beautiful. What's the rush?"

At the end of the alley a man turned and walked towards me.

"A pretty girl like you shouldn't be out here alone."

I walked backwards, my heart in my throat.

"Where are you going, beta?" he asked in a soothing tone.

I stumbled over a pothole.

"Careful, gorgeous. You'll hurt yourself."

I shivered. My mind flashed back to the long, gloomy winter two years ago.

The noise of the streets faded into the background, leaving me alone with the sound of his slow breath. The man reached out and grazed my cheek. I stood frozen in fear. No one else was near. I was just a girl.

The man whispered in my ear and I shuddered. I stared down at my feet. A tear rolled down my cheek. In my head I cried for Tarun. Where was he? My lips, pressed together in fright, would not allow a sound to escape. It was as if an explosion had gone off a few feet away and left my ears hearing nothing but a dull ring. Why didn't I run?

As the man came closer, I remembered Tarun's face from that winter. He took the blow for me that day.

Tarun's mouth dripped with blood. He screamed at me from the ground.

Run, Ruchita! Run!

This time I did. I turned and ran. I ran because I wished I had that winter. I ran because I wished Tarun hadn't bled for me. I ran because I wished I were free. I ran because I *was*. I ran because I wouldn't let anyone take that from me.

WARNED
(Mukti)

I escaped into the dark night and held my breath as I passed the main house. They were tucked in, dreaming sweet dreams, safe from the dangers outside.

I hated them. I wished they would quiver under the night sky and cower in fear of the morning. They didn't know the feeling of sleeping next to skeletons each night.

Someday I would shut them up in our cage. I'd lock them up like birds and give them one seed to share, so their pestering beaks would have to fight over it. I would chain their wings so they couldn't fly. If they tried to chirp I'd tape their beaks so they were never heard. They'd be like us: trapped. They'd be winged birds unable to fly.

Focus, Mukti.

I had to channel my anger. I searched for the hole that Jawn had cut in the barbed wire. I crawled through, scraping my arms on my way through. Barefoot, I walked along the narrow path in the mountain for two hours until I found the eucalyptus forest. The prickly twigs and leaves crunched under my sore, blistered feet. I felt a tingle on my right cheek like a tiny feather tickling me. I slapped it and found my hand with a dot in the center. Mosquitos. They were the other ones to blame for my sister.

The thought of not making it back in time scared me into a run. I looked in front of me to find streets full of rickshaws and motorcycles burping exhaust into the atmosphere. One of the myriad shops had the medicine I desperately needed for my sister.

I clenched the smooth bill to make sure it was still in

my hand. I smelled the sweet scent of its rough paper. I wondered how many people had held it before me. It was crinkled and faded, but the face of India's peacemaker, Gandhi, was clearly visible. I clenched my fists, took a deep breath and walked into the city. I smelled the wonderful odor of freshly roasted and dipped sweets and hungered to take a bite.

It hit me suddenly. I was free.

I could escape and never look back. If I didn't go back to my village and used this money to go to a city far away, I could start over. They would never find me. A bus stopped in front of me. It was almost empty. I reached for the handle but stopped.

I ran through the streets and into a little shop, thinking of my sister and only my sister. Two men looked down at me from the counter.

"What do you want?" One rolled his eyes.

The other snickered.

"As if she could even afford anything," the other mocked.

He reminded me of Shubar. I *hated* Shubar.

"You're right. I probably can't afford it."

I waved the bill in the air. The man bit his tongue.

"Wait! Wait! Come back!"

But I was already running through the streets again.

I struggled to maintain my balance on the uneven

concrete slabs. Paw prints were permanently marked in the cement from wild dogs that had walked on it when it was still wet. The open-door shops were filled with people chattering while sipping their daily darjeeling milk tea.

When I spotted another pharmacy, I spun around and took in my surroundings. Suddenly the city felt a thousand times bigger. A panic overtook me. I wished I had a shawl. The dark night sky was filling with grey storm clouds.

The little shop was about to close. I watched the owner shutting the gate. Bolting towards the shop, I accidently knocked him to the ground.

I helped the shocked man up and apologized. Terrified he would yell at me, I prepared myself for another rejection. Instead, he smiled sympathetically and brushed himself off.

He looked tired, with dark circles under his eyes. He seemed quite young for a pharmacist and was lanky and small-boned. He readjusted his glasses and gave me his attention.

I started pleading my case. "Sir, I need your help. My sister has malaria. I don't know how much longer she has, but she keeps getting worse and worse. I need something that will break her fever."

My throat closed up and tears welled in my eyes.

"I have just the thing. You're in luck," he said as he walked into the shop and opened a cabinet. "I was running low on these as monsoon season brings a lot of malaria. They're some of the last ones I have." He handed me a tiny white bottle with a label in a foreign language. "This is the best I've got. It will help break the fever. It's Rs. 200."

As I examined the bottle he asked, "What are your sister's symptoms?"

"She hasn't been able to sleep the past week because of her constant chills. She has a bad cough and high fever."

"All right. I would keep her out of the heat and in doors with ice on her head. Make sure she stays very hydrated and give her two tablets in the morning and two at night."

He started going through his cabinets, stacked with hundreds of different medicines. He took out a dark brown bottle labeled cough medicine.

"To help with her cough."

"Okay. Thank you."

"All right. That will be Rs. 350."

When I handed him the bill, he asked, "Why are you alone out here at this time of night? It's not safe."

"My mother had to stay with my sister," I replied uneasily.

"And your father?"

I squeezed my eyes shut. "He isn't around anymore."

"I'm sorry. It's getting late and I have to get back to my family," he said. "I wish that your sister will get well soon."

A feeling of overwhelming gratitude came over me, and I wanted to show my full appreciation. I bent down to touch his feet, but he pushed away my hands, saying he didn't deserve such praise.

With that, he locked up the store and I faced the open street. The heavy raindrops pelted my back. My face streamed with water, and my hair was pasted to my skull.

Once I was deep in the forest, all light disappeared except for a few beams of moonlight that shone between the leaves overhead. My ankles were covered in mud. My clothes were dripping wet. I clutched the medicine in my hand. The bottle pressed into my skin and reminded me to keep going.

The rain eventually stopped, and the sun came out of its hiding place, casting a pleasant orange glow on the forest floor of crumbling leaves damp from the storm. When I reached the edge of the forest, I saw the entire sky again. To my left, the moon sank behind the mountains of granite. To the right, I saw a faded light emerge from the horizon. I trekked to the edge of the mountain, and the ramshackle cement huts, far below, came into view.

The unstable stone shook beneath my feet, but I continued to run as fast as my body could carry me. Finally I found the barbed wire and crawled between the pointy thorns, scraping my arms again in the process. I felt the stones beneath my feet begin to grow hot from the sun, and I knew I was too late. From the side of the mountain, past the main house, I sprinted towards the cement shacks. When I reached the quarters, I pressed my hand against the cement wall to catch my breath.

The entire quarry was huddled together in a crowd. I approached them, unsure of the tragic scene transpiring in the distance. Their beading eyes warned me to walk away. But I couldn't, because I too was caught staring at the man before me, unable to tear my eyes away.

"Is that Mukti?"

"Was she gone too?"

"What will they do to her?"

I felt myself losing my balance and stumbling backwards. Sandhya saw me and told me to join the crowd before I was seen apart from it. But I didn't care.

Siddharth's arms stretched behind the tree, hugging the trunk backwards like the symbolic martyr sacrificed over a cross. His neck hung over his body, unable to bear the weight of his head. Scorched skin covered his frame. I thought he was dead, but his chest slowly rose and fell. Blood trickled down the edge of his limbs, and the tracks of his tears were visible on his bloody face.

I didn't understand. What could this man have done to deserve this? My eyes filled with tears.

Suddenly there was a rustling in the crowd. A girl's cry pierced the air. I saw someone being yanked by the hair and dragged.

Siddarth lifted his head just enough to watch his little girl be taken away from him forever, sold to the Dalals[17] like a dog[18].

Priya pulled Arjun and Raj to her chest, hiding them from the atrocity. Arjun was crying. Beside them was Sandhya's mother. She was crying too. But hers were tears of anger.

The quarry grew hushed as the jamadars scolded us. How dare anyone try to escape after all they had given us? Did we expect to find a better place? This was all we had. We were

---

[17] Dalals- Traffickers; those who recruit the girls and also boys (for bonded labor) and sell them to the maliks for profit
[18] True story

nothing in this world. We were born to work the land. How dare we try to escape and not pay back our debt?

Siddarth had suffered terribly for his crime and ingratitude. His body, electrified, would never recover from the singe of that day. He had watched his daughter trafficked into sex slavery, and he had done so still chained to a tree. He had to accept the fact that he would never see her again. He would barely be able to live without her.

Tamara was the girl. I wished I could have comforted her that moment, but how could I? I didn't even speak the same language. Yet, maybe that was the meaning of true human connection: the ability to connect and exchange emotion even without words.

Suddenly it seemed as if everyone was looking at me, as if I were the next victim. I pushed through the crowd to get to my sister and give her the medicine, ignoring their fearful stares.

I wasn't next. They couldn't have known I was gone.

My stomach tightened into a million knots. My head spun as the lack of sleep suddenly caught up to me. I was running to escape the wrath of Shubar and Darshan.

I ran straight into them.

Ro's words filled my head. *Find your confidence, Mukti.*

I tried. I squeezed my fists tight. I looked Shubar and Darshan straight in their faces and braced myself.

Shubar spat on the ground in front of me, barely missing my dirt-encrusted feet. He bent over until his face was just centimeters from mine. His large, hairy nose practically touched mine. I pulled back in disgust. He smelled of cow dung and cheap beer.

"Where the *hell* were you this morning?" Shubar roared.

I took a step back.

"And don't even *think* of lying to me. You know what I do to liars."

"I was in the back fields cutting granite cobbles." I almost burst into tears. I looked down at my feet.

Shubar jerked his head back. "Are you lying to me?"

"I was in the back fields cutting granite cobbles," I said again.

I didn't want to end up like Tamara.

"Look at me!"

Reluctantly, I looked up. His hand rose and smacked my face. It stung from the blow, but I didn't cower. My insides burned with anger. How many times would he beat me? How many times would he order the jamadars to tie men to trees and electrocute them?

I know I was expected to bow down to the almighty masters. But I had just watched another innocent man beaten almost to death for wanting to be free. And I had spent the last week praying for my dying sister.

I stepped forward.

"Why would I lie to you, sir? What would I have to hide? You've taken such good care of me. You know my loyalty lies with you. Why would I want to go anywhere else? This place is my paradise."

My sarcasm caught him off guard. Darshan hadn't looked at me once.

"Darshan, grab me my whip," Shubar commanded.

Darshan hesitated, "Bai, you don't need to do this. You've already made one example today."

"I said get me my whip!" Shubar snapped, turning towards his brother. Then he looked back at me. "Clearly, this one hasn't learned."

Darshan stood still. His eyes darted between Shubar and me. My eyes pleaded with Darshan—my only chance.

"WHAT ARE YOU DOING STANDING THERE? GET MY WHIP BEFORE I WHIP YOU!"

The hairs on the back of my neck stood up. I felt myself cower back into my shell.

But Darshan held his ground.

"No. You disgust me."

"How dare you talk to me like that?"

Darshan turned and left.

"Where are you going?" Shubar screamed.

"I'm leaving!"

Shubar chased after him, leaving me standing there in

shock.

I found the strength to walk the rest of the way to Priya. I brushed my sister's cheek and felt her forehead. Her temperature seemed to have dropped a bit.

I kissed her cheek and hugged the peas. Hugging them felt like coming home.

Raj was the first to speak. "How did you do it? How did you get the medicine?"

I smiled, showing my big, tainted teeth. "It's a secret."

I lay down beside Priya and held her hand in my lap, brushing it gently as I repeated what had happened with Darshan and Shubar. I smiled proudly.

Priya frowned. "Mukti. Oh, Mukti. How foolish of you!"

"But it's a good thing, Priya." I forced back angry tears. All I wanted was for her to be like Ro, just once. I wanted her to listen to me and understand. Clearly, this was impossible.

"Why do you always have to cause so much trouble? Oh, Mukti. You know I am just saying this because I care. Did you not just see what happened today? Shubar will have you killed."

She didn't understand. She never would. I stormed outside and grabbed the hammer, slamming it into the rocks. With each blow I looked across the quarry. There was no shade anywhere. There was no hope for the sun to set. *Slam. Slam.* No water. *Slam.* No hope. *Slam.*

The quarry became an oven again as the sun rose in the

sky. My feet burned on the intolerable granite. I began to cry, knowing I had no choice but to let my feet blister.

That night the wind howled wildly. I tossed and turned in bed. I rolled over and cuddled with Priya, playing with her hair. Outside, I heard the dirt crunch beneath heavy steps. I thought maybe a wild dog had wandered into the quarry.

The steps entered the shack, and before I knew it a hand was grabbing me and pulling me away. I screamed into the night, waking everyone in the quarry. I struggled in Shubar's grip, trying to break free as he dragged me outside. I was already dead to him.

Priya had caught up with us now and held onto me, begging Shubar to let me go. His boot smashed into her face, knocking her to the ground. Stumbling all over the place, Shubar struggled to take me outside as I kicked and screamed. He smelled of rum, armpit and vomit. He shoved me face-first into the dry stone. My forehead stung as my skin was ripped, and I hit the rocks. My body flipped and Shubar got on top of me. His weight push me down. He was drunk, but he was still much stronger than me. His fists barreled down at me.

"This is all your fault, *gandu*! Darshan is leaving because of you!"

I spit in his face and repeated Darshan's words: "You disgust me."

His chubby hands grabbed my throat and banged my head against the rock. I saw stars. They smiled at me. They *smiled*. How could they? They looked at me as if all were beautiful in this world. Like they were my friends.

Yelliddaaney Devaru? Where is God?

Because Devaru certainly wasn't with me. I screamed at the sky. *Is this my fault? Did I do something to deserve this in a past life? Is this my punishment because I'm a Dalit? Can I be done yet? Please, let me be done!*

Silence and the sound of my skull hitting the ground were my only answer. My lungs cried for air as my body went limp. The stars faded into the darkness. I choked on my own blood. I saw the faces staring outside the open windows and doors, cowering behind the cement bricks. No one would risk it. They looked at me, and I looked back. I kept fighting. I wouldn't let him take me down easily. All I could taste was blood and betrayal.

His hands choked around my neck like chains. My lungs shrunk, and my body squirmed in a panic. I never felt so weak, so alone. Suddenly I felt a massive weight taken off me. My throat opened and air flooded in. I turned over, gasping. I saw Ro's face hovering above the water. She smiled at me with her pearly teeth and pink lips. Someone lifted me off the ground and supported me. I heard a man screaming at Shubar, who lay unconscious on the ground.

"Are you okay? Mukti, can you hear me?"

I recognized the voice, but couldn't put a name to it. I felt myself being lifted and carried away. Where were they taking me? I tried to look up and see who was holding me. Everything started spinning. My eyes closed.

They snapped, and I saw the stars. I heard the wind whispering. I tried to listen, but I couldn't hear its secrets.

Blackness.

TRUTH
(Ruchita)

My father was in Chennai on a business trip for two days. The house had never felt so empty, and yet Daeva was still there. We were learning to tolerate each other.

I heard strange noises from her room last night. At the time I didn't think much of it, but this morning I saw a man sneaking out of her room in a rush, which made me wonder if my father knew he was there. My father never mentioned him, either. I didn't hear him come in, which is weird because I could hear everything in this house. I didn't really know what to think of it yet.

Monday, August 22, 2005

I am starting to look normal again—like a real girl, as my father would say. On the other hand, my father doesn't know that I haven't been practicing Kathak. I've been avoiding starting lessons for weeks, but I'm running out of excuses. I know my father won't understand the real reason.

I also haven't been back to the city since...

I'd rather be with Daeva than be out there alone. I'm not something for the world to take and use at its will.

Besides, staying inside has given me the chance to read, and as my father is gone most of the day, I find my books to be an easy escape.

I put my journal down and ventured into the garden. My skin hadn't felt the sun for days and my body needed to move. Besides, I could see from my window that the weeds had taken over the garden once again. If I didn't pull them out, *they* would become the garden. I sneaked out the side door and breathed in the fresh air. After an hour amongst the little green enemies, my wrists started to ache and my stomach begged for me to feed it. I put down the shovel and wiped the dirt from my hands.

When I came in, I saw Daeva on the couch.

"You're a lovely writer, Ruchita," Daeva mocked.

I heard the flapping of pages. My feet stopped in a panic. What had she done now? I turned around to see her hands flipping through my life page by page next to the crackling fire.

"That's private! What are you doing?" I yelled.

"I seem to be the star in your recent entries. You certainly have a lot to say about me, don't you?" Her pointy tongue slipped in and out through her teeth.

"You have no right to go through my journal! Give it back!"

"Don't forget whose house you're in. Anything in my house, *is* mine," she smiled, continuing to flutter through the pages.

Suddenly her fingers grazed a page and ripped right through it.

"*Aaahhhh!* What are you doing?" I felt like she had torn through my own skin.

She tossed the page into the crackling fire. The flames screeched with joy. Sweat began to bead on my forehead. She had the ability to toss my entire life into the flames with a flick of her hand.

"I never meant for you to read it. I'm sorry, really. I didn't mean to hurt you."

She chuckled. "Oh, honey, I'm not hurt. Your words can't hurt me," she scoffed, turning the pages slower now. "*But*...I will hurt you if you tell your father what you *think* you saw."

"What are you talking about?"

"Don't worry about it, beautiful," she snickered. "Well, worry a little. It would be a shame to see your pretty face go to the flames. Your father would be so disappointed." Her lip pouted in a fake frown. "What could he do with you then? You'd be a useless *Dalit* without your pretty face. Just like your book would be if the flames caught it."

She ripped out another page and fed it to the fire. The paper shriveled as the edges turned black. Soon there was nothing left but smoke. My stomach pressed so tight it could fit into my fist.

She tossed the journal at me and slid out of the room with a grin still on her face.

I clutched my journal as tears fell down my cheek in bitter relief. I ran out of the room, slipping on some of her slime on the way out. Before I hid my journal, I flipped through the pages figuring out which pages she had burned.

Saturday, August 13, 2005

<u>My Future</u>

Since I've been back, my mind only travels

forward, to the future. Despite wanting to enjoy my life now and soak up every moment of freedom, I can't spoil my future by wasting my present. I keep reminding myself that I escaped for a reason: because I wanted to be more than a beautiful face, but it takes more than wanting something to get it.

I can keep studying hard like I have been, but if I never find the courage to ask Baba to enroll me in a new school, what's the point? Staying here is driving me crazy. The other day I saw an advertisement about a boarding school in Bangalore and couldn't help but be intrigued. Mukti and I had dreamed of going off to school together when we were little. It was just a dream on a rooftop, but today it could actually be real. The campus was enormous, beautiful and, best of all, far away. I love my father so much, and it has been amazing reconnecting with him, but the longer I stay here, the more I fear losing him…and losing myself.

If I stay here, I'll never be more than Daeva's extra pair of hands, and I didn't run away to become someone's doll again. I've been that before. I've seen that life, and it's not for me.

When I came back out of my room, I saw my father's car in the driveway.

"Baba! How was your trip?" I ran up to him and gave him a kiss.

"Wonderful. How is my gorgeous girl?"

I smiled. "Great, now that you're home."

I wanted to tell him. I really did. But I couldn't tell him

Daeva knew who I really was, because I was afraid he would take my journal away.

Daeva called from the kitchen, "Come join me for dinner!"

We followed the smell of hot dhal and rotis to the dining room.

As Daeva and my father made small talk my mind flew off again. In my head I was walking through the gardens of a boarding school, carrying my school books and wearing a clean-cut uniform.

"Ruchita! Ruchita!" a voice interrupted.

"Yes, Daeva?" I answered sweetly.

She turned to my father. "Think about it, Hakesh, She's already fourteen. She's gorgeous. When's a better time?"

I tilted my head, confused. "What are you talking about, Baba?"

He faced Daeva. "I don't know, Daeva. She's still quite young, and she just came back home. What's the rush?"

"There's no rush, dear. It can be a very lengthy process, that's all. Before I met you, my father went through this with me, and it took months just to find a worthy match."

"Well, that's because no one could possibly be worthy of your beauty," my father flirted.

I wanted to vomit.

"Stop playing with your food, Ruchita," my father

scolded.

"Sorry."

My father whispered across the table, "Let's discuss this later. Alone."

I was already listening by now, though, and heard him anyway.

After dinner I went into the garden. I sat on a soft mound and let my fingers run through the moist dirt. My fingers found a lone white flower. I plucked it and started twirling it. I didn't understand why the petals were so important. It was the stem that managed to hold up the pretty petals. Besides, the flower could exist without the petals, as it was the stem and roots that gave the flower life. I watched a bee buzz over the patch of flowers, attracted to the soft white beauty. I sighed and looked back at my flower. I wondered what it would look like without its petals. I plucked off each one until it was nothing but a bud and stem.

"Much better," I smiled.

A few days later I was in the garden again and overheard a conversation between Daeva and Baba. It was more of a fight. Both of them were screaming now.

"How can you expect me to keep her in my home?"

"She's my daughter!"

"She's a Dalit!"

My heart stopped. My father must have told Daeva the truth.

"You don't understand! You've never had a child! You can't just throw them on the street!" Baba yelled.

"You're one to talk!"

Smack! I thought he hit Daeva.

Baba screamed, "How dare you use that against me! You *know* I didn't have a choice! I was in the slums with no money. We were dying."

"Face it Hakesh. If it was so hard for you, you never would have done it. *You* started this mess by letting her back in. Now you clean it up! I don't care how you do it, but find a way to get *rid* of her!"

Tears rolled down my face.

I stopped listening.

I couldn't listen anymore.

The world around me was silent.

CHAINED
(Mukti)

I woke up to the feeling of a wet cloth dabbing my head.

Premela! She gave me a hug. As always, she filled me in on what my memory couldn't.

Darshan had been the one who stopped Shubar after Raj sprinted to the main house to find him. I asked Premela to help me to the bathroom. I wanted to look at myself in the mirror. I wanted to remember what I looked like.

Afterward, Premela escorted me back to the sleeping quarters and set up a cot for me to rest in. My brain failed to command the rest of my body on how to move. She said I wouldn't have to work as long as Darshan still had any say in the matter. I replied that I didn't think I would be of much use. She explained that for each day I was injured my debt grew only bigger. At this rate I would never work off our family's debt. Darshan was kind enough to give my family a loan for my treatment, but now our debt had tripled.

I wanted to cry.

We were never getting out of here.

Premela was still speaking but I couldn't hear a word she said. I stared at the chipped cement, and my thoughts floated towards my sister.

"Priya? Where's my sister? Is she okay?" I begged Premela.

She pointed to my left.

I tried to wiggle to look over my shoulder, but my head felt like a slab of granite. It was impossible to move its weight.

Priya was asleep beside me.

My face felt like a piece of soft clay that the entire quarry had stomped on. My skull ached, and every once in a while I seemed to forget how to breathe, so I would fall into a sharp panic.

Sandhya stayed in the room with us. I watched her looking into the distance, twirling her hair, ignorant as a bug. I wanted to scream. I wanted to shake her until she understood, but she never would. Sandhya would never feel the anger that burned inside me, because she had never felt freedom before. I couldn't blame her, because she would never know the difference between drowning and swimming. She's been drowning her entire life. She's never reached for the surface. So to her what's the difference? This was just her life.

I closed my eyes and pretended to be with Ro again. We were on my rooftop laughing and crying over our lives.

"I miss you, Ro."

"Oh Mukti, if only you knew how much I miss you too. I have so much to tell you."

"Me too, Ro. Me too."

"Like what?"

I looked into her eyes. She always looked so confident. It was as if she knew exactly what I was going to say.

"Don't be the girl they want you to be, Mukti. Be the girl you want to be."

"Who do you want me to be, Ro?"

"I want you to be whoever makes you feel free. If you let them confine you in the spaces they put you in, you'll never find me."

"Where are you?"

"I'm waiting for you."

"How do I get out of here?"

"Be the girl you've always wanted to be."

"I've always wanted to be you."

"But who am I that makes you want to be me?"

"Everything, Ro!"

"Then be those things," she said with a wink as if it were the obvious answer.

"Mukti? Mukti!"

A small stick jabbed into my sides repeatedly.

"Mukti!" Sandhya screamed, shaking me out of my reverie.

"Sorry, what?" I asked, startled.

"Shubar is coming. We need to get you out of here."

I let her lift me out of my cot and onto my unstable feet. My knees buckled, and I immediately fell into her arms. A mixture of fear and frustration over my inability to walk brought me to tears.

"Oh, Mukti. It's okay. Come on. We just need to get out of sight and to the other side of the mound."

"I don't think I can, Sandhya," I cried.

My mind flashed through images of Shubar's fuming face and his foaming mouth dripping over me. I could still smell his hot, drunken breath, and a panic shook my insides. My head throbbed and begged me not to let him bash it to the ground again.

Sandhya managed to get my arm over her shoulder, and she half-dragged me out the door. My feet struggled to hop over the ground, as we passed through the quarters.

Ro's words still lingered. I knew what I had to do. I just had to do it.

Out of the corner of my eye I saw a figure move in the distance. My head jerked in that direction and I made out a small shape.

"Sandhya?"

"Yes."

"Look over there."

Cautiously, she watched too. I moved my fingers to my lips and we crawled around a mound of crushed stone.

The figure moved out from hiding and stepped in front of the barbed wire. He scared a flock of rock doves, perched on the barbed wire. They took flight, showering the sky with frantic wings.

It was Jawn!

Fearful he might be caught by a jamadar, I waved him over to join us. An amiable smile greeted us. His face was clean-shaven and I couldn't help but stare at his teeth. They were perfectly white and straight. I covered my own smile with my hand.

I struggled to introduce Sandhya because my head still spun. I didn't notice the other man beside him until Jawn introduced him as his translator.

The translator spoke our tongue. "My name is Balaji. John and I work at an organization called Ajadi. We'd like to ask you a few questions about your work here."

Sandhya spoke up quickly, "We can't talk. We will get in trouble."

She tried dragging us away, but I pleaded with her.

I faced Balaji and mumbled, "Quickly."

All of his questions seemed fairly basic. I didn't see his point in talking with us. He asked about our working conditions and our families. And I realized he already knew the answers to the questions he was asking. It all seemed redundant, until he asked his next question.

"Have you ever thought about leaving?"

We both stared at him with blank expressions.

"We'd like to help you. You have rights. You're children, and under the law you are protected. You should be in school, not working under these harsh conditions. You have the right to be paid for this work." He slowed down, realizing he was throwing a lot at us. "We want to help you leave this quarry. And rebuild your lives. India passed a law 30 years ago, banning this type of labor. We want to help free you from this work."

It felt like another trap. I wanted to leave, but I didn't want my head to bleed against the rocks again. My heart screamed, *"Escape!"* But I couldn't push past my fear.

He kept talking, but his soothing voice didn't mollify the danger he was spitting at us. "We want to free your entire quarry. It won't be easy. There are many of you. Before we can take any action, we need someone from the quarry to plead your case to the magistrate. If we take one of you back, just to ask a few questions, we can get the approval for a raid. Your loans will be paid and you can find other work with fair pay."

I turned to Balaji. These men had no idea of what they were talking about. "You can't trust the magistrate! They hate us. We are Dalits! They will laugh at us. They are friends with the landowners here."

Sandhya was nervous for other reasons. "No. We can never leave. It is too dangerous. We pay off our debt first. If we are caught leaving they will be beat us or have us killed."

Her words scared me more than the men's. I didn't want to stay here the rest of my life. I didn't want to wait for Shubar's hands to beat me to death.

Then I thought about Priya. "I have a sick sister who I can't leave. She has caught malaria and is very ill."

John spoke to Balaji, who translated, "The sooner you come with us, the sooner we can get your sister to the hospital with proper medical treatment."

"I can't afford it. If I take a bigger loan, my family will never be able to pay it off."

149

My heart thudded. I wished so badly I could bring her to a hospital. Priya had sacrificed so much for me, and I wanted to do the same for her.

Sandhya yanked my arm. She wanted to leave.

I continued to question the man. "What do you want from us?"

He answered sincerely, "We want to help you."

"Why? Why us?"

"You don't deserve this life."

I thought everyone believed Dalits deserved this.

I don't deserve this.

I tried to convince myself it was true.

The quarry started spinning. The mountain in the distance disappeared. The sky looked grey. Sandhya pushed me up, but I kept falling. I was falling into the water.

I heard a voice above the surface whisper, "I'll go with you."

No, Sandhya! You can't!

I was screaming, but nothing came out.

"They don't notice me, Mukti. Shubar would know the second you left. You need to take care of Priya and yourself."

I squeezed into her arms and pleaded with my eyes. It took all my strength not to pass out. I watched her take her hands off my shoulders and turn to the two strangers. Soon she was just a dot in the distance.

My feet slowly dragged me back to the cement shack. I felt like a leaf clinging on to its branch while the wind blew wildly, trying to knock me off.

Priya was still in her cot. Tears welled in my eyes. There was nothing I could do but stay with her so she knew she wasn't alone. Her cheeks, puffy and hot, beaded with droplets of sweat. I decided to braid her hair away from her wet face. We both needed strength. I fingered through her dusty hair and folded the three plaits into one, and then did the same to mine.

I pulled myself up into my own cot.

When I woke up, the peas were already in our sleeping quarters. They gave us their food portions for the day, as Priya and I were unable to work for our own.

"Raj, no. You need it more than me."

"Mukti, please just take it."

"We'll share," I suggested.

When we finished the small ration of ragi, I told them about Jawn and Balaji. It was hard to get my words out in full sentences, but they understood me. They'd always been brighter than me. After everything the peas had been through, nothing seemed to take them by surprise. They simply did what they were told.

My head felt like a thousand bricks again, and my body refused to carry them. I struggled to get up from the cot.

"Don't worry, Mukti," Arjun said, placing his hand on

my forehead. "We'll bring everyone to you tonight."

Word spread fast and by the time nightfall arrived the quarry was anxiously waiting. Arjun helped me as I limped outside, while Priya slept soundlessly in her cot. Everyone pretended to be asleep, as I spoke with the elders and heads of families.

My hands shook as I struggled to keep them steady at my sides. I looked back and forth at the faces in front of me. An elderly woman groaned. I knew some people still believed the rumors that Sandhya's mother had started. I knew I would never be Priya. I'd never be adored or respected. But I didn't care anymore. I was sick and tired of trying to be what everyone wanted me to be. I was tired. Just as tired as they were. I'd been beaten and yelled at and beaten again.

I needed to get out of here.

I was determined to get out of here. I needed to save Priya, and every other innocent person on that quarry. And I so badly wanted to be with Ro again.

If you're confident, they'll follow you and believe in you too.

Ro would've said something like that.

I shook out my nerves and turned to the group.

I began by explaining my first encounter with Jawn and then my escape to the pharmacy. Trying to keep my head up, I shifted uncomfortably.

"Today, Jawn and his friend stopped by the quarry again. They said something that at first sounded crazy. It sounded like a trap. But it's not! No matter what you think at first, you have to hear me out and then hear them out. This can change our lives. It will. And I really hope…and believe that if we all come together, we will be free from this quarry in less than two days."

Huge outcries erupted from the group. They all broke out into conversation. Half of the people couldn't understand what I was saying, because they didn't speak Kannada. So translations were being passed around too.

But I was far from done.

I raised my voice to be heard. "They work for an organization. Ajadi. They save people like us and take us back to our villages. They help ensure our freedom. The government guarantees it and will help us rebuild our lives." I stopped and took a deep breath. "Sandhya agreed to go with them to the magistrate…to give them proof of our situation."

My voice started to shake. Sandhya's mother's face lit up in flames. Her eyes widened. She hated me.

"They are coming back soon. Sometime within the next few days. I don't know exactly when, but I know that this is our one chance. This may sound insane, and that's because this *is* insane. But living in this quarry for another second sounds even crazier," I raised my voice again because people kept talking and shouting over me.

"We have to work together! We can't turn on each other! We can't leave anyone behind! I don't know how you got here, or where you came from, but I know that I miss my home and I miss my family and my friends. I miss going to school. I miss being treated like a human being! I miss living without the fear of being beaten every day! I want to wake up every day and know that my family is safe. And happy."

I looked at the group again, only this time I made eye

contact with everyone. I hoped that even those who couldn't understand my words would read my expression and feel the hope that radiated from me. Because hope was the last thing we had.

"Every night I go to bed and dream that tomorrow will be different. Every morning I wake up and hope that it will be my last here. What do you think about when you're working out here? I think about another life. I imagine the day that I'll get to feel human again. I imagine the day I'm not treated like a piece of dirt. The day that my sister is healthy again! The day that my brothers can run around and be kids again! I want to live again in a world where I am treated like a human being. A world where we are all free."

A young man in the back asked a question. "What happens if they fail to get us out? If we don't escape? What will happen to us?"

His comments took me by surprise. I never thought about it, and I realized I didn't have an answer for him. "I don't know...I..." But I did know something. "That's the risk I'm willing to take."

That was the truth. I didn't know what would happen if we failed.

"This *Mosagaara*[19] is setting us up in a trap. Shubar and Darshan are testing us! How could we ever trust you? You're with them!" Then Sandhya's mother turned to the crowd and yelled, "She's going to get us all killed. We can't trust her!"

Her long yellow fingernails pointed at me. In her head I was a traitor. She looked a hundred years old. Her stomach rolls hung out of her dirt-brown sari. Covered in hairy moles,

---

[19] *Mosagaara*- Deceiver

her face looked as if it had been stretched apart and then crinkled up again like tin foil. She never smiled, but then again a lot of us had forgotten how to smile. I could feel her energy from the other side of the quarry. As one of the originals, she had immense influence here too. I used to avoid her as much as I could because she hated me, but I knew she loved her daughter, Sandhya, with all her heart.

"Do you think Sandhya is a traitor? Because last time I checked she was the most loyal person I know. She's never set foot outside this quarry in her entire life. Think about that. *Never*. And yet she trusts in these men enough to risk her life to see that world out there. She knows it is a thousand times better than this hell in here. So fine, believe the rumors about me, but know that Sandhya was never given special treatment. You are all my family, even if you don't think I'm yours. And my sister Priya, she's your family too. And I can't bear to lose another one of you. We've all lost someone. We've been suffering for so long that we can't even keep track of time. I'm tired. I'm so tired. Please. I can't do this another day, and I can't watch any of you suffer another day with me."

The quarry had gone completely silent. I heard a few sniffles. I knew the children were listening in behind the cement walls.

My heart burned. "And the jamadars. And Darshan and Shubar. This is our chance to get *revenge*. This is our chance to watch them suffer."

Revenge. It rolled of my tongue like sweet jalebi.

I couldn't stop then. "We don't deserve to be treated this way, and they don't deserve us! We have rights! We're human! I want to make them feel the pain that we've felt. We deserve to live again!"

I was crying now.

A roar rose up. My heart pounded. Adrenaline rushed through my veins. Hands punched the air. The air filled with a soft chanting; even the silent ones showed fire in their eyes. I quickly quieted them down and finished what I had to say.

"We can't speak of this. We can't let any of the jamadars get suspicious. I don't care how far out in the fields you are, we can't whisper about it. We can't take any chances. I will be here with Priya. When John and the rest of Ajadi come, do what they say. Until then, hold onto this hope, because this hope will keep us going."

With that, I watched the quarry disperse into the grounds amid nervous chatter. Everyone left except for one. Sandhya's mother placed her hand on my shoulder. There was an anger in her eyes that I couldn't understand. I couldn't look away.

I comforted her. "Sandhya is strong. She'll be okay."

But that wasn't her concern.

"I don't want to leave. This place is my home and my only home. I don't have anywhere else to go."

I watched her sit there like a bird born without wings, never knowing it could fly, while I trembled with my wings chopped off, remembering what it was like to soar.

Tears filled her aging eyes, "I don't know if Sandhya ever talked about her father. He was such a good man. He really was, and so brave too. But it was his bravery that got him killed, Mukti. And your bravery is dangerous. It will get us all killed. My husband escaped here too. He even made it halfway across the country before they caught him. And when they brought him back…they tortured him. They threatened him with death every day. Instead they made him into an example. *They* did it to him in front of everyone."

She said "they" as if more were involved than I was aware of.

"They? As in Darshan and Shubar?" I asked.

"No. There used to be more," she said with a sigh. "I've been here a long time, Mukti. A very long time. I have seen much more than you will ever see. So yes, Shubar has always been here, but he was not always alone. He used to have multiple partners who ran this quarry. And they were just as vicious, willing to do whatever it took to make money."

Her lips quivered. She stared into her lap. The wrinkled creases in her forehead betrayed years of stress and sorrow. I reached out to hold her hand in mine.

"The first years of this quarry were run by a mob of men. When my husband," she gulped just saying the word, "escaped, Shubar became paranoid. He was afraid that others would escape too, and as a solution…it was a terrible thing…he put all the men in chains. He bound shackles to their ankles. Each weighed a basket of granite. They were forced to live in these for *years*. It was cruel. I had to watch them in pain, suffering every day. The chains caused rashes around their ankles, and we had no way to heal them. Our men eventually died. My husband died before the newspapers found out, when Shubar was forced to get rid of the chains[20]. All of his partners fled in fear. That's when Darshan came to help out."

She sobbed into her lap. "My husband died a week before the men were unchained. Only days before they were

---

[20] True story that happened in 1996

157

freed! If he had just held on…maybe he could have…"

She clutched her stomach in pain. I squeezed her hand and rubbed her arm. She rocked back and forth as her teeth chattered. Her glossy eyes stared into the distance, but they weren't looking at anything in this world. My head tried to wrap itself around the story and imagined the quarry twenty years ago.

"Don't you see that this is why we need to leave? They can't make us live like this. Shubar shouldn't get away with this. This is your chance to get revenge on the man who put you through   hell!"

"That man was my husband. He was Sandhya's father! Don't you understand? Don't you get it, Mukti?" She looked straight into my eyes. "He's dead! They chained him like a dog! You haven't seen what they're capable of! He tried to escape once and look what happened! What makes you think you can? What will they do to my poor Sandhya? Tell me! Because I can't bare to lose her too!"

She shook me while screaming in my face. My insides shuddered. I didn't know what to say. What could I say? I couldn't save her from her own fear. From her own past. If she wouldn't leave, neither would Sandhya. I let her shake me till my brain turned to sludge. The chains closed around my ankles and bound me to the ground. Sandhya's mother was already chained. She couldn't move, and now neither could I.

FUTURE
(Ruchita)

I woke up with excruciating stomach cramps. My mouth stretched wide, fighting the idea of being awake. I stood up to go to the bathroom, but remembered to grab my journal hidden underneath my pillow. As I reached down to pick it up, my heart skipped a beat. A pool of red soaked my sheets. Panicking, I stripped them off my bed. The clock read 6:58. I didn't have much time before my father would come to wake me.

Footsteps tapped against the floorboards outside. Daeva's and my father's muffled voices filled the hallway. Terrified, I threw the sheets back on the bed, realizing I couldn't bring them into the hall with me. Their voices faded as they returned to their bedroom. Quickly, I tiptoed to the bathroom to find a wet rag. I opened the cabinet and searched for a cloth, but my shaking hands knocked over Daeva's beauty products. I struggled to put them back on the shelf with unsteady hands. My head snapped towards the door when I heard my father calling my name. I dropped the rest of the bottles and sprinted to the bathroom door, but it was too late. My father was already in my room.

I wanted to cry.

"Ruchita? Ruchita! It's okay, honey! Where are you?"

I stood in terror at the bathroom door. "Here," I whispered.

My throat closed. My lungs pulsed frantically. Tears filled my eyes, and before I knew it Daeva had run over to give me a hug.

"Oh sweetheart, it's okay!" She wiped the tears from

my face. I pushed her hand away and ran to my room. I tried tearing up the sheets but found them too resilient. I scrunched them up and threw them in the trash instead.

"Ruchita, calm down. It's just a part of becoming a woman."

"I don't want to be a woman! I'm a girl!" I screamed with tears flooding my face. "I'm a girl! I'm a girl!"

I pushed past my father and sprinted into the garden where I hid behind a bush, beneath the window seal. I sobbed into my hands. This couldn't be happening. It's too soon. This would ruin everything.

Daeva's soft voice floated over the window seal. I hadn't realized the window I'd been sobbing beneath was open.

"You know what this means, Hakesh."

"I know. I know. It's just so hard to let my little girl go."

"They've been asking about her constantly since the wedding in August. You said once this happened, you would agree to the proposal."

"I know, Daeva! I just didn't think it would be so soon!"

I gasped. Suddenly it all made sense. I remembered the wedding so clearly now. That family kept staring at me, and I didn't know why. Daeva had been talking with them throughout the ceremonies. I couldn't believe it was already happening.

I couldn't wait any longer to ask my dad about sending

me back to school. I had to do it that night, and if I didn't convince him then, it would be too late.

I paced up and down the hallway for an hour before I mustered the courage to approach him. His broad shoulders were hunched as he read today's newspaper, not noticing me until I stood right in front of him. Daeva softly hummed in the kitchen.

"Yes, dear?"

I took the magazine from behind my back and made my proposal.

To my disappointment, my father had no interest in sending me back to school.

He let out a painful, reluctant sigh. "Oh, Ruchita. I don't know why you're so caught up with this school business. You have to realize that you have so much more potential. Why would a beautiful woman like you want to stay locked away in some library studying?" The word *woman* stung my heart. Just a day ago I was his gorgeous *girl*.

"You could be creating beautiful children and supporting a husband who would do all that hard work for you." I looked away. He would never understand. He continued speaking in a disappointed voice. I hated that voice. "I don't understand it, Ruchita. You have to trust that I know what is best for you, and that I am doing everything because I *want* the best for you."

"And what's that?" I asked nervously, because I already knew the answer. As of this morning, I could finally be married off. To my despair, that's exactly what my father told me.

But I was even more nervous, because I knew it

wouldn't be the first time he would send me away. I had tried to ignore what I overheard the other week. I'd never be able to. Those words would stay with me forever. I'd never shake them off.

"No, Baba! Please don't do this to me. I don't want to!" Tears welled in my eyes again. "I'm not ready. Please!"

I buried my face in his chest and clung to him. He was supposed to protect me. His strong arms wrapped around me, making me feel safe momentarily, but then he opened his mouth again and all of my fears returned.

"His name's Ramesh Ramamurthy."

"Stop! I don't want to hear this, Baba. Please. I'm still a girl. I swear. I'm still a girl!"

He rocked me back and forth in his lap. "There comes a time in every girl's life when she has to grow up."

I heard a feminine voice chime in, "It's a wonderful thing to be a woman, Ruchita. You'll grow to love it."

I looked up and glared at her. She was the one forcing my father to let me go. I knew he didn't want to. Not again. I started to bawl and collapsed onto my father's chest.

"Hakesh, let me talk to her. It's a girl thing."

She reached out to me. The only reason I let go was because she used the word girl.

We went into the bathroom, and I was actually glad she was there with me. I wouldn't have known what to do. She made it into a bit of a joke and made fun of my father a bit for being a "man" who'd never understand these things. We

162

bonded over the fact that only we could know these things.

"Thanks. Really." I blushed. I really did appreciate her words.

"I know you think I'm trying to get rid of you. I'm not. I've loved having you around the house."

I raised my eyebrows dubiously.

"No really!" She laughed. "It gets lonely when your father leaves all day. We should hang out more."

A part of me wanted to make amends with her. But the next four days I spent most of my time avoiding my father and Daeva. I couldn't help it. And they did a good job of doing the same. Anytime I walked into a room, Daeva and my father were silent.

When I passed the kitchen this time, though, they called for me to stay.

"Ruchita, we have some exciting news!" Daeva announced.

"I don't have to get married anymore?" I prayed.

"No," my father responded, annoyed by my persistence. "The Ramamurthys are coming over tomorrow, and I need you to look your best and behave your best, like the elegant young lady I've taught you to be."

I didn't have the strength to fight back anymore. I nodded and went back to my room to sulk.

I hate this. I hate how I have no control over my own life. I don't want to meet this family! Beauty is the most horrific burden a girl can have. If I ever have a girl I hope she's blessed with an ugly face. Maybe I'll burn mine. Daeva had already suggested it. That'll scare them away.

Where's Mukti when I need her? She would feel the same way. If she were here we could run away together. That way we'd never have to be married off to some man. We would live happily every after. Mukti and me.

But I don't know where she is, and I can't run away alone or I'll end up in that alleyway again. I'm so scared of that alley. This marriage is like an alleyway in itself. Either way I'll be tied to a stranger.

Oh Mukti! Where are you?

Tomorrow became today before I had the chance to push it out of my mind. Daeva had helped me put on a new sari. The colors shifted from the head to toe, starting in reds and oranges and transitioning to dark yellows and greens. My hair was braided back neatly, exposing my bare face that Daeva had marked up with her makeup.

"You'll look more mature," she said.

I didn't want to look mature. I was still a girl. I felt so self-conscious.

Once again, I was on display.

I was in the bathroom staring at myself when I heard the knock on the door. My shaking fist wiped away my last tears. Daeva would yell at me if I ruined my makeup. I stared again into the mirror. This wasn't me. I had been trying to find myself ever since I came back, and yet here I was again as my biggest fear. I took one last breath before I positioned myself in front of the door with my father and Daeva by my side. I couldn't calm down.

"Just a few hours and it will all be over with," I told myself, but my shaking hands remained unconvinced.

The door opened. I saw the mystery man's hazel eyes and was locked in. Without realizing it, my palms pressed together and my head bowed in respect. Both families moved to the living room, so I knew it was my job to then serve the tea and sweets. I couldn't help but stare at him and his gorgeous eyes. I tore myself away, trying to be as graceful as possible.

I walked to the kitchen to pick up the serving tray and wished it weren't china. When I lifted the tray, my hands wouldn't stop shaking. Just centimeters off the table, the tea spilled.

"Ow!" I screeched, yanking my finger back as the hot drink burned my skin.

The pot crashed to the ground.

"*Aiyyoooo!*" Shoot!

I wiped the tea off my sari. I was sure the commotion could be heard from the living room. My face dropped in shame. Ramesh wouldn't want a wife who couldn't even carry a tray of tea.

Daeva darted into the kitchen.

"I'm sorry. I'm so sorry, Daeva! I swear I didn't do this on purpose. I'm just so nervous. I can't stop shaking. Why can't I stop shaking?"

Her arms wrapped around me in a warm embrace.

"Breathe, beta. It's going to be okay," she said soothingly, patting me on the back.

I looked over her shoulder confused, expecting to see my father, but he wasn't there.

"Why are you being nice to me?"

"I was in your shoes once, too."

"But your marriage with Baba wasn't arranged," I said.

"Well," she said pulling out a chair from the table, "your father wasn't the first man who tried to marry me."

"Really?"

"Really." She pulled me beside her. "In fact, I handled the whole situation much worse than you did."

I looked down ashamed.

"It's natural, Ruchita. Look at me. We all go through it."

She stopped short at her last sentence. I could tell she was holding something back.

"What?" I asked. I wanted to know.

"Well, I didn't go through with mine."

She paused and wiped the tea off her hands.

"I didn't show up to the wedding. In fact, I took some of my father's money and flew up to visit my friend in Gujarat."

"You can do that?" I asked excitedly.

She laughed. "Don't get any ideas." Then she turned serious again. "I stayed in Gujarat for a few months until all the tension died down, but my father never spoke to me again. He wouldn't even look at me when I visited him a few months ago…and now he's gone."

"I'm so sorry, Daeva."

"Listen to me, Ruchita. I knew that man wasn't right for me. I got this feeling in my gut. I knew it from the start. I wouldn't force you to marry a man you truly felt uncomfortable with. You can be honest with me, and we can work it out with your father if this arrangement isn't right, okay? Stop putting so much pressure on yourself. This should be exciting for you! You're about to meet the man that you could be spending the rest of your life with. This family is very special to me. I trust them. The question is can you trust me?"

"Well, he is kind of cute," I said shyly, feeling butterflies in my stomach.

She laughed and kissed me on the forehead. "Come on. Let's go."

Daeva pulled out a new tray for me, and we walked back into the living room.

The father of Ramesh looked at me with concern. "Is everything all right?"

"Everything is splendid," Daeva reassured him.

I smiled as I served the parents, trying to make up for the disturbance, and when my eyes met with Ramesh's, I almost dropped the tray again. He laughed softly, making me blush. I sat down in between Daeva and my father, thankful that I didn't have to hold anything anymore. I looked up to see Ramesh still staring at me. He hadn't stopped since I'd been in the room. It made it hard to look back at him. I wiggled in my seat. The parents continued talking, while Ramesh and I sat in silence. The whole thing was so uncomfortable.

When the Ramamurthys finally left, we congregated in the living room. My father's face beamed in excitement.

"So? What did you think? Shall I accept?" he asked with such enthusiasm that I couldn't bear to disappoint him.

The only thing that truly bothered me was how much older Ramesh was. I understood I couldn't marry a boy, but I still felt uncomfortable with the idea that my husband would be ten years older than me. I felt conflicted. I hated the idea of being married, but now that Ramesh was a real person, and gorgeous too, it made it so much harder to hate him.

"Yes," I finally answered, letting out all the air inside of me.

My father jumped up. "Great!" He started walking away when he added, "Oh, this will be such a wonderful way to get the whole family back together! Ruchita, my love, you make me so proud!"

I went to bed early, so Daeva and my father could

discuss the arrangement. Three months ago I never imagined this is where I would be: engaged. And yet the more I thought about it, the more I started to like the idea.

I could be married.

I grinned at the thought.

Friday, November 4, 2005

Life has been surprisingly calm at the house ever since the engagement. I've been waiting for some big fight to stir up drama, but Daeva and I have been getting along really well lately. I think our talk made us see each other in a new light. I actually have a lot of respect for what Daeva did. She peeled back her scales, and I found out she wasn't so snaky after all. The only thing that is disturbing my new peace is the man I caught Daeva with. I haven't brought this up since that day, and I'm scared to. I probably never will. I don't want to risk anything that might harm our new relationship. We've even been hanging out together too! Last week we went to the hair salon together. It's been really fun planning this wedding with her.

Yet, all of this wedding planning has made me busier than I expected, and I realize I haven't written in almost two weeks. I guess I've been writing down my wedding plans and ideas, but I haven't had a chance to gather my thoughts about all of this. The truth is, all the excitement in the air has rubbed off on me, and I think I'm finally happy with the arrangement. I'm excited to start a new life, and maybe Ramesh will even let me study on my own instead of shaming me like Baba.

I think Daeva is calling. I'll write again soon, I promise!

My head was buzzing with a Hindi song that had been playing in my head for hours. I was alone in the house with Daeva again, as my father was on another business trip. I walked into the kitchen where Daeva stood engrossed in a phone conversation. She motioned for me to come over.

"Who is it?" I whispered.

She winked. Of course. It was the Ramamurthys. Who else?

Curious, I leaned my ear to the phone to listen to the voice. Daeva swatted me away. I laughed and waited patiently on the couch for her to finish.

Finally, she hung up the phone and motioned me back over.

"The Ramamurthys have organized a special ceremony for you and Ramesh and would like us to join them later tonight."

"What kind of ceremony?"

"I don't know. They said it was a surprise, but a ceremony is a ceremony so we should look nice, shouldn't we?"

I smiled, "I can wear that new purple sari we got together!"

"Perfect!"

The Ramamurthys sent a car and driver to pick us up. The ceremony was being held at the other end of the city, so we were told to prepare for a long drive and Daeva brilliantly suggested I bring my journal so we could keep planning the wedding. I gladly took it with me. The feeling of being on the inside of the car instead of tapping on the outside was still hard for me to get used to. For so long I had felt like an outsider, peering into the lives of those behind the tinted glass. Now I was one of them.

The car smelled of the flowers hanging from the rearview mirror. Daeva and I rested in the back seat, humming to the music coming from the car speakers.

I looked out the window as we passed the little teashops. We drove past vendors selling mounds of cherries and coconuts, and boys balancing and rolling tires with sticks. Old men with their heads wrapped in rags sat in meditating position. They had red chalk bindis stamped between their eyebrows. The white cloth skirts wrapped around their hips matched the skirts on their heads. I watched a legless man push himself down the streets on a skateboard. I swallowed the saliva that crept back up my throat.

As the wheels kept spinning, the scenery started to change. We weren't in the city anymore. In fact, there were no more people in sight. The further we went, the thicker the plants grew. Mosses and vines started to cover the road. I could barely see the path anymore. Tree branches created a tunnel above us, obscuring most of the light, and only the occasional ray of sunshine peeked through the thick leaves. The shadows cast by the trees danced around the car as it bumped up and down.

I jolted when a large branch scratched against my window. Suddenly other branches were scratching the windows, too. They screeched like nails dragging across a chalkboard. Their pointy nails seemed to want to grab me through the windows, and I felt a familiar trapped feeling return. I clutched my journal. The wind howled, picking up leaves, spinning them around and blowing them against the windows, hiding the already barely discernible road ahead.

Daeva asked the driver where we were, but he didn't respond. His face remained expressionless. The windshield wipers pushed aside the myriad leaves that fell on the glass, but they kept falling. The breeze whispered my name. *Ruchita.* Daeva's eyes looked fearful, but neither of us dared say a word.

Suddenly the car halted to a stop.

"What happened? Why did we stop?" Daeva asked.

She grabbed my hand. We both sat there petrified. Leaves hid my view of the outside. I could swear I saw something dark move in front of us.

"I'm getting out. Stay in here, Ruchita." Daeva's voice trembled like the wind.

I couldn't stand being all alone in the car with no outside view. I rolled down my window, as another shadow flashed across the front glass. I looked out Daeva's window to see if it was her, but everything was suddenly still again. I realized the driver was no longer in his seat.

"Ahhhh!" A scream shook the air. I turned towards the door, ready to get the hell out of there, and was met by two eyes. A charcoaled man grinned. His eyes were white as the moon. He smiled, showing pointy yellow teeth, and reached for me. A shrill scream escaped my throat. I pushed myself to the other side of the car and tried to roll up the window, but it was too late.

Half of his body was already inside, reaching for me. My hand struggled to find the door handle. Through the mass of leaves, I saw another pair of eyes. I screamed so loudly the city could have heard me. The wind howled outside, shaking the branches.

I was trapped.

I kicked the man's hand as hard as I could. He yelped. Then he faced me again. He yanked on my leg. I fought with all my might to escape his grip, but he was too strong.

Suddenly I was ten again, being dragged through the slums. How was this happening again? Why me?

By now other hands were pulling me out of the car, too. I clung to the seat with all my might, screaming at the top of my lungs. But the rustling of the wind drowned out my helpless cries. No one could hear me. I flipped myself over and felt my knees scrape against the sharp glass window. Tears flooded my eyes. I could scream at the top of my lungs, but no one would hear me. I was pulled through the window. My nose smashed against the glass.

The air was thick. The wind blew my hair against my face, further blocking my view. Leaves jumped towards me as if I were a magnet. In the distance I saw a familiar face. It was expressionless. The leaves swarmed around her.

"Daeva?"

I escaped the man's grip and tumbled over the forest floor, crawling towards her. But my body dragged backwards, as the wind howled through the leaves.

"Why are you doing this to me?" I sobbed.

My fists banged against the forest floor. I kicked and screamed, but it was no use. Blood came out of my nose, filling my mouth with a bitter taste. I tried to spit it out but only choked on dead leaves. The men taped my mouth to mute my cries. What was the point? No one could hear me anyways. I felt my arms pulled behind my back. I tried to stand up and run but had no balance with my arms locked behind me. I managed to move about two feet before I fell flat on my face again. My nose burst into excruciating pain.

It hurt to cry, but I cried anyway. I kept fighting and kicking and screaming. I could feel the rope digging deeper and deeper into my wrists, but I didn't care. I didn't stop fighting. My body fell numb. I couldn't feel the pain anymore. I couldn't break free. I struggled against the ropes for another hour, in vain until I lost enough blood. They already had me wriggling beneath in their strings.

I wished I never woke up.

OXYGEN
(Mukti)

Dawn kissed the horizon. The granite mountains appeared behind fading shadows. The giant rocks, rounded like boulders about to tumble down into the quarry, were slowly being chipped away. I wondered how many more mountains had existed when Sandhya's mother first came to the quarry. And I wondered how many would be left if we kept chipping away at them.

"Jay Shri Ram[21]", I muttered as I finished my daily prayer, this time with a little more emphasis and a lot more hope.

I paced back and forth outside the cement room. It had been a few days since I addressed the elders of the quarry, and I had gained my balance again. Now I was trying to figure out how I would tell Priya. Would she think I was crazy? Maybe I should have talked to her first. Priya always seemed to know what to do in these situations.

I put on my nicer Panjabi dress today. Actually, I had been wearing it the past week in the hopes of looking my best when we escaped. Then I laughed at myself, remembering that both dresses had tears and bloodstains on them now. Neither was nice.

My head pulsed, as I leaned against the wall. I took a deep breath and stumbled through the door to Priya's side. Her eyes were bloodshot. She looked worse than ever, sweating up a storm. The twins sat in the corner. They fiddled with their fingers not saying a word. If the peas weren't talking, I knew something was definitely wrong, so I pressed my palm to her forehead and felt my skin burn against hers.

---

[21] *Jay Shri Raam-* said at the end of prayer, translated as Hail Lord Rama, Hindu Diety

175

"Peas, why don't you go run around outside for a bit? Maybe find Sanat and help him with his load."

They nodded and scurried out.

As they left, Priya's body began to shake. I jumped backwards in time to dodge the vomit she spat up.

"Mukti, I don't feel good. The med-medicine stopp-ed working. My ton-gue- is so dry," she stuttered.

I dug up the bottle of medicine and gave her another pill. It didn't go down easily without water.

"Everything is fuzzy. It doesn't feel right."

I turned away from her, not knowing what to say. My hands trembled. I wiped my sweat with my dirty shalwar. Priya continued shaking, and I knew I had to tell her about Ajadi. She needed something to fight for, something to hold onto in case I wasn't enough.

Out of habit, I started playing with her hair and emulated her fingers' movements. She had shaped and tightened the plaits in my hair for almost thirteen years. When I was done her breathing had slowed. She was calmer, and I knew it was time.

A tear trickled down my cheek. I couldn't imagine losing her a day before freedom.

"Priya?"

She slowly rolled over. "Mhm."

"I'm so scared," I whispered.

Her eyes filled with tears, too.

"I...I'm going to miss you so much. But I don't want to miss you. I want you to fight through this."

She sniffled. "I'm trying, Mukti. I'm trying so hard. But it hurts so bad. All I want is for it to end. And it's never-ending." She started to sob. "I just want to die."

"Don't say that. Please. I need you."

"I love you so much, Mukti. I'm so proud of my sister. I don't think I'd be here if it weren't for you."

"Priya," I cut her off. I needed to tell her everything now in case it was my last chance. "When Papa died I know how hard it was for you. And when Mama left you had to take care of everything yourself. When we were younger I never understood what you were going through. I didn't understand why you wouldn't play with me. Or why you would never be happy for Ro and me. But I get it now...I really do. And I'm so sorry. I'm so sorry I was hard on you. I'm sorry I wasn't there for you. I'm sorry I didn't help out more. I'm sorry I was mad at you for it. You were just doing what you had to do. And I know now that it didn't mean you loved me any less."

I wiped my tears. "I hate this place so much, Priya. I hate it so much. But the one thing I love about this place is having you back. I got my sister back, and I'm not ready to lose you. I have this bad feeling that when we leave this quarry, I'm going to lose you all over again."

I kissed her forehead, and she reached for my hand. I knew she accepted my apology. She just couldn't say it.

We sat in silence for a few more minutes until her shakes subsided. I continually wiped the tears that kept coming.

I was scared. I was scared for so many reasons. My heart filled with heavy water. I felt myself drowning as I sunk deeper and deeper into the water. I struggled to reach the surface—the glimmering reflection in the distance. I could see the light dancing on the water but couldn't reach it. It faded more and more until I was surrounded by extended darkness. My body couldn't fight the fall. I needed my rock. I needed Ro to pull me out of the water.

"Mukti," she finally spoke. "What do you mean *when* we leave here?"

I sighed, "Look. Don't be mad. I just didn't want to put any more stress on you. And you would've done the same for me. When you got sick, I ran away to the city to buy you the medicine."

"Mukti! Where did you get the money? You didn't steal it did you?"

"No I didn't. A man gave it to me." I grinned. I couldn't help it. "A man you've never seen. His skin is like…like the paper we used to write on at school! It's like he's never been in the sun before. And he didn't speak like us. He gave me 500 rupees! I hid it and decided I'd only use it for an emergency. And when you got sick I used it for medicine. Anyways, the same man came back last week with another man who spoke both of our languages. They're going to help us!" I lowered my voice to an excited whisper. "We're going to be free."

"What are you talking about, Mukti? You're not making any sense."

"They told us they're bringing in a police force. Oh, the good kind! Not the bad ones we know. Then they're taking us back home, and we *can* go back home. Because we will get a certificate that says we're free! We can live in the village again, Priya! We can have a real life, and the best part is..." I stopped, realizing I had raised my voice. "They can save you. They're taking you to a hospital! Then you won't have to hold on any longer. You'll come won't you? You'll go with us back home?" I started rambling. "It just doesn't feel right without you helping me by my side. I keep second guessing myself and I realized I just needed you. I needed you to help me figure it out. You've always been the one to figure it out."

"Mukti. I-I don't know. It's not like that doesn't sound nice. *Every day* I want to go back home. But that doesn't mean we will...I've accepted by now that we never will, Mukti. We just never will."

The heavy weight fell on me again. There was so much pressure on me to save my quarry. I needed Priya. I needed her to pick up the weight.

Priya motioned for me to come closer. "Mukti, you are the bravest person I know. You're so full of hope and confidence, and it makes me happy knowing you haven't lost everything by coming here. You're still a child at heart."

My shoulders slumped. A child? She thought I was being childish?

"I'm so proud of you. You don't need me to tell you what to do anymore. Sometimes following yourself is the hardest thing to do, but wherever you go, I'll follow."

"So you'll come with me?"

"Of course I'll go with you," she said with a smile. "But stay here with me right now. I don't want to be alone." My sister reached out and kissed my hand. She felt her braided hair and shut her eyes to fall asleep.

I woke up the next morning with the noise of two peas screaming in my ear. To my left, my mother was leaning over Priya, pressing her palms to her cheeks. It took my ears a few seconds to wake up, but when they did I still couldn't hear what the twins were screaming at me. I shook my head and tried to fully wake up, but my head had blocked off all sound from entering my brain. My lips burned yet they felt numb too. I realized I was on the floor.

"Mukti! Mukti!"

I started to make out what they were saying.

"Mukti, they're here! They're-! Hurry! You- get out! Darshan and Shubar- gone-couldn't arrest- let's go!"

It felt like a million needles were poking through my scalp, but I managed to piece together the information. Then I turned to the doorway and saw Sandhya! My nerves shook with sudden excitement, and somehow I shot up like a spring and hugged her.

"I was so worried! Are you okay? What happened? What did they ask? Where did they take you? Where is Jawn?"

Sandhya hugged me back and told me to be quiet. "We have to focus on getting Priya out of here. Darshan, Shubar and the jamadars left before they could arrest them. They must have figured it out or seen them coming. Either way we don't know where they are and we need to leave before they come back!"

I panicked. "Who's going to carry Priya?"

Sandhya pointed toward the door. "They're here to help."

Three men gently picked up Priya and walked out as

quiet as mice. I held her hand all the way out, then kissed it goodbye. I had to find everyone else.

"Where are you going, Mukti?" Arjun shouted after me.

"I'll be back soon! Take care of Priya."

I saw police standing outside of the barbed wire. They were armed. I searched through the crowd of people running frantically. Some were still raiding the sleeping quarters, trying to find their families, while others crammed into the vans.

Across the field I spotted Jawn and Balaji arguing with a man.

Sandhya and I rushed over to help. "What's the matter?"

"He refuses to come with us," huffed Balaji. "He says this is his life and he won't go."

I explained that some of these people didn't have anywhere else to go. But Balaji persisted. I begged them to drive a van up to my sister. They wouldn't be able to carry her far enough in time. Jawn took Sandhya and me towards a van already half full.

I opened the door and heard screaming behind me. Arjun was sprinting towards us, warning us about something. From behind we heard gunshots. Shubar was shooting at the van with a rifle.

I screamed, ducking.

We had to get my sister and my brothers. We couldn't leave them behind.

I hopped in the van and yelled, "Drive! We have to get my sister!"

"We can't! The bullets will flatten our tires. We'd all be stuck here!" the driver screamed.

We sped forward anyway and almost ran into the two men carrying my sister.

"Are you crazy?" Jawn yelled at the driver.

The bullets shattered one of the windows. We all ducked. Everyone screamed. The van turned around, acting as a shield for my sister and brothers. I jumped out and helped the men move her to the back. The van drove forward and I held onto the door as it took off.

I gasped. We were all safe.

For now.

More gunfire echoed through the air. It was like a Diwali festival, with sounds exploding in the sky. The difference was we were fleeing for our lives. I peeked through the shattered window to see policemen dodging bullets coming from Shubar and Darshan. There were other men I didn't recognize.

How were we going to get out of here? I looked at Jawn. His forehead creased. If he was worried, I knew I should be too. But at least I was with my family. I glanced around to see that everyone was accounted for. Everyone was—except my mother.

"Arjun! Raj! Where's is Mama?"

They froze. Tears filled Raj's eyes.

"It's okay you guys, we'll get her. We'll find her." I was screaming on the inside, though.

We had to find her. I wasn't going to leave without her. Balaji told me to stay inside, but I was already off and running.

"Mama? Mama? Where are you?" I cried so hard the tears blurred my vision.

All I could hear was the gunfire as I searched through the cement buildings. It had finally hit me. The fear. I realized the danger I was putting my quarry through. I was risking all their lives. I had risked my own family's lives. I was trying to save them, but maybe I was just hurting them more.

All the memories of my mom came back to me. I was just a little girl when she helped me put on my first pair of shoes. They were small pink sandals with a little silver buckle on top.

I could feel my mother's arms wrapped around me when my father died, as Priya knelt over his body for hours.

I missed her already. My body ached for her gentle touch. I just wanted to hold her hand again.

I heard Shubar yelling death threats. He threatened to beat our families and kill all the children.

"Get back here, you filthy animal! I'll have you chained for the rest of your worthless lives."

I saw him grab a little boy and pull him up by his shirt until his eyes were level with his.

"Who do you think you are? Huh?"

The boy was terrified. Shubar dropped him in the dirt and started kicking him. The boy got up and ran away in time.

I zoned out, not hearing the rest of his words. He was the animal. He was the one with no heart. Even though Shubar's bullets were still piercing the air, families were yelling, and children screeching, all seemed to fall silent when Shubar stopped yelling. I lost sight of him in the dusty air. I spun in a circle with my heart pounding.

Then I saw him—five meters in front of me with a gun to my mother's head.

I stood, petrified. I couldn't move. I couldn't scream.

"I know you're the cause of this mess. Everything starts with you!" Thick saliva spat from his mouth. "You try and turn my own brother on me? Listen to me *gandu*[22]! You bring these men into *my* home? And you think you can get away with it?" He chuckled. It brought me chills. "Stop this madness or I'll kill your mother! I'll blow this bullet through her brain! *Huchchi…..Ninna Thaayinaa illey Kondhu Bidtheeni!* I will kill your mother right here! I will! I'll do it!" he hollered.

My mother kneeled on the ground, her hands clenched over her head. Her arms trembled, and I could hear her soft whimpers. Shubar spat on her. My legs felt like jelly. I trembled. This was my all my fault. If my mother died it would be my fault.

"What do you want me to do?" I begged.

My mother fought Shubar's hold, but he was so much stronger than she was.

---

[22] *Gandu*- filthy, dirty

It was hopeless.

"Call that man over. And don't call for help or she's gone."

I believed him. It wouldn't have been the first time he'd murdered someone. He kicked my mom in the back so hard it sounded like thunder. She wailed in pain. I didn't know what to do. I didn't know how to save her. He would probably kill her anyway. He would kill me too.

Behind the building I saw a shadow move. It was Sandhya's mother! She must have followed me out of the van. I started to step backwards when I heard a thud. I saw her hand raise and crash into his skull. Shubar fell to the ground. Blood trickled from his head.

I hugged my mom so tight I could've stopped her breathing. Her eyes kept blinking, trying to brush back the tears. I didn't fight them. They poured out.

"Run to the van quickly and tell everyone to hurry and get out of here," I told my mother. "I'll be right behind you."

I stared at Sandhya's mother. "You saved my mother." I bent down and touched her feet. "I don't know how to repay you."

She shook her head. "You would've done the same for me. Besides, I've been wanting to do that for years."

She turned around and kicked Shubar one last hard time.

"Is he breathing?" I asked.

She shrugged. "I don't want to put my head down there

to find out."

Her hands were shaking. They still clutched the bloody rock.

I picked up the gun and turned around to leave when I saw Darshan. He was mad. No, he was horrified. I couldn't blame him. If I had seen two women leaning over my brother's body, I would've felt the same way. He muttered under his breath. I enjoyed watching him like that.

"What did you do to my brother?"

I pointed the rifle at Shubar's head.

"He's not dead yet, but if you tell your men to stop firing and let us go, maybe he'll survive. I haven't decided yet. Maybe I'll spare yours. You've been...decent...recently. I guess."

All my fear was gone. This was *my* time. This was what I had been playing over and over in my head every moment I spent in this quarry: the moment I would get to watch *them* suffer.

Darshan didn't move. His eyebrows arched. His lips pursed in thought.

"What are you waiting for? Go!" I yelled. I didn't have to pretend to be mad. I was pissed.

Darshan didn't budge.
"You don't have the guts!" he sneered.

Sandhya's mother ripped the gun from my hand, pulled back the trigger and shot into the ground.

"Get out of here before I kill you myself!"

Darshan put his hands in the air and ran. He screamed for his men to stop. Shubar was awake. I kicked him and told him to get up and walk. He tried to take the gun from Sandhya's mother, but she slapped his hand away and hit him in the head with it. He didn't try anything after that. The gunfire had stopped and it seemed like the war was over, but it wasn't yet. Not quite.

"Get everyone in the vans! Quickly!" I said.

Sandhya's mom shoved the nose of the gun into Shubar's back and urged him forward. She was muttering something dark under her breath. We slowly walked towards the van where Jawn and my family waited. All the other vans and buses had left. When we were inside and the door was shut, Sandhya's mom dropped the gun.

Shubar was no longer a threat.

The van sped through the wire-fence gates that had once caged me. A flock of pigeons blocked the road ahead, but the driver didn't slow down. The birds fluttered their wings and took flight.

I looked back at the quarry. The open cement buildings suddenly seemed harmless. They were no longer the boxes caging in disease and rain. Dust still blew through it, shifting in the wind. I blinked. I saw the pink main house and almost laughed. It looked tiny against the vast fields and rocky hills. I couldn't see the oval window that Shubar used to watch us through. Without thousands of hands working the land, the quarry was a barren landscape.

I took a deep breath, letting the air fill my lungs. I felt myself being lifted out of the trembling, dark water. As I reached the surface, I sucked in the oxygen.

It tasted like freedom.

GLITTER
(Ruchita)

I should've burned my face when I had the chance.

Tuesday, March 20, 2007

I don't know why I bother filling these pages anymore. I should have let the ink spill over them a long time ago. I used to write so I could remember. Now all I want is to forget. I want to forget how I got here, that I am here, and everything about here. Here is worse than anything I could imagine. I close my eyes and I see darkness. I hear its voices—its screams. And when I open my eyes I see darkness. I hear its whimpers and moans.

At least in death I'll find silence.

I've tried to let the ink spill over my pages twice, but I didn't cut the blades deep enough. I bled, but I've bled before. Nothing here is new. I feel the same strings pulling me, but I'm not dancing anymore. They've got me moving under their weight, but there's no rhythm. I've forgotten what music is, unless it's girls weeping in the day and screaming in the night. I've forgotten what feeling is, unless it's a constant numbness that stifles my body and chills my blood.

I've given up on waiting. No better day is coming. Each better day leaves with each wind, catching its sweet breath as it runs out that door—the door we are forbidden to leave. I don't blame the wind for fleeing so fast. I wouldn't want to stay here either. This place could give even the wind chills.

189

My body shakes. The toxic powder courses through me, and I lose all control. I hate it. I want to scream. But I have no voice. Last night they grabbed Vanhi for the first time. I couldn't watch, but I couldn't look away, either. I watched them jab the needle deep into her wrist. Why did they have to go straight for the heroine? It's given me the most feeling I've had in months. I can almost feel pain again—almost.

If I escaped this eternal numb, bullets of pain would be shooting up and down my right arm. If I knew I'd be writing again, I would've cut the left wrist.

I put down my journal and examined my wrist. The new scars almost hid the old ones. I didn't know which one I'd prefer to see everyday. The circular gashes reminded me of how I got here. They were like the ropes' shadows. And the cuts from my blade reminded me of why I'm still here—because I can't escape.

Even death won't take me yet.

A girl's scream echoed through the corridor.

"Give me the pills! I need the pills! Please!" Anita tumbled into the brothel screaming.

I rushed to the doorway where the girls were crammed to watch the scene unfold. Anita trembled on her knees, bowing down to the snickering malik[23] above her. She fell to his ankles pleading, sobbing. Mahabala kicked her to the floor, showed no mercy.

---

[23] Malik- Brothel owner

"Please, I won't leave again. I promise. I'm yours," she begged.

Her words made me wince. *I'm yours*. My stomach churned. Waiting for the vomit, I looked away for a moment, but my stomach had nothing to give up. I looked back at the haunting scene. I wanted to scream and tell her to stand up, to fight, but my own trembling hands mocked me. They laughed at me. I laughed at me. If I were in her shoes I knew I wouldn't fight either. I would take the blows and wait for the bleeding to stop.

Mahabala smiled. "I know you won't, sweetheart."

He knelt down and gently lifted her face off the ground to widen her jaw. I watched the white drugs fall into her mouth like sweet drops of sugar.

I had lost my taste here. I only had memories of it, like when Mukti's father used to buy us chocolate in the city. But it was a bittersweet memory now, because I realized Mukti was probably in a dollhouse somewhere too. The houses filled with water. We were both drowning, and neither of us had the strength to get back up. The only thing we could do now was stop struggling and let the current take us.

I shoved through the crowd, disgusted. Everything about this place was repulsive. I found a quiet space and sat down. My mind immediately went to Vanhi. Oh sweet Vanhi. The needle reappeared in my head. I tried to shake it out, but I knew her fate was no different. Deep down I always hoped she would escape her doomed fate, but I should have known better. Every last bit of light slipped through my fingers, and I found myself reaching into the darkness.

I opened up my journal and found my first passage about Vanhi.

Fire

They busted open the door. Her screams bounced through the halls, growing louder and louder, until she was thrown to the floor in front of me. The little girl crawled backwards into my lap, cowering from the keepers. She couldn't be older than six. I rushed forward to hold her. The door slammed behind the men, leaving everything silent.

That night Thalia and I calmed the girl down, brushing tears from her delicate face. She fell asleep fast in my arms as I cradled her like my own child. Losing my own control, I cried myself to sleep, weighed down with sorrow.

Her name is Vanhi, meaning fire. Don't be fooled by her first night here. She's the bravest, strongest girl I know. Nothing shadows her light. Her ball of fire blazes inside her every day and no one can blow it out. Her wild temper and her outgoing personality outshin the rest of the dolls in this dollhouse.

Vanhi hates being told what to do and never ceases to throw a fit. Her tantrums cause the keepers so much trouble, and they will only put up with them for so long. They gave her opium to make her have sex with the customers when she first arrived. When she throws her fits, they still do.

She's just a baby. Her chubby cheeks attract so many pinches that cause her to squirm in annoyance. She has stunning aqua eyes that still mesmerize me. The first night, when I picked her up off the floor, her eyes met me with desperation. She needed me.

Today Vanhi told me something that surprised me.

"Ro, if anyone's gonna get out of dis place, it's definitely gonna be you."

Her words gave me a new strength that I hadn't felt in a while. But it quickly vanished, and I wished she didn't have so much confidence in me. I hate feeling obligated to hold onto something I don't believe in anymore. I don't believe in hope, and I wish she wouldn't hope for me. But I'll never tell her to stop. I never want her to lose the spark that the rest of us already have lost. Somehow she manages to keep some of her innocence, and I see how this preserves her. Vanhi's bright flame flutters every time she laughs or smiles, and I'll do anything I can to keep it glowing because I know I wish I still had that spark. Mine died a long time ago. It died when I was sold for the second time. It died when I lost my arrangement, my home, my father and my hope. I know I will never get out of here, and if I did where would I go? Who would take care of Vanhi? Who would stop her from burning herself to cinders?

Vanhi was the only light in the darkness. We lived in fear, not knowing what would happen next. And yet, the routine was monotonous, predictable. We woke up, cried because we were still alive, because we remembered yesterday, because we remembered there was a tomorrow. We split into our different sections, found an empty stall and waited. We waited for the unbearable—waiting was the worst part.

I didn't remember my first time. I didn't remember much of my first weeks actually. But it all came back to me in flashes.

The first thing I remember was waking up in the back of a car: ribs shattered, eyes puffy, dried blood stuck to my face. The dalal[24] yanked me into a restaurant and said if I acted obediently they would give me ice cream. I didn't feel like fighting anymore. My ribs poked through my muscles, and left me in intolerable agony as I struggled to breathe. I could barely move, let alone fight back, so they fed me ice cream as some sort of treat, but I remember crying because swallowing made my broken ribs jab me inside. They forced me to keep eating, and I remember vaguely sitting there as the room turned in circles. They had laced the top of my vanilla ice cream with opiates. I was knocked out for the many days it took to bring me to the brothel[25].

Next came the gharwalis[26] in the dark room. Two fingers snapped in my face.

"Wake up!"

I blinked hard.

"Can you hear me?"
Where was I?

I blinked again, hoping to wake up somewhere else.

My eyes opened and I was surrounded by a swirl of glitter, powder, and judging eyes. Brushes smacked my face. I felt my skin slowly suffocate under the thick powder. Then my eyelids sank beneath the black liquid. Terrified, I squeezed them shut as brushes dotted my lids.

"Open your eyes," a woman's voice commanded.

---

[24] Dalals- Traffickers; those who recruit the girls and also boys (for bonded labor) and sell them to the maliks for profits.
[25] Based on true stories of trafficking
[26] Gharwalis- House madams, managers

I tried but my eyelashes were dripping with black mascara. Suddenly I felt my body spinning, as though a million hands were stripping my body of clothes. Shackles clasped my wrists and ankles. Metal chained my neck. Finally, my eyes found the strength to break through the darkness. A mirror was shoved in front of me so I could see my bedazzled body glimmer in the reflection. The sparkling bangles, hanging off the ends of my limbs, flashed in the glass. Anywhere else I would have admired their intricate beauty, but here I felt chained down like a prisoner. The mirror shimmered in front of me. I hated myself. I hated the doll staring back at me.

My old dance teacher's words whispered in my ear.

Beauty is pain. It's the price we women pay to be glamorous.

I remember complaining before each recital, hating dressing up. Once again I felt like a plastic doll. The longer I looked at myself, the more my body struggled under the ponderous weight. I couldn't carry this new mask.

December 2005

Glitter

Paint, powder, glitter
Henna, lipstick, glimmer
Mascara dripping thick
Paint me with your lies
Draw me like a fool
Dress me like a clown
Pick me up to knock me down

Just a glance
Look in that mirror
Look at me
Who am I?

195

What they want me to be
A doll
A puppet
A girl
A woman
A toy
Entertainment
A false, tormenting statement:

Power.
You have it, I get it
Can I go now?

Is there a place you have to be?

No.

Then lay back down
We're not done here

There's no timer
No
Just an alarm in my head
Ringing, screaming
Wake up!
But I can't
It's not a dream
It's my endless reality

Can you see me?
In this darkness
Are you blind?
Can I be seen?
What do you see?
'Cause it's not me
It's what they want you to see

It's the lie
It's the game
It's the glitter in the way
This is not me
What you see
Just a dolled up piece of meat

They shoved me on stage. I watched the girls in front of me be stripped naked before the audience, to be judged and admired. I was up next. A hand shoved me forward onto a pedestal, like a cow for sale. A man took off my clothes. And I let him. He spun me around so they could price me and sell me off to a valuable bidder. And I let him, because what could I do? I let them judge my beauty and worth as a human being, just as I had been judged all my life. I let them sell me once again as I had been all my life.

Flash. I was with Thalia. A feeling of comfort came over me. She was the only one who could make me feel safe, and she had been there from the beginning. She was my moon in the middle of the night. Thalia had guided me along my way and taught me everything I had to know about this place, including my dreaded responsibilities. Although assigned as my "sister," when her duties as an adhiya[27] were done she remained my best friend.

My first few weeks in the safe room were spent being comforted by her, as my nightmares woke us up each night. Soon, however, the room became a place where all of our worries were put to rest. Sleep became my favorite escape, and I shared that brief moment of relief cuddled up with Thalia.

I missed her dearly. I missed each moment with her.

---

[27] Adhiya -literally meaning "half" are the prostitutes who are half-paid and have accepted the lives as prostitutes. They usually started as slaves. They also assume the role of older sister in the brothels and convince the new slaves to obey and take care of them, doing such things as tending their wounds

Her beauty mesmerized everyone, and I should have known it would only be so long before she was taken from me. Everyone was, but it didn't mean it hurt any less. I missed running my fingers through her silky black hair. I missed her motherly hugs and sweet words of comfort. She was the mother I never had, and I hated them for taking her away from me.

August 2006

I'm really worried about Thalia. She's been gone for days now and we still haven't heard from her. I thought she might be in the infirmary, but Ashrita, fully recovered now, returned with no news of her. It's weird falling asleep at night without her beside me. Vanhi cries for her every night too, wondering where she has gone. I spend my nights cuddling with Vanhi, wishing Thalia was there. Wherever she is, I hope she is safe and it is a better place.

It was a week after Thalia had disappeared when my biggest nightmare came true. Even Thalia's warning hadn't prepared me for such a terrible night.

September 2006

The Frozen Cell

There I was. Amidst the nightmare I can't describe. It's the insanity that rips you out of your own skin and then shoves you back in it. It's the frustration that drives you into walls. My mind wandered from death to life to death again. I was forced to crave death without being able to die.

Eternity, the cell was, as I trembled on the floor, trapped for hours. The cold cement walls echoed with endless screams of past sufferings. They were haunted with the girls' stories, many of which were clawed into the cement walls. I could hear their nails scratching the cement, but no matter how deeply they dug, the wall remained.

After the first few hours, I started to hear voices. I realized they were coming from my own head. I tried to sleep, but sleep refused to come to my rescue, so I lay awake staring at the wall for hours, forced to remember.

At least I was untouchable inside.

Eventually I could map out the entire dollhouse room-by-room, corridor-by-corridor and stall-by-stall.

The dollhouse was an untouchable world, locked up each night by the keepers. They watched us from above and played with us with their strings. Each morning the keepers would pluck the puppets, perk us upright, and place us in an unsanitary cot. It was like being dragged through a public bathroom, but stone replaced the stalls and curtains hid those inside. The curtains may have been brightly colored, but they didn't fool anyone about the darkness inside.

It wasn't for a couple months when I learned the truth about Thalia's mysterious absence. A strange girl tapped me on the shoulder and pulled me aside. The petite skeleton looked like insanity. I didn't want to talk to her at first, but when I realized she knew something about Thalia I pushed aside my fear. The girl leaned in closer until I could smell her hot putrid breath.

"I hear you've been looking for Thalia. You didn't hear this from me, but…" she leaned in closer and whispered even softer, "she didn't escape. The malik took her for himself. That disgusting dog," she spat like a hysterical witch. "He wanted her all for himself."

It all made sense, then. The malik always had a special eye for her. His stare knotted my stomach, but Thalia never seemed to notice. He never came downstairs much, but we heard him from below. The ceiling would shake from his pounding stereo, and we could hear the faded laughs and screams above it. Thalia, more than any of us, hated him. We hated them. I couldn't imagine how she felt living under that roof every night. My heart throbbed for her. I hoped she was in a better place.

When I begged on the streets the moon used to give me a sense of sanity in the construction site. I'd lie beside Tarun and stare at it. The glimmer reminded me that there was something more to life than begging in the streets. There was another world out there that I could be a part of. It was devastating not being able to look outside and see the moon shining above me. I used my pen to draw a fake window in my journal and traced a moon inside the box.

I needed something to admire, and the cold walls were no inspiration. I used to dream about leaving and escaping every night when I was with Tarun, but back then I had a life to run to and a future to run from. Now I am in the future that I ran from so long ago. And I no longer have a place to escape to. Death is the only light left at the end of my tunnel.

March 2007

I've lost all sense of hope. There is nothing in this world left for me to hold onto. There is no window of opportunity I can look outside of to see the moon and stars twinkling. My dreams have faded. I can't remember what they were anymore. A sad hum rings in my ears as the song has slowly grown softer and darker. Each day passes more and more slowly as I drag my body, waiting for death to come. I've become the stone walls that surround me. Nothing moves me. Nothing inspires me. My walls are chipping away, but I haven't crumbled yet.

Somehow I'm not ready to crumble yet. I want to leave, but I don't want to disappear. I don't want to be forgotten. I can't let myself fade to nothing. I can't let this world move on without me, as if I never existed. I did exist. I do exist. And yet how can they know I exist when my body will be burned to ashes, leaving my story to die with me?

I hope someone, someday, will hear my story so people outside of these walls will know the truth about the world they live in. I want them to know that people like me are here, and that we're sold, trapped, abandoned, beaten, starved, drugged and, most of all, silenced. We're hidden. We are the invisibles. No one sees us, but we're still here. We still exist. We still walk the same earth, breathe the same air, admire the same sky, dream of a future better than our own. We have two eyes, two hands, two feet, one heart, just as they do, but we don't live the same life.

We are treated like toy dolls, as if we don't feel, as if we don't hurt, as if we aren't human. But we do feel. We do hurt. We are human.

I know I'm human, but if I am, why do I feel so lifeless? Like a puppet, empty and powerless? Was my sole purpose in this world to be put on display? Is my story not worth hearing? No. I refuse to believe that. I am just as human as the rest, and it's about time I started to feel like one again. As long as I still have a voice in this world, I'll keep screaming. And maybe, just maybe, one day I'll be heard.

FIRE!
(John)

John Hanson was a little boy growing up in the big city. Manhattan was crowded and noisy. Among the tall strangers and towering skyscrapers, he always felt small. He fearfully held the hand of an adult as he strolled through the bustling streets, afraid of getting lost in the crowd. From his small apartment, full of antiques and ancient paintings, he'd watch the interesting people go by. He'd admire the colossal billboards on the buildings. At night he watched the city turn into a magnificent light show, filled with glimmering windows and spotlights searching through purple skies. He'd watch the transition from the live night to the dull morning. The people would soon be rushing, late for work. He'd laugh as he saw them spill their coffee, usually from the nearby Starbucks that had a line stretching around the corner.

He would wait patiently for the sun to set again, so the skies could turn to oranges and flashy pinks. Soon the city would awaken and John would sneak out of his room past his bedtime to gaze at the wonders of Manhattan. Men and women dressed in cocktail dresses and tuxes tried to get an empty taxi. Smoke rose from hot dog and pretzel stands on street corners shared by homeless people smoking in their puffy jackets.

When his city became a snowy wonderland, John melted inside. He loved watching the delicate snowflakes land on the windowsill. He loved sticking out his tongue to catch the falling ice. However, what made this time of year really special was his family. Every year, no matter where they were in the world, his parents would come back for Christmas to spend time with their boy, John.

He adored his parents, Natalie and Marshall, but held a grudge for abandoning him to live with his grandma for most of the year as they travelled the world to do their work. John never did understand why he couldn't travel with them, and his heart would ache for them to be back in his life. Patiently yet anxiously, John would sit in front of that small apartment door and wait. When Natalie and Marshall slowly creaked the door open, he hurtled across the floor and tackled his beloved parents to the ground. He had missed them so much.

There came the time when John packed his bags and flew far across the globe. The eleven-year-old boy stared out the airplane window and waved goodbye to the city lights. The only life he had ever known was gone forever, but it was John's dream to travel with his parents. He'd sacrifice anything to be with them, and so for the rest of his life he moved from country to country, city to city, village to village, and he never looked back. The world was a dangerous unknown, but John's family took any and all risks for their passionate desire to help people.

As a kid, John didn't always understand why he was missing out on little league baseball and school dances. He didn't always understand why he was living in small villages with people who didn't even speak the same language. He didn't always understand why he had to sacrifice his life for others, and he didn't realize how extensively his experiences were influencing him. But on November 15, 1987, he knew everything he had ever sacrificed and everything he would soon risk were worth it.

His feet deep in mud in a field in Thailand, John looked at the abandoned site in panic. Flames burned the rice mills and scorched the bordering plantation. To his left his mother Natalie sobbed, refusing to leave.

Marshall shook her frantically, trying to shake sense into her stubborn heart. "Natalie! We have to go now! They'll kill us!"

"I'm not leaving without him!" she shot back.

She squeezed the little boy's hand, refusing to let go. His dusty black hair was filled with debris and his eyes with fear. John's parents' escape plan had failed, and the boys on the plantation were trapped. They had to leave them behind, but Natalie knew what would happen to them when we did.

Sprinting back to the car, with the little boy in tow, Natalie, Marshall and John ran for their lives. Once they were inside the rundown vehicle, the mob of angry plantation owners surrounded them. They banged their sticks and threw rocks at the windows. Marshall tried to speed past, dodging cattle and sheep, but the men followed, screaming and wielding torches. A flaming stick crashed into John's window, shattering the glass and starting a fire inside.

The car swerved out of the way of a brick wall. It flipped onto its side and John's head slammed into the roof. He screamed as his shoulder dug into the glass-shattered ground. John saw the hot red blood staining Natalie and Marshall's faces. Suddenly, the car metal felt burning-hot against his skin, and he realized the cotton-covered seats were on fire. The air grew thick and tight. Black smoke stung his eyes. He couldn't see past the front seat.

Groping and fumbling, John found someone's hand, its rough texture comforting. He was torn from the car and left lying on the ground, coughing and gasping. A dozen hands patted his clothes, stopping them from catching fire. He blinked hard and saw half a dozen dark faces spinning around him. He turned towards the flipped car and watched the flames engulf it.

He screamed helplessly, "Mom! Dad! No!"

Struggling to get onto his feet, he watched the group of

boys risk their lives for his parents. They dove into the burning vehicle until his mother's curly almond hair appeared through the broken window. Burns covered her parched bloody skin, but she was alive.

The little boy stared at John. Hadn't he been in the car the whole time? Soon he was beside him. John knelt to his knees, crying and hugging the little boy. How could he thank all of them?

His heart sank when he realized the boys wouldn't be leaving with them. They couldn't save them from the life they lived. The enslaved orphaned boys had led them to safety. Now they returned to the chains that bound them to the fields forever.

John looked down to see the little four-year old Thai boy still holding onto him desperately. He didn't let go until he was adopted and named his little brother, Tommy.

To this day, Tommy inspires John to keep fighting for children enslaved around the world. He wanted to continue his parents' legacy and risk everything he had for those who had risked their lives for him. John would do anything for his family, and that day, with feet mud-deep in the rice fields, surrounded by burning mills and a scorched plantation, he realized he had brothers and sisters all around the world.

REFLECTION
(Mukti)

We drove through the secluded quarries for an hour before reaching paved road. We passed the abandoned fields and dried rice patches. Our bodies bounced in the van as we traveled over the rocky ground and rebreathed each other's air. Out the window I saw the sky filling with clouds. Rain was on the way. It would soon be drowning the quarry.

I clenched my fists, waiting for the city.

The van filled with a warm thickness. Sandhya's sweaty arm rubbed against me.

Balaji broke the empty silence.

Apparently we weren't free yet.

"Freeing your quarry is not simple. It can be a lengthy process. It takes multiple steps, but luckily we've already finished the rescue. Now we'll go to the district magistrate and file for your release certificates. Each of you will explain your case—how long you were there, why you were there, your conditions, etc., and then we can continue on to the rehabilitation process."

Balaji was about to speak again when a loud yelping from the back of the van interrupted him.

Priya, with a face redder than mendi chalk, was gasping for air. The first aid kit's thermometer read 105 degrees. Heat radiated from her skin as water escaped from her pores. I clutched her hands with all my might.

My mother started mumbling, "My baby. My baby girl. Please, I can't go on without you. You're still my little girl."

The driver changed routes and squeezed by the rickshaws in our way. An echo of wild honking bounced through the line of traffic. But no one moved. There was so much traffic.

"How far away is the closest hospital?" I felt panicked.

"Without traffic, twenty minutes, but with this traffic it could be more than two hours."

I wanted to scream at him to find some kind of way. Tears smudged my dust-covered face. Why did Priya have to be the one to get malaria? Why her and not me? I heard the mumbled prayers from the back of the van. I couldn't pray anymore. I had already prayed too much. I needed something else to hold on to. Where was my rock when I needed her?

The tires screeched and suddenly we were off the road. People jumped out of our way as we skimmed by a local fruit stand. Mangoes toppled into the street. The angry vendor started throwing fruit at the car and the driver had to use his windshield wipers to clean off the splattered mango.

We turned onto a private road with tall gates. The lazy security guards were distracted, chatting away. Our car skid past them and onto the road. Everyone in the van admired the surrounding mansions with gardens full of golden fountains shaped as animals and gods. The main house was a rundown shack by comparison. Flustered and embarrassed, the guards chased after us with angry fists.

"What are you doing? Where are we going? Have you gone mad?" Balaji screamed at the driver.

Another man explained, "This is a private community. He's taking us through back routes to skip the traffic."

The van accidently slipped off the road and drove over a manicured lawn, chopping up the grass. Two women wrapped in purple saris jumped out of the way. They had giant scissors in their hands to cut the blades of grass. I could see the other gates now. We were so close, but they were shutting.

I just gained my freedom. I couldn't be put behind bars again.

My head hit the top of the van as we ran over a speed bump.

My sister had stopped yelping. I think it was because she didn't have the strength to anymore.

She had to hold on. We were so close.

"Just a few more minutes. Please, Priya. Stay with me," I whispered into her ear.

The car swerved and I knocked my head against the window again. We were back on the paved road. My head was in colossal pain. I didn't know how many more blows my skull could take. Suddenly, everything started fading. The lights went blurry and I found myself falling. Falling. But I was sitting down.

Blackness.

The van jolted. I woke up in a haze. It was like a dream.

"Hospital?" I asked again, but couldn't hear myself.

I read Balaji's lips: "Not. Much. Longer."

Shankar was a fast driver, and I appreciated him speeding for us. But I wished he hadn't knocked me unconscious.

Priya murmured something, but I couldn't make out what. I put my ear to her lips, and she whispered faintly: "I...can't... please...Raj...Ar-jun," I only heard bits of words. I didn't know if it was because of my hearing or her shortness of breath. "I love you."

Then she went silent. Her eyelids closed. I saw a tear fall.

"Priya, hold on! Please! Don't leave me. I need you! Priya! I love you," I screamed. My head rang.

The peas stared at me blankly as tears streamed down my cheeks. My mother pressed her palms against Priya's cheeks, praying.

Finally I was free. Finally we were free. *Devaru Yekay avalannu nannindaa dooraa maadutthiddaaney? So why is God taking her from me?* Was that my punishment? Had I done something to deserve this? My chest hurt. I felt the entire quarry weighing on my heart. I felt Shubar strangling me. I watched the life being sucked out of my sister, and I could feel it being sucked out of me, too.

In the distance I saw the white building.

"Priya we're almost there!" I cried. "We're at the hospital. We need you to keep fighting. You can do this, Priya. You've fought for so long. Fight just a little longer."

The van came to a stop.

"John and I will carry Priya in from here," Balaji said, carefully picking her up.

She seemed lighter than a handful of grass.

I watched them run as fast as they could to the emergency room. I couldn't stay in the van. I chased after them. Cars honked for the van to move.

My brain banged against my skull and I felt myself slipping. I barely made it to the emergency room. I stumbled in, panting—everything spinning. Suddenly I felt the wind get knocked out of me. I clutched my stomach.

Blackness.

The emergency room smelled of blood and sweat. It was a narrow hall with white and blue marble tiles. Ten small chairs were lined up against the wall. People crowded in everywhere, sitting on the floor and leaning against the walls. The children's emergency room was on the left. It had ten bed stalls separated with white stained curtains. To the right was a crowded room. Chaos is the only word I could use to describe it. I sat in the middle of the hall, feeling lost.

There were at least fifty people around me, sitting on the floor waiting, sobbing and sleeping. I jumped out of the way of a man on a gurney being rushed to surgery. He had a bloody gash running from his right arm down to his upper leg. I could see his shoulder blade sticking out. My hands covered my mouth to stop the vomit.

I tried to find my sister, but instead saw John talking to a doctor holding a clipboard. A warm hand grabbed my arm. It was Balaji.

"Where is Priya?" I cried.

He was calm. "She went into that room. They are taking care of her right away. The hospital knows John from all of the work he's done. He's brought a lot of patients here. They're going to take care of her. Don't worry."

"How do you know she's going to be okay? Did they say they could save her? Can I see her?"

His mouth kept moving, but I didn't hear any words come out.

His eyes looked at me with concern. "Mukti, you don't look too good. Are you okay?"

I blinked hard. Did he say something?

"Here's the doctor. You can ask her the questions," he added, still concerned.

I saw a blurry doctor in a white uniform walking towards us. The room started to spin. She said something in a sweet voice.

"I'm her sister. Will she be okay? Where is she now?"

"We're pumping fluids into her system. That's all I know, but I can show you where her room is. You won't be able to go in right away, but you can wait outside."

The three of us followed Doctor Parvati to Room 201. Balaji supported me to prevent me from falling while John talked to the other drivers on the phone. They were meeting us here. So many needed treatment.

I was fine, I convinced myself. I was here for Priya.

The doctor knocked on the door. A nurse in sky-blue clothes with a cotton mask opened it, and I peeked in. Priya lay in a bed limply with a tube system connected to her. I pushed past the doctors to her side.

Her eyes were half open. She was barely conscious. A black monitor beside the bed kept beeping. The other doctor in the room saw me staring at it. He told me that if the line ever went straight it meant her heart had stopped. I glared at him. *Seriously?* My sister was on the verge of death. Then he added that he would do whatever he could to make sure that didn't happen.

Priya was sweating so much. An IV pumped minerals and fluids into her system that were meant to revive her. My eyes swelled with tears. At least she was free. If she died, she would die free.

The doctors tried to push me out of the room. They needed to figure out how to break the fever. I wouldn't move. My feet were nailed to those glossy tiles. They tried to drag me out, but I struggled out of their grasp. I was surprisingly strong. I kicked and screamed until they let go. If my sister was going to die it wasn't going to happen with her all alone in a room full of strangers.

Suddenly nurses came in with tubs of ice. Doctors and nurses hurried around the room while my sister lay perfectly still. I watched the monitor beep. The green lines descended. A nurse lifted her body and carried her to a tub of ice. They stripped off her clothes and submerged her body into the vessel.

Priya shook. Her body shifted and jerked. Doctor Parvati smiled, a good sign. Everything else in the room seemed to fade away. It was only Priya and me. I knew she was scared.

"Mukti, it's time to go," I heard a voice say.

I was grabbed and dragged back. My head felt like a

million fireworks going off. It was so painful. I couldn't struggle anymore. John and Balaji were outside waiting. Balaji was the one on the phone now. Raj and Arjun sat beside them with their hands in their laps. To their right were Sandhya and her mother.

I let Arjun sit in my lap and held Raj's hand. They had gone through a lot in the past few days. I looked around and realized my mother wasn't there.

I didn't have the strength to worry anymore. My skull pounded like pots and pans falling down stairs. Ever since that night, my head had never stopped screaming.

"Where is everyone else? Where did the drivers take them?" I asked Balaji, who was off the phone now.

"On their way here. Another doctor is going to give the rest of you medical checkups. Mukti, I think you should go first. They are already with your mother and the other two men now."

"Lokesh and Nira," Sandhya chimed in.

Balaji pointed down the hall. "Speaking of the doctor, here he comes."

My vision started to fail. I balanced against Sandhya as we moved into a different room. We went into a transportation box that magically moved us upstairs.

When we arrived in the room, we were each put in different beds. I fought my body's instinct to sleep. Doctor Vrajesh put me through all sorts of tests.

I failed to get through most of them because I couldn't focus for long periods. He had me read letters on a wall from a distance, but I could barely see past the first row. He stopped me when he saw me growing frustrated by my inability to see. Next, he placed a set of headphones on me and said to press a button when I heard a beeping noise. With all of the commotion and traffic outside the window, I couldn't hear a thing. Eventually he gave up on that test, too.

He was very concerned about my head bruises and the pain I described to him. I told him how I struggled to breathe and stand on my own.

He noticed the cuts and bruises from the first granite incident, and I told him that story, too.

"You can look away if you want," Doctor Vrajesh suggested as he pierced a needle through my skin.

"No thanks," I said, wanting to watch.

"You're very brave," Doctor Vrajesh said, impressed. "Many children cry because of the pain."

"I don't cry over the small cuts anymore," I responded dully.

He wrapped my wrist with tape to secure the IV that pumped fluids into my body. Once the doctor left, my head fell onto my pillow. Sleep won.

I woke up to voices. A different doctor hovered over me.

"Are you awake?"

I blinked hard.

The woman explained that I had a severe head

concussion. For the next few weeks, I had to stay away from bright lights and remain in bed.

All that information seemed irrelevant the second I saw Priya. She looked so beautiful walking through the hospital room with the assistance of a nurse. It took me a moment to understand the sudden change in her appearance. I soon realized it was the new life coursing through her.

I shifted to a sitting position so I could see her better. To my left, my mother was asleep in a cot, but where were the peas? I asked the doctor to unplug my IV so I could go to the bathroom. To my amazement I found running water! It poured over my rough hands and face, soothing me.

I looked up at the mirror and stared at my reflection. I tried to figure out why I looked so different. My cheeks and lips were fuller. My eyes dazzled. I thought that I looked a little more like Ro—the girl I used to know. Maybe it was because I wore a real smile. Or maybe, just maybe, it was because for the first time in a long time I was free.

GAMES
(Ruchita)

The next day I woke up feeling dizzy with a tingling in my chest. I ignored it. There was a new hum amongst the dolls today as gossip spread like wildfire. The Commonwealth Games were coming to New Delhi[28], so a group of girls was being sold to new dalals.

Fear swept through the brothel. The young women dreaded their fates, knowing the dollhouse was no safe haven but fearing the dalals more. Dalals knew exactly how to break their girls before selling them. They broke our bones to break our spirits, so we became subservient to our customers and our maliks. If we were beaten enough, we would lose all hope and any fight left in us. We'd believe prostitution was our lives, and we could never be anything else. We'd never run away, and therefore we'd be sold at a higher price.

Vanhi came to me crying that day. Her face was swelled up like a puffy poori. She wept in my arms as I held her scratched and bloody hand from that afternoon.

Asahyya. Disgusting.

That was the only word I could think of. Vanhi, so tender and sweet, being thrown into dens for the dogs to hound on was *disgusting*. I carefully examined her pink raw hand and found myself imagining her in the stall, digging her nails into her own skin to divert herself from the pain. I winced.

I knew her pain. I knew everything she was going through. It made listening to her so much worse, *because* I knew.

---

[28] Commonwealth Games -the Commonwealth Games increased sex-trafficking and the sale of sex slaves tremendously. Construction for the games also forced thousands of laborers into bondage.

Her hair stuck to her wet forehead and caught in her mouth as she struggled to speak. I barely heard her story between sobs.

"I just couldn't Ruchita!" she shouted. "He was repulsive! I would rather die!"

Her body heat rose. I felt like I was trying to tame a fire, but the flames inside her were uncontrollable.

"Beta, Beta. Breathe. Vanhi, you're going to be okay. Everything is going to be okay."

"How can you say that, Ro? You *know* it's not going to be okay! You *know* that!" She screamed, grabbing my shoulders and shoving me back and forth. "Nothing is okay! Everything is wrong. Everything is awful. I want to leave. I miss home, Ro! I miss home! Take me home. Ro, Please! I don't want to go back in there. Please. Ro, Please." Her screams faded to a sob.

I wished with all my heart I could take Vanhi home, but Vanhi couldn't be saved. None of us could. Even outside this brothel we'd be dolls. We'd be roped to misogyny. We'd never be free.

A new fear crept into me. *The Commonwealth Games.* Vanhi was the most valuable girl in the brothel, priced the highest because of her purity and age. Would they take her away from me? The one piece of my humanity left? I realized I didn't have much time to comfort her. I didn't want them to break her, as I knew they would, and mold her into a lifeless spirit, meek and obedient.

"Vanhi, you are the strongest person I know. Remember when you first got here and you told me you would never let them hold you down? You said you would never let them be stronger than you? Well, hold onto that strength right now. Don't let them see you weak because they don't deserve to see you defeated. I know this is hard to understand, but sometimes to win you have to stop fighting. Vanhi, listen. You can't fight back. Show them that you are strong by being in control. Let them lead you out of here like a champion, and even if you don't feel like one, don't let them see otherwise. You can't throw a tantrum. It'll make you seem weak, and you're not weak. You are strong. We've been through this before. You're not alone, but you know what's coming, and you have to be okay with that. They'll be here soon, so prepare yourself. Be ready."

Vanhi looked at me with fiery eyes. She lay perfectly still and placed her hands on my shoulders.

I hoped my words could make a difference in those final moments. "Don't resist them. We'll be together soon. Maybe they'll take me with you. Fighting back will only make it worse. Please, promise me you won't resist them, Vanhi? Please?" I stared at her, pleading.

She nodded and threw her head against my chest. Heavy footsteps echoed in the hallway. I looked up to see the two dalals coming our way. I saw the nasty whip. My heart sank.

"Let her go," one of them commanded.

I clutched her tighter. It was a mother's instinct, and yet I knew there was no point. She was stripped from my arms. Vanhi clung to me, begging for me to hold on. But my frail arms had no strength.

This time Vanhi was drowning. I watched her sinking from above. My hand plunged into the water and reached out to her. I tried to lift her up, but felt her slipping through my fingers. Every part of me wanted to save her, but I felt myself letting go. I hated myself for letting her go.

As they turned the corner, I heard a thousand cracks in the air like fireworks. The sound of the whip smacking against her fragile skin echoed off the walls. Her screams carried through the halls, past the doors, into the city. My eyes flooded with tears. Hearing someone I loved in pain was a million times worse than feeling the pain myself.

I covered my face with my hands. I bawled until my body ached. Suddenly, my hair was yanked from behind. I let them drag my body through the hallways. I was thrown onto a cot that reeked. I was there for hours. Twenty men came to me.

The next day the mothers inspected us. They ripped through our hair, spread our legs, flipped us over, pulled our ears. If we passed, we were yanked into another room where a group of girls had already been dolled up. It was our turn. I hadn't thought much of any of it, as these checkups were common, until I saw the sweat dripping down Maya's face.

The Commonwealth Games.

Were we the ones chosen to be trafficked to a new brothel?

I searched the room for Vanhi. To my disappointment, she wasn't one of us. My already broken spirit cracked a little more. I needed my fire. I needed my light.

The next day was an eerie dream. It had been two years since I had seen daylight. The barred windows in the dollhouse were almost never opened. Although the evening in Mumbai was only dim, my eyes cowered from the brightness. I looked up at the dilapidated brothel. Green vines curled around the bottoms of the windowpanes, intertwined with violet flowers. The rusted brown paint was chipping, giving the building a

220

vintage look. I had never seen the outside before.

I followed the dalals to the bus. We were shoved into the back. Almost all of us settled in obediently, but one girl started a fuss. She began screaming, struggling to break free of the dalal's grip. The dalal grabbed her arm and snapped it[29]. I watched in horror as Samarya bent over in terrible pain. I clutched my own arm as though it were mine that was broken. Samarya was forced into the bus. The rest of us sat in silence, listening to her soft sobs but refusing to make eye contact. Some of the girls huddled in each other's arms, sniffling.

I looked out the window.

Where was my Vanhi?

My heart froze as I remembered a girl I once knew. Suddenly it made sense that I was so attached to Vanhi. Because Vanhi *was* Mukti. She was the same light needing me to be strong.

I watched a limp body being carried to the bus.

Oh, my dear, sweet Vanhi. What had they done to you? Her petite frame was lifted inside. I ran over to see her. I felt her chest. It slowly rose and fell. I exhaled in relief. She was alive, but they had drugged her.

I told them to leave her with me to tend to. Her body fell gently on my lap, and I stroked her hair. It could be days before she woke up. But as long as she was breathing by my side, I could breathe too.

The bus bounced through the streets, past roaming cows and noisy mopeds. It wasn't long before sleep wrapped

---

[29] True story

221

me in its arms, and it wasn't until late at night that I woke up.

When I opened my eyes, I saw Vanhi breathing heavily. I pressed my palms to her cool cheeks and whispered for her to wake up. Her eyelids fluttered but didn't open. I sighed and looked back out the window. It was pitch dark out, so there wasn't much to see. But it inspired me to imagine a world of my own.

The dim moon hid behind the smoky clouds, providing me with hope. It had been awhile since I had seen it, and now I couldn't tear my eyes from it. I watched it appear and reappear through the clouds, dreading its disappearance.

When the bus pulled into the crowded train station, I could tell we were far outside of Mumbai's city lines. A dalal made us wait patiently, as he argued with a man behind a guarded glass window, trying to buy our tickets.

Hundreds of travellers shuffled by in a rush to catch their train. We watched them and filled with a strong temptation to run into the crowd and never look back. But we knew we had nowhere to go. We had no money to buy our own ticket to safety.

I watched the dalal bargain with the man behind the glass. The ticket keeper eyed us suspiciously. I could only imagine what was going through his head when he saw a group of fifteen girls, beaten, starved and trembling in fear. But the second the dalal slid him an envelope filled with money, it didn't matter. The man turned a blind eye. I wondered how much money was in that envelope. I wondered how much money it took the man to justify the selling of fifteen girls like cattle.

Yet every man, woman, and family that rushed past us convinced themselves the same thing.

An ear-splitting whistle sounded through the station and shook the grounds. Suddenly a massive, dark-blue metal machine tore along the tracks. The girls were terrified. Vanhi trembled in my arms.

The dalal pushed us forward and suddenly we were swept into the crowd of people. As the passengers hurtled into the metal carts, all remaining air was pushed out, leaving no room to move or breathe. I felt the sweat of a stranger rub against me. I shivered and clutched onto Vanhi as if my life depended on it, afraid I might lose her in the rush of people. Although trapped in the same cart, the four dalals kept a firm eye on each of us. We knew not to run.

I rolled my eyes.

We had nowhere to go.

I spotted an empty seat and lunged for it. An elderly woman shoved me out of the way, trying to claim the same seat. I shoved her back. My legs wouldn't last longer than five minutes standing upright. Her mouth opened as if to yell at me, then she saw the girl in my arms. She backed away with a soft look.

The train jolted forward, and a second later my body caught up with it.

"Ro?" A gentle voice whispered.

I looked down and saw a glossy-eyed baby staring up at me. Tears began to trickle out of the corners of my eyes.

I smiled down at her. "Hi, Vanhi."

My fingers ran through her hair, down the sides of her cheeks, and traced the bottom of her chin.

"We're together?" she asked.

I nodded. "We're together."

She pulled her body up from my lap so she could rest her hands on my shoulders. Our eyes locked. I stared at this angel in front of me and wondered how someone so sweet and pure could end up in a cycle so cruel.

"Ro?"

"Yes, Vanhi?"

Vanhi stared at the passagers in the train. Then she looked up at me, red in shame.

"Ro, I don't want to go back."

I looked at the top of her head resting against my chest. "Go back where?"

She played with the beads on my kurta. "Home. I don't want to go home."

"Vanhi, beta, we're not going home."

She looked at me with pleading eyes. "Yes, we are Ro. We're going to my home."

"We're going to Delhi, Vanhi."

"Delhi is my home, Ro."

"Oh?"

She rattled the beads on my shirt nervously. I could tell she wanted to tell me something. Her chest rose and fell hard.

"I used to live in the slums with my family—with my father and mother, and brother Aja, and Ramesh, and Babu Masa, too. They all worked on the same construction site. They were building new apartments for the city. I didn't go to work with them usually, because I was little. But one day the landowner promised my father I would get half wage for the same work. So I went with them the next day…and…and that man really liked me…He gave me extra food and promised other things, too. Eventually he got me alone…and he began to touch me." She choked on the words. "He would tell me not to say anything. He threatened to hurt my family if I ever told, and so I didn't say anything. I didn't want him to hurt my family…He kept…It went on for a couple of weeks. But when I finally told my mother…"

She stopped. Tears streamed down her face. My heart sank. She was just a girl.

"She told my father. And…and he asked me if it was true," she gasped between breaths. "And I said yes."

Her face fell into my chest. I wrapped my arms around her tightly, trying to comfort her, but knew that no matter what I did, I could never take her pain away. She would live with that pain forever. I knew how hard it was to relive that past, and even more to share her story out loud. I admired her courage because I too knew how hard it was to do.

"He slapped me and said, 'You're a disgrace.' He said he was so ashamed of me and asked how I could do this to him. I told him I didn't want it to happen, but he said I was a shame to the family and now I could never be married. So he…" She stopped again, and I began to cry too because I knew exactly what she was going to say next. "…he sold me to the dalal."

I wished she'd never told me. I wished I could erase

225

that memory, but I would never, never forget her story[30].

Vanhi looked up with her glassy eyes and asked, "Is your family ashamed of you, Ro?"

"I don't have a family."

We spent the rest of the train ride in silence, breathing in the rank, musty air and pondering our futures. I thought about my almost-past. I wondered what Daeva had told my almost-family, the Ramamurthys, when I went missing. She probably convinced them I ran away in fear of the marriage, and my father probably believed her too. For hours, I wondered what my life could have almost been, and I wondered if Mukti was happy or if she too was thinking of her almost-could-have-been life.

---

[30] True Story

UNCONSTITUTIONAL
(Mukti)

The radio buzzed in the background as we drove over the dirt roads. Priya snored behind me, waking up every so often when we bounced over a pothole. My elbow rested on the windowpane and my head against the cool glass. I gazed at the stars. The dark night captured me, isolating me from reality, and my eyes flashed back to my reflection in the mirror.

Was that really me, Mukti? Was I that girl staring back at me?

Then my eyes flashed back to the wild dog darting across the road.

We were far from the city lights now and completely surrounded by wilderness. The vehicle's front lights dimly lit the road ahead, but the darkness overwhelmed everything else. The Ajadi Center felt so far away and the night so long. We had been driving for hours and didn't seem to be gaining any distance. My mind fell numb to my thoughts.

I listened to Priya's calm inhaling and exhaling. The sound of her breathing was like a lullaby to me. Just knowing she was alive was enough to make me feel peaceful. Yet my mind wandered back to the hospital mirror. I looked at my reflection in the car window.

"Mukti," I whispered.

I looked at the faint reflection, hoping to find a strong, confident leader but instead saw a naïve girl, scared of the literal and figurative road ahead.

"Mukti," I whispered again.

It sounded ordinary. I didn't want to be ordinary.

The past few days replayed in my head. It all seemed like a distant dream, a figment of my imagination. I looked back out the window at the stars. We would be arriving any minute now. The entire quarry would be there.

I was terrified. It would be the first time I saw them since we escaped. I had no idea what they thought. They had been settled in the Ajadi Center for two days now. Balaji said they had been fed, given medical treatment and a place to sleep. The center was the first rehabilitation site for former *slaves*, as they called us. There were a few teachers who came in to give school lessons to the children, but the center would be only a temporary solution for our quarry. We couldn't stay there forever.

Lights appeared in the distance as the car turned onto a new street. We came to a stop before a large gate and were told to get out.

"Careful of the mud," Balaji warned as I stepped outside, almost slipping.

Shankar and Balaji had described the Ajadi Center, but it was nothing like I envisioned it. The facility was much larger, filled with a dim light and chalky buildings that surrounded a grassy courtyard. The warm air embraced my body. The moment my foot touched the ground I felt an immediate sense of security.

My heart jumped out of my chest as the night erupted with applause and screams of joy. The entire quarry had woken up to welcome us. Boys and girls swarmed me, and the elderly, who'd once despised me, now kissed my feet in respect. My heart filled with a joy that almost brought me to tears. I had never felt so loved. The community huddled around us crying, laughing and praying. Priya was welcomed by a hundred hands blessing her with good health while my mother was in the embrace of another woman. We stood there, stunned.

Eventually the birds flew back to their nests, and my family was escorted to our rooms. When we arrived at our door, Balaji handed us a shiny metal object. I held it in my hands, confused.

"What is this?" I asked.

Raising his right eyebrow he answered, "The key to your room?"

He took the key and twisted it in the knob. He flicked on a switch and light appeared! All of us stood in shock, taking in our new room and its amazing features. The peas immediately jumped into one bed, claiming it as theirs.

"Mukti! Mukti! Look we have our own bed! Look how cool!" Raj's face lit up in excitement.

Priya and I collapsed on the other bed. Before I could discover the bathroom with running water, my body had sunk into a deep sleep.

The next morning began with a loud knock at the door. I opened my eyes, seeing a haze of white and orange puffs. I stumbled out of bed and ended the insufferable banging at the door. Outside stood a man, sweating beneath the sun.

"Are you Mukti? You are very late!"

"Yes—"

"They need you immediately! You were supposed to be at the vans twenty minutes ago! They're leaving to go to the district magistrate."

Suddenly it hit me. The sun was glaring in the sky and the center was already bustling with activity. It must have been late morning. Someone was supposed to have woken me!

"Where are the vans?" I asked.

"I'll show you."

He motioned for me to follow. I left the empty room in a rush without getting ready.

We went past the gates of the center and into the muddy streets where everyone was waiting, probably for me. John looked at me with irritation.

"I'm so sorry! I didn't wake up! I didn't have time to get ready or any—"

Balaji cut me off, "Don't worry. You are here now. Let's go."

We all crammed into one van, and I realized I would once again be trapped in a vehicle for hours. The district magistrate was on the outskirts of the village.

There were only four to represent the quarry at the magistrate, and I didn't know the others very well. One of them came from Tamilnadu and didn't speak Kannada, so we had never talked before. The other two always had worked on the other side of the quarry.

We waited for another fifteen minutes in the driveway before I got annoyed. Why did they rush me here if I would be sitting in a car? A man in the back started humming to pass the time. Balaji, John and another man were discussing something outside. I cracked the window, hoping to hear their conversation.

At first they were speaking that other language I didn't understand. But then Balaji spoke to the other man in the language I understood. "Shouldn't we go to the Panchayati Raj Institute first? That is where we have gone for almost all of our cases."

They argued a little in the other language.

"No. This is too big. We need to go straight to the district magistrate." Balaji translated for the other man.

This as in us? As in our quarry? My stomach twisted in knots. What if we had gone through all of this just to show up at the magistrate and have the door slammed in our faces? They wouldn't believe us. I knew it. Why would they? What were we to them? They despised us. We were the filth polluting their streets. We were Dalits.

Balaji stumbled back into the van and prepped us for the day.

"We are headed to the district magistrate now where we will start the process of legally releasing you. There are basically four major steps. First is identification and awareness, which we've already done. Now there is release, which is what we are going to do at the magistrate. We plead our cases with the four of you as witnesses. They will explain the law and you will answer a few questions. If they believe our case, we will have to file for release certificates. The third step is the rehabilitation process. After everyone is legally released, the government will provide a certain amount of rehabilitation funds or opportunities that will provide you and your families with a stable income to live on. This process is not simple, and it is not quick. It can take years for certificates to be filed, and some may be released while others are not. We have gone through this many times and know what we are doing. But I have to warn you that this can be frustrating. We need to be patient."

He turned back around in his seat and watched the road. I asked, "What about the fourth step?"

Balaji turned around. "What, Mukti?"

"You said there are four steps."

"Yes?"

"But you gave us only three."

"Oh. Well, the fourth step is retribution, but we aren't focusing on that right now. Besides, retribution almost never happens."

"What is it? Why not?"

"It's when those who committed the crime get punished."

"Oh. Like revenge?"

His eyes narrowed.

"I guess."

I sank back in my chair and grinned, imagining Shubar behind bars.

When we finally arrived, I was surprised to see that the district magistrate's office was no more than a small white building. Not very intimidating. We walked up to the door when suddenly I heard a riot of people swarming the building,

232

which was hidden behind a massive tree. Its wizened branches stretched far out into the sky and gave the place an eerie feeling.

I looked up in awe. There was no wind, and yet the tree seemed to be shaking. Suddenly a black object fluttered, then another and still another. Hundreds of bats were hanging from the branches and started screeching. I shuddered in disgust and scurried through the door.

The air inside was cold, but other people's body heat made the room stuffy. While everyone else was shoved around, as if in the way, John and Balaji were immediately welcomed and treated with respect.

The four of us spent twenty minutes trying not to be swept away by the crowd. I struggled to stand in place as the ground moved beneath me. Finally, a pudgy, round man came out to greet us. He gathered our group and brought us to a tiny room with corners stacked with papers, books and typing machines. The man sat behind a desk hidden by stacks of documents. We stood in the back of the cramped room and waited to be called.

Panting, the pudgy man stated the law and described the system of bonded labor.

"The bonded labor system basically has three distinct elements. One: bonded labor exists as a type of master-servant relationship. Two: there exists a debtor-creditor relationship, where the laborer is the debtor, and the creditor is the master. And three: the master uses force where the servant is compelled to work and does not have the freedom to exercise his will. This is a legal definition. Bondage exists in any relationship that has those three elements."

He continued, speaking in long, annunciated breaths.

233

"The abolition of forced labor falls under part III of our constitution, dealing with fundamental rights. Furthermore, India is signatory for a number of conventions of the International Labor Organization and the United Nations that forbid forced labor, slavery and slave trade. The Bonded Labor System Abolition Act of 1976 aims to eradicate the evil totally. We are here today to enforce this. We will be asking each of you a number of questions to make sure that you fall under this category of bonded laborers."

My eyes bulged. *What in the world did he just say?*

He interviewed Ramesh first, which was unfortunate. Ramesh had been shaking since the moment we left the Ajadi Center. One could smell his fear from the other side of Karnataka.

"Don't worry. You can tell the truth. No one is going to hurt you," Balaji tried to comfort him.

"Tell only the truth," the pudgy man repeated in a monotone voice. "Minimum wage on average is Rs. 6000 per month, and standard work day is 8 hours, with minimum rest while at work of 30 minutes every five hours. Were you given decent working conditions and ensured a decent standard of living?

"Sir, the master was very fair. He treated us well. We were fed. I only working off debt that I told to work off. I borrowed money, and because of loan I work seven years. But he treated us with fair."

I grinded my teeth, wanting to strangle the man. Why was he defending Shubar? We weren't treated fair. Some died under the conditions, and we weren't paid at all!

John and Balaji frowned. Finally, the man finished up

with Ramesh and moved on to the other two men.

To my utter surprise, they answered the questions the same way. I waited furiously. When was it my turn?

The man started by asking my age.

"Thirteen."

"Did you know that Article 24 prohibits child labor under the age of 14 years old in the constitution?"

"No."

Then he continued his usual speech, "The act defines bonded labor as someone who has or is presumed to have had a bonded debt. Have you entered into an agreement with a creditor, in which in order to pay off this advance, obtained by you the debtor or by any relatives was in pursuance for any customary or social obligation or by reason of birth by any particular caste or community?"

Although I didn't understand half of the words he said, I comprehended enough.

"Yes, sir. My family and I were told we had to pay off a debt, and we have been working in the quarry ever since. We don't know how much we have paid off."

"Were you for a specified or unspecified period of time, without a wage or given nominal wages for your labor?"

"I was not paid for my work. I was working off the debt."

"And did you have to forfeit freedom of employment or other means of livelihood?"

235

By now I just knew to say keep saying yes.

"Did you have to forfeit the right to move freely throughout the territory of India?"

"We could not leave or we would be captured again and beaten."

"Did you forfeit the right to appropriately sell at the market value anything to pay off the debt?"

"There was no way to pay off the debt other than to work in the quarry. We had no choice."

He scribbled down a few more notes and wiped drops of sweat from his forehead. The sweat stains under his armpits seemed to grow with each passing minute. The man turned to John and Balaji, gesturing that we were done here. I didn't feel relieved. I thought sharing my story with the magistrate would feel uplifting, like I was freeing myself from my past. But I felt numb. My body was empty. I didn't feel like I had shared any story at all. I just added data to his books. The man in front of me didn't know my story. He didn't feel my pain. He just wanted to get on with the rest of his day. We were just another paper on his desk. How did I know he'd even help us?

My knuckles turned purple. I clutched the edges of my chair and spoke again.

"You call us slaves. I don't feel like one. We weren't *people* under their power. No, we weren't slaves, because we weren't even human. We weren't even animals. We were pieces of property, objects—there for them to beat, rape and spit on. They killed our families and friends and tortured our men and women. I watched my brothers lose the life inside of them. I watched my mother's back break against the weight of never-ending labor." I looked up at the man, to see if he was listening.

He was. "But you didn't see those things. I did. I'll never stop seeing those things, because every night I'll wake up from my sleep and scream. Because I'll still get nightmares. Because I'm afraid that those dreams will be my life again. So, sir, if you have any kind of human heart inside of you, you will see that we *are* people too. We're human. We feel and we hurt and we break and we suffer just as any human being does, and if you have the power to bring an end to my pain, please, sir, I'm begging you, save me."

A tear crept towards the edge of my lid, lost its grasp, and fell to the floor.

The pudgy man reached across the desk for my hands. But he pulled them back and stared at me.

"I will do everything I can."

He led us outside into the crowded hall where he handed a document to Balaji and made his final remarks. "As you know, they are considered bonded laborers unless the creditors can prove otherwise. If they chose to defend themselves, you will pursue that in a separate procession."

I looked back and forth between the man and Balaji.

The feisty crowd pushed past me.

We weren't free yet. I knew that much.

MINE
(Ruchita)

"Ow!" I screeched, as someone carelessly jabbed a needle into my arm.

All of the girls were perched on tables as our new gharwalis[31] injected us with a new drug called steroids.

The pudgy gharwali looked at my concerned face and said, "It's for the westerners. They like their girls plump[32]."

I looked to my left to see Vanhi cringing at the needle.

Who were these westerners?

It wasn't long before I found out. The Commonwealth Games had attracted hundreds of tourists from all over to the city of New Delhi, and they weren't just there for the games. They wanted more. And to my misfortune, they got what they wanted until they were satisfied. Then their large white bodies shut the curtains and exited the brothel.

The drugs that the gharwalis pumped into our systems had short-term effects that were already visible. Our bodies already had more shape to them. But no one knew the long-term effects—and I didn't know if we'd live long enough to see them.

A day after our arrival, I was introduced to an adhiya[33] who happily guided me through the brothel. She showed me my room, which consisted of a cot, dirty sink and grimy walls plastered with pornographic posters. It was on the third floor

---

[31] Gharwalis- House madams, managers
[32] Based on true facts. Prostitutes and sex-slaves were given steroids for the Commonwealth Games.
[33] Adhiya- half-paid prostitutes. Take on older sister roles in the brothels

of the brothel as we—the young and trapped—were kept in the back, hidden from the police and social workers. Even if the police did find us, monthly bribes kept their mouths shut.

My elder sister was very chatty, and it wasn't long before we were deep in conversation.

Ayesha, the adhiya, spoke about her past in half-broken Hindi with a sense of odd pride. I could understand her Hindi, even though it had been awhile since I took lessons with my father in Nirega.

"I'm from Nepal. Hundreds of us are taken from Nepal's villages and brought to Varanasi. It's the initial destination before we're spread out among India's red-market cities. Like Mumbai and here, New Delhi! I have been with this malik[34] for almost six years now. Two years ago I was freed from my travel debts, the fees that I owed to my dalal for transporting me here. Accepting my life as a prostitute was the best decision I ever could have made."

"Really?" I asked, intrigued.

"Mhm. Now I am an adhiya. I am paid half of the money I earn from customers, and I give the other half to my malik."

"How do you become an adhiya?" Maybe I could become one.

"I accepted my fate as a prostitute, and now my malik allows me to receive half the money for my work. It's more complicated than this, though. One day I want to become a lodger, but I have already been working two years as an adhiya and have almost no savings."

---

34 Malik- Brothel owner

"Are you really paid the half he promised?"

"I am paid my half, but the malik charges me rent for my room and for food. And also now that I am free, I have to pay the police bribes myself. Sometimes it can be up to 8,000 rupees!"

I liked Ayesha a lot. Her bubbly personality balanced with my lack of spirit. I enjoyed her stories too. She was one of the few girls willing to share them. With her help, I became a streetwalker within my first few weeks.

She enticed me with her wild past. "The police raided the streets where all the brothels gained never-ending business. This time, though, they didn't take bribes. They arrested all of the prostitutes and put us in prison."

Her story shocked me. "They arrested you instead of the gharwalis and maliks?"

"Yes. They blamed us," she said, wiping the blood from my oozing cuts. The gharwali had recently beaten me with a splintered slab of wood because one of my customers had complained. I winced as Ayesha pulled out another splinter, "Don't worry. Our maliks paid for us to come back. I was in prison only a week or so.[35]"

She told her story as if it were normal. And it was. Hundreds of girls were taken everyday and sold into this business, and each day the girls trapped in this cycle were getting younger and younger. The younger they were, the less likely they were to catch diseases such as HIV. Ayesha told me that, too. She seemed to know everything.

The first few weeks in the new brothel were torturous. I

---

[35] True story

240

was forced to listen to my friends be beaten and beaten and then beaten again. They were beaten until they had no more bones in their body to break. It was the gharwalis' way of ensuring their trust. I was already lifeless, though, and I had no intention of leaving, so I didn't experience too many. I accepted this as my life a long time ago. I wasn't a slave to these men. I *chose* to let them use me.

Ayesha taught me how to act in front of the gharwalis and maliks too, so I gained their trust even faster. The moment the dalal sold me to the malik, he sensed my shattered spirit. The malik found my loyalty alluring and upgraded me to a streetwalker, a pretty prestigious role. I wasn't thrilled to be a streetwalker, but I didn't mind it, either. I did what I was told and didn't think much of it. I did fear being given a pinjara[36], though. At least in the brothel I could be with Vanhi.

When the last customers left, Vanhi wandered to my room and crawled into my cot.

"Ro, guess what?"

"What, Vanhi?" I tried to sound enthusiastic, but my voice was dull.

"One of the customers today said he worked for an NGO. He asked questions about me and this place and said he wanted to help me! He said he wanted to help save us."

My chest rumbled in anger.

"Kalli!" You dummy!

"What?"

---

[36] Pinjaras are cage-like one-room brothels on the streets

I squeezed her head between my hands and shook it.

"Vanhi, don't ever tell those men anything. It's a trap! The malik plants these men in here to test your loyalty! You must tell them nothing! If you answer their questions, the gharwalis will punish you! Oh, Vanhi! What have you done? What will they do to you?"

Vanhi began to cry. "I'm sorry, Ro. I'm so sorry. I didn't know."

I placed her head against my chest. "It's okay. Don't worry. It's okay, Vanhi. Shh. Shh. Hush. Don't cry."

The next day I woke up with a weird feeling. My stomach felt not heavier but fuller. Everything inside me seemed to change. Nothing felt right.

I walked downstairs by the front lobby where customers ordered their "meals". I listened to the conversation between a man and gharwali.

"What would you like, sir? We have all types."

"Do you have Nepalese? Preferably young."

My heart relaxed. I was safe for now.

"Yes, we have a whole floor full," the Gharwali answered with a wink.

"Ayesha!" she shouted.

Within seconds a group of twelve girls lined up in front of the customer, awaiting his choice of meat, which was ironic because he was probably a vegetarian.

"Her," he said, pointing at a thin, timid Nepalese girl. There was always a big demand for her type. The Nepalese were all like this: thin, timid and speaking only a little Hindi.

"You'll enjoy her."

"Nadia, take him upstairs."

The little girl grabbed his hand and led him through the halls.

A few more days passed, and I started to feel sick in the morning. I tried to keep it to myself so they wouldn't throw me into the infirmary with the ill. For the first time in my entire life I was late. I had never been late before—not until this week.

Sitting in my cot, I realized my life had changed forever. A small light had found its way to me through the darkness, and I was so grateful. But the longer I lay there, the more terrified I became. I remembered what they did to girls like me. They forced pills down their mouths and killed the light inside of them. I held my palms gently over my stomach and prayed that my only light wouldn't be taken from me.

A man entered my stall. Instead of turning my emotions off so I felt numb, I felt angry again. The man disgusted me. The gharwalis disgusted me. I wouldn't let them hurt my baby like they had hurt me.

That night, after bearing the weight of eighteen men, I forced myself to stand strong again. Everything Ayesha had trained me to believe, I pushed aside. Soon hope brought me to the hole in the ground that I had avoided for so long.

It was still there waiting for me: my journal.

My Light, My Freedom Child

I finally have a reason to live. I have a purpose. I've been sitting in darkness for too long, waiting. I don't know what for. Maybe for death. But life found me first. A new life. One that is living inside of me. And I won't let the world take it from me.

Truthfully, I'm scared. I'm terrified. I feel so alone in this, and yet I know I'm not. I'll never be alone again. I wish Mukti could see me now. I wonder if she'd be happy for me. But of course she would be happy for me. And then there's Vanhi. She once told me that if anyone was capable of making it out of here it was me. I never thought I could. I never had the will. I think this new light will guide me. Maybe this is Devaru giving me another chance. All I know is I can't give up now. I am going to make it out of here. Until then I'll have to hide my light. I can't let them see my shine or they'll drown me with darkness.

I want to bring my baby into a world where it can be free. I want it to breathe the air of the real world and not the stench of this dollhouse. I won't let my baby experience what I have. I want my baby to see the sunrise over the rice fields from the safety of a stable rooftop. I hope my baby has the fire and strength that Vanhi has.

If she's a girl I'll name her Vanhi, and if he's a boy I'll name him Swaraj, meaning freedom. Because every day my baby will remind me of what it means to be free. My baby will be my freedom child.

Down the hall a rustling noise disturbed my thoughts. A man was pulling a small figure through the corridor. I saw the body twist and turn, trying to escape the firm grip. I piled the dirt over my journal and peered into the corridor.

"Ruchita!" a familiar voice exclaimed with joy. It was Vanhi! I felt a gust of joy every time I saw her.

"I'll take her from here," I told the gharwali.

He let her go with a scowl. Soon she was in my arms. I squeezed her tight.

"Ouch! You're hurting me!" she yelled.

I laughed. "Sorry. I just missed you so much!"

"It's only been a couple of hours, Ruchita. Get a hold of yourself," she teased.

Vanhi jumped up and kissed me on the forehead.

"Are you okay? You are surprisingly energetic." I looked at her with concern.

"I don't know! I woke up with a buzzing feeling in my head, so they gave me some pills to help my migraine."

I sighed. They had given her opium again.

"What?" she asked, reading my face.

"Nothing."

I felt a pang of guilt.

I was going to leave her.

How could I? She was like a daughter to me. I couldn't sacrifice one child to save another. And yet I knew I couldn't take her with me. The thought of leaving her behind would haunt me forever. Like I had left Tarun. She would think I abandoned her. I wondered if he thought that, too. How could I put her through that? What if she starts to think that I'll come back for her? Should I? No, I couldn't. I already loved the light inside me so much. I needed to protect it.

There was no sense of time in this dollhouse. Each night a hostile wind filled the stalls, and I knew it was time for me to go outside. I rushed to the glitter room where my body was once again transformed into the ideal doll. My body spun into a golden sari so tight that I could barely breathe. The icy breeze chilled my overexposed body.

"Ouch!" I screamed. My hair was yanked from behind and pulled into a tight bun on top of my head. I choked beneath the powder and groaned as my eyelids were lathered with thick black eyeliner and mascara.

My body was their puppet, but my mind remained calm and aware. Every moment was essential. I had to start planning now.

A new group was escorted outside the dollhouse into the bustling streets. The doors opened, releasing a blinding light that took a couple of minutes to adjust to. The sun was just about to set, and the hum of the streets was building.

I searched the roofs of houses for hidden goondas[37] and maliks that stood silent above the shops. They would be my biggest challenge. I remembered how the goondas reacted to a man shoving and touching Nadia. With no hesitation, the guard put a gun to his stomach, making him retreat with his

---

[37] Goondas- big thugs, strong men

hands in the air.

There were no more problems after that.

On the roofs, I saw women unclipping dry clothes from strings hanging outside their windows. Monkeys scavenged for scraps of food or sat on the roofs in groups, picking flies off of each other's hairy backs. I heard Bandhura next to me flirting with a young man. She was dressed in a pink outfit lined with silver. Her rosy pink lips whispered something in the man's ear as he grazed her upper thigh. He followed her off the sidewalk and they both disappeared. After thirty minutes of avoiding customers and intensely searching, I spotted three men who could possibly be goondas. The only way to validate my assumption was to find them again tomorrow. Eventually I was forced to find a customer as my malik scolded me for standing around.

Later that night I wrote down a plan.

April (I think it is near the end) 2009

A Plan

I can only hope this will work. I only get one chance. I'm going to disguise myself as the mannequins outside the shop nearby. As the maliks often drift off into conversation, I can slip away long enough to switch outfits with a mannequin and run into the darkness. We wear the same sari every night, so the guards recognize us by our outfits. Hopefully by the time the guards come to yell at me for standing still, I'll be gone.

I don't really know what I'm going to do once I escape, but I can only plan so far into the future. Maybe I'll go find Mukti. For now I have to focus on *hiding my pregnancy. I only have a few more weeks before my belly will give me away.*

I started to get anxious about leaving. The closer the day came, the longer the days seemed, and yet the wait was only the smallest obstacle. Whenever I thought of my baby, my heart expanded and pounded until my ribs hurt. She was *mine*. No one else could control her. I kept imagining my baby as a girl, and yet I wanted nothing more than for my baby to be a boy. A girl would never be safe in this world. If I had a son he would never have to live in the constant fear that I lived in.

I fled to the abandoned closet that guarded my life story. I dug up the hole and held my journal in my hands. My fingers ran over the thick skin of the cover and through the decaying paper. I felt a relief and comfort. My journal had always been my release. If I couldn't tell anyone else, at least I could tell my journal. When I wrote in my journal, a part of me felt like I was telling my story to the world, like someone was actually listening. Maybe I was crazy for thinking that someone might actually care about what happened to me, but a part of me felt obligated to share my story. Another part of me felt like I was sharing it with Mukti, because we told each other everything. My journal became that rooftop. It was those lazy mornings that we'd spend hours talking. Mukti had been with me through everything, even if she didn't know it. A part of me couldn't let her go, and so my journal was my way to talk with her even if she couldn't hear me.

I forgot to tell you! Only a few more weeks and this nightmare will all be over with! I can't believe it!

Vanhi knows I'm pregnant, but she doesn't know I'm trying to leave. I just wish I had someone on the outside helping me. There is only so much I can see from the inside, and it would be so comforting knowing that someone, anyone, was watching out for me on the outside, someone who could protect me and my baby if we needed help.

I know once I escape, I will be alone for a while, but as long as my baby is on the way, nothing else matters. Once the stars appear in the sky and the moon switches places with the sun, it will be my cue that it is finally time. Nothing can stop me now.

I heard approaching footsteps in the hallway. My heart beat louder and louder. I didn't react fast enough. The closet door was slightly open, and it was too late to close it now. Panicking, I tried to hide my journal back in the ground, but the man was already in the doorway.

"Who are you? What are you doing in here? Get out!" the malik ordered.

I tried sitting over the hole but knew I was caught. Everything I had worked so hard to hide was now fully exposed. I cowered as he grabbed the journal.

He pushed me aside, revealing the hole in the ground. He dragged me outside and threw me to the ground. I tried to crawl away, but he stepped on my ankle.

"Ahhhh!"

I heard my bone crack under his weight. Then he was on top of me, raining his fists on my face. The taste of blood filled my mouth. I knew he was screaming, but I couldn't hear anything. I couldn't feel anything, either. I screamed anyway.

I woke up in a stall, trapped and hopeless. I shivered in the stiff cold. I don't know how, but I knew it was raining outside. I just had a feeling. Maybe the rain would wash away the sins of this dollhouse.

I lay on the cot, unable to move. Every part of me hurt. I looked down at my arms and legs and saw dark blue bruises. I checked my arms for any signs of injections. I didn't know what drugs would do to the baby. Tears froze on my cheeks. My skin burned even though my body shivered. I had no idea how long I had been here.

I felt like I was drowning. My journal floated above the surface. The ink ran and blurred the pages. I didn't even reach for it. I just stared at it. My tears mixed with the salty water. Was I even crying?

A clock ticked in my head. Time stood still, but it kept ticking. I wanted to scream, but my lips stayed shut. I cried, wishing sleep would save me again, but I lay there awake.

Frozen. Trapped. Lifeless.

MAZE
(Mukti)

Days seemed long again. I woke up everyday and saw his face. He was supposed to taste freedom. He was supposed to be living his life. It wasn't fair, and I was to blame. I failed my first case and lost the life of a precious boy. I hadn't looked in the mirror since the sit-in. I would be too ashamed of the person looking back at me. She was weak, scared and insecure. John encouraged me to get back up. He gave me the opportunity to research different cases almost every day, but the fear of failing kept me down.

I ran to my drawer and held the certificate in my hands. Its once-rough edges were now soft and thin. My fingers traced over my picture in the top left corner, and I reread the words. My mind flew back to the day I received it. An immediate flush of joy ran through me. There was no other feeling in the world like gaining your freedom.

That day felt so distant now, and yet the same feeling of relief came back as I held the certificate in my hands. I remembered the reason I came to Ajadi. The moment I held that release certificate I knew what my future held for me. It was that day that I walked up to John and Balaji and asked if I could work with them, because I wanted to free those who were still trapped. I wanted to inspire others to gain back their rights. What I wanted most was to share that same feeling of relief and joy with others when they held their own freedom in their hands. I wanted them to know they could be their own person, because all of my life I had felt like someone else's. That day I realized I was whoever I wanted to be.

Everyone deserved that feeling.

I stared at my certificate, remembering why I came to Ajadi and the person I wanted to be.

I went to the mirror hanging on my door. Every morning I used to look at myself and think about the person I wanted to be. Then I compared her to the girl staring back at me. I pulled my hair back to see my scars, the majority of which had faded but would never fully disappear. I didn't want them to, either. They were a constant reminder of my past: a past that I couldn't forget. As long as I remembered my past, I would continue helping people who still lived it in the present.

I opened the drawer by my bed. Inside I saw my two most precious possessions: a bracelet and a note.

The day Ajadi let us leave the rehabilitation center I went straight home to my village, Nirega. I skipped through the village homes in hopes of reuniting with my one true love. Everyone greeted and welcomed us home—everyone except the girl I yearned to see the most. The girl I had prayed for every day for the past five years. Ro was gone, and I had no idea where she was. The villagers told us she left not long after my brothers did, and they hadn't been back since. When Laxmi Masi heard we were back in the village she raced to find me and hugged me. She pressed something into my palm.

I looked down confused when she closed my hand into a fist and cried, "She told me to give this to you if you ever came back. I was so afraid you'd never return."

The next few days were filled with emptiness. My mother and sister readjusted to village life with ease. I sat on the rooftop wondering about my lost friend. We did a Ganesh puja on our house, blessing our new home for security. The entire village came—everyone except Ro. My sweet Ro had vanished, and I had no idea how to find her.

I did have a token of her remembrance, though. And I'd keep it forever.

Mukti,

I've torn out a piece of my journal in hopes that one day you will read this. My father is moving us back to Bangalore. I don't know where in the city, and I don't know if we'll ever come back. I miss you every day. I still sit on the rooftop and write in my journal, but it isn't the same without you by my side. A half of me is missing without you here, and yet I know you will always be with me wherever I go. I hope that I am with you too, keeping you safe and strong.

If you need a reminder, wear this bracelet around your wrist, and know this:

I am with you.

Forever and always,

Ro

The bracelet was just like Ro: beautiful and strong. I spun it around my skinny wrist and felt she was with me. I put it back in the drawer for safe keeping. I knew she would be there when I returned.

That day the Ajadi headquarters was busy as always, buzzing with workers, the sound of papers rustling, ringing phones and of course a sweaty, overworked John. He ran by flustered, chasing after another volunteer. I had been there for hours already and just sitting in my chair was driving me mad.

I had been promoted to work with the marketing campaign for Ajadi. I helped raise awareness to bring in donations and start fundraisers. Trying to keep a smile, I worked hard at my job, knowing it was just as important as the others. But really, I wanted to get back in the action again.

On my way home, I looked at the small shops along the road. They seemed tired today. Sad clouds covered the sky, allowing no sunshine. It was almost monsoon season again, when the skies would cry out all of the world's sorrows, flooding the streets and slums. The birds would be scared back into hollow trunks. The monsoon would take its revenge on our cities at night and forgive our sins by morning with a blazing sun that soaked up the damp sidewalks.

A ray of sunshine through the curtain woke me. I sat up and stretched. I was incredibly excited. Today I would ride the train all the way to Delhi with a group from Ajadi! We were attending a slave labor conference with activists from all over India. Last week I found the courage to ask John for something to get me more involved again, and he gladly invited me.

The conference was held in a massive hall filled with hundreds of activists gathered to hear speakers tell their stories. After the speakers finished, the people broke out into contentious debates, discussing the most recent events and progress made on the issue. Ajadi proudly boasted of our success, reminding me of just how little I had achieved myself. The conference was empowering, and I felt proud to be among the many amazing people from all around the nation who were fighting for the same cause.

Afterward I walked back to the hotel with some of the other Ajadi workers. I left the hall with the same empty feeling in my stomach that I came with. I decided to wear Ro's bracelet to the conference in hopes of finding her confidence, but I forgot I was wearing it. As I strolled down the sidewalk, I spun it around my wrist. The day was murky and unclear. Shadows ran up the walls and faint voices gossiped in the teashops. With each step I heard a flop from my flappy shoes as I dodged the brown puddles. I let my hair down. It made me feel freer.

Around the corner a man threw a pile of garbage into the street. I sighed at the rubbish-filled sidewalks, knowing that although the rains would wash trash out of the driveways, it would never completely disappear. Pollution always filled the city. Without it, it would be empty.

I looked closer to the trash he had thrown out. I noticed red stained blankets, broken bottles, fruit peels and rice bags. The man turned and walked away. He took a few steps before reaching into his left pocket and tossing a book into the pile. Who would throw away a book? It reminded me of Ro's journal. My heart ached as I thought of her. I waited for the man to disappear back into the strange building before I searched through the mound of trash.

"Mukti, where are you going?" Rajesh asked.

"I'll meet you back at the hotel," I reassured him.

When he turned the corner, I knelt down and picked up a leather object from the pile. The old rough-backed book was filled with stained pages, printed with a million words—a million Kannada words. I examined it carefully in awe. Could it be? Each page was a different shade and material. Some writing had been scribbled on the ends of newspapers, while others were ripped napkins, paper bags or dried leaves squished inside.

I wondered if it could be. I knew the chances were one in four hundred million, and I feared being wrong.

I returned to the hotel, clutching the journal tightly to my chest as if someone might take it from me. I felt the need to protect its stories and hidden identity. The fragile pages could easily fall out and I could lose a glimpse of a life. When I reached my room, I sat on the stiff bed and went numb. I shed a tear, leaving a wet spot on the white bed sheet. Why was I so scared?

Carefully, I opened the journal and studied the writing. It took me awhile to recognize the tattered leather and blue-ink handwriting, but when I did, my heart was overcome with joy.

The first few passages were clearly written when she was young. The spelling and handwriting were a child's. They were the passages she wrote when we sat on the roof together for hours, watching the sun rise and set. She loved writing about her passion for dance and the small things in life that were important to her then. I could hear her voice as I read her stories, and soon I was there with her. I was watching her feet move across the floor, I was running by her side against the icy cold wind as she escaped, I was crying with her when she discovered her father had remarried, when she realized soon she would be married. I lived through my best friend's entire life as though I was there with her the whole time.

My heart ached, I felt myself grow pale, and I set the diary aside. I couldn't read anymore. My heart couldn't take it. I couldn't bear to watch my other half suffer. All this time I had been praying for her safety and happiness, but she had neither. Guilt overwhelmed me. How could I have let her suffer for so long? I never searched past the village for her. What kind of a friend was I? She would have searched every square centimeter of India to find me. She would have known something was wrong.

My tears fell on the white bed sheet.

My eyes adjusted to the dimness of the room. The sun had already set and the clocked flashed 11:42. Her words sang in my head. I could hear the sadness in the notes. All my life I had been jealous of her beauty, and now I realized her beauty was a curse.

Eventually my guilt subsided, and I realized I had found her—my other half who had been missing from my life for so long! I opened the curtains and stared at the bright stars.

"Thank you," I whispered.

Something, far above me, had guided me here and taken me to her journal. It wanted me to save her. My mind flashed back to the day she pulled me out of the river. She had saved my life, and now it was time for me to save hers.

Sleep never came. I got back up and scanned the pages again. A small circle fell in my lap. It was a scrunched-up piece of paper with a poem on it.

I wake up today to an empty world
I walk the empty streets
I see empty cars
Empty trains
Empty shops
Empty rain that doesn't wash the wrongs away

Streets flooded
Fuller by the day
With empty people
Hiding from the pain

Am I blind?
Or is there just no color in the sky?
Maybe they see something I don't
A false reality
A falsely colored world

But no matter how hard they try
To paint the world full of colors
The darkness remains

They can try and paint me too

But they'll never take this darkness away
I drown in it everyday

As I read through her life, I experienced her highs and lows. Eventually the highs stopped altogether, and I found myself losing her. Everything that made Ro who she was slipped into a deep depression. She lost her confidence, her strength and her hope. She was no longer the rebellious wonder I had worshipped. With each word I could feel the life being sucked out of me, just as I felt it being sucked out of her.

My life is a maze
Each year locks me in further
The walls climb higher
The maze twists deeper
I look and see walls
Dead ends, locked gates, crowded empty stalls

The moon blushes through an open door
I find my way back home
I solved the maze!
I finally solved the maze!

A light flashes
I stare at a mural upon the wall
It was my life
Each crack, each splinter

A laughter boomed
And the walls shook around me

Crashing, shattering
The mural fell
My life split to pieces

The blank wall stares back at me

It mocks me
I had never left the maze
I was born in the maze
My life was the maze
My life will forever be
A maze

I flipped to the last pages and read her last words.

A week from tomorrow is my escape. I have hope. I refuse to live another day with makeup plastered over my face, pretending to be something I'm not. I'm not a slave. I'm a human being. I'm a beautiful girl who doesn't deserve to be misshaped by others. I won't let them touch me anymore. They can't control me, and they can't take my baby.

I feel so alone in this darkness and yet I am not. The moon shines through the dim room and reminds me that somewhere out in the world my sister Mukti is with me. Even if I never see her again, I know she is thinking of me and that she would love my baby as much as she loved me. I can feel Mukti's spirit in my baby, and I know that he or she will have her compassion. It gives me courage and strength to know I will never be alone again.

Whatever it takes. That's what I'll do. Whatever it takes to let my baby breathe freedom. Whatever it takes to let my baby learn to walk on ground that isn't shaking beneath its feet. Whatever it takes to one day teach my baby to write in the light and not in hindering darkness.

All I can do is give my child freedom. I can give it all of my love and all of me. I will make sure to be the loving parent that mine forgot to be.

We deserve a life. We deserve freedom. Maybe one day the world will meet us, and we won't be forgotten.

I sat in silence. No thoughts. The air was still. Her entire journal was written as if to me, as if she knew I would read it one day. Most of the passages were written like a conversation, and I knew she was speaking to me, Mukti, her other half. It was like we were on the roof together, and she was telling me everything I missed and everything she wished I was there for. She told me how much she needed me, and now she needed me more then ever. I shut the journal and sucked in a deep breath. I needed Ro, too.

I looked at the sky. A crescent moon gleamed in the night. My head rested against the wall, and I shut my eyes for a moment. There was the pitter-patter of rain on the rooftops. I clutched the book with both hands to make sure it was real.

I had to tell John.

He was two rooms down from me. I knew he was probably asleep, but I walked over anyway.

A faint light flickered beneath his door. A black shadow appeared and disappeared. My hand still held Ruchita's journal. I knocked on the door.

"Who is it?" a stressed voice asked.

I swallowed a mouthful of saliva. I didn't know why I was so nervous. John would want this for me. Then I wondered if he would tell me this one was too much.

"It's Mukti, sir," I said shakily. The door opened to reveal John's hotel room. Papers plastered the floors and his laptop beeped with new notifications every two seconds. A dead plant bent over, its stem sagging on the cluttered floor.

I had been learning and practicing English for a while now, but every time I had to use it I felt my nerves come back.

Looking around I asked, "Is it a bad time?"

"Never. Did you enjoy the conference?" he asked, already back at his desk.

"Yes! It was amazing. Thank you again for the opportunity."

"Of course."

He turned towards me in his chair and waited to hear the reason I came.

It took me a moment to gather my emotions. I didn't know how to explain everything at once, but finally I began.

"When I lived in my village," I started, "I had a best friend named Ruchita. She was like my sister. We were raised inseparable. Until of course...well, the day my family was sent to the quarry. But even then I thought of Ruchita every day and wondered where she was and how she was doing. Of course, I assumed she was still in my village, but when we were released and my family went back to Nirega, Ro wasn't there. She didn't know if I'd ever come back, but she left me a note with one of the villagers saying she had moved to the city. I hadn't heard from her since."

"Mukti, where is this going?" John asked, getting restless. He didn't need anyone wasting his time.

I handed him the journal and tears filled my eyes.

"She used to write in her journal every day. She wrote down everything. Her entire life is in there." I looked up at him with hope in my eyes. "I found that journal today in a pile of trash on the way back from the conference...It's hers. It's Ruchita's."

He looked at me, confused. "But we're in Delhi. You're from a village outside of Bangalore."

I exhaled a short breath. "She was trafficked." The words barely left my lips. It was hard to believe the horrific truth.

"Oh." His face changed. He began to understand. "I'm so sorry."

As my eyes streamed with tears, I explained, "She's pregnant."

He remained silent.

"I know it's asking a lot, but..."

John cut me off, knowing where I was going. "Mukti, I'm sorry but it's too dangerous."

I stood there stunned. I never believed he would actually turn me down. "But, I don't..."

"Look," he said with a sigh. "There are so many things. For one, this case is in Delhi and you live in Bangalore. But more importantly, you don't understand this kind of business. Sex slavery is extremely dangerous and so big in this area that even if we did try to save her, we would never find her. There are thousands of coerced prostitutes, and the reality is that by trying to help her we would probably hurt her even more. I know this must be hard to hear. I can't even imagine the pain you're feeling, but there's nothing we can do, Mukti."

"Isn't that the reason thousands of sex slaves suffer? Because we're too afraid to get involved? We're letting them *win*, John!" I screamed back. "Everything Ajadi does is dangerous! Anil *died*, John! On *my* case! I know it's dangerous, but if we don't try and help they're going to die anyway!"

My hand clasped my mouth in terror. How could I be so disrespectful?

I quickly apologized. "I'm sorry. I'm so sorry!"

With my head down I left the room. I left the journal with John in the hopes that he might meet the amazing Ro and read her beautiful yet tragic story.

Delhi's humidity choked me. The slow, droning fans did nothing to assuage the deathly heat. The rain only made things worse, as it trapped the heat inside. As I took off my shawl, a rustling sound caught my attention. A crumpled paper had gotten caught in my shirt when I protected the journal from the rain. I lit a lamp and took a closer look.

To my surprise there was no writing, but instead something like a picture, like a maze. I almost tossed it aside thinking it was another doodle but realized it started to look like a detailed map. There were a few words scribbled in boxes and spaces that I recognized from her stories, and once I read the word "Doll House," I knew it was a map of the brothel. I clutched the map tightly, feeling a new hope. I couldn't give up on her yet. I had to keep fighting.

I fell on the limp bed and sank into the mattress. I watched the candlelight flicker off the walls and dance on the roof above me. Slowly, I was lulled to sleep.

FOREVER AND ALWAYS
(Mukti)

The flickering candlelight soon became the morning light that glimmered through the pale curtains. The sun sparkled, reminding me I had a reason to be excited again. Determined, I braided my hair, slipped into my shoes, wrapped my shawl around me and walked out with determination in my step.

The monsoon air whipped me in the face when I stepped out the door, knocking me back a few steps. Humid and putrid, the air caused my Panjabi dress to glue to my sweaty skin. I groaned when I stepped in a warm puddle from last night's showers. I lifted my leg and squeezed out the wet ends of my pants. Taking a deep, controlled breath, I wasn't going to let the bad weather determine my mood. Today was going to be a good day.

The Delhi office had a different vibe this morning. I found a large block computer and searched for groups that worked to prevent sex-trafficking. I couldn't find one. I grew frustrated when I realized the industry didn't publicize itself. It would have been too dangerous. The mobs would hunt them down. Through local safe houses, though, I was given possible contacts for an organization that could help my case.

The first few phone calls led to more contacts and more numbers, but I soon realized no one was willing to help. By nightfall my throat hurt from pleading for help over and over again. I looked at the last scribbled phone number. This was it. I said a prayer under my breath before I picked up the phone. My heart sank when I got a man's voicemail. Almost in tears, I got ready to pour out my last cry for help to this machine. I could only hope someone out there would one day hear me.

Beep.

I left him my name and Ajadi's contact information. All I could do now was wait.

I spent my next two days glued to the phone, refreshing my email every minute and scanning my texts. John got fed up with my nagging and told me to go take a walk.

He gave me back Ro's journal. He hadn't so much as glanced at one of her stories. Still, I felt relief when I grasped it. I felt like I was with her again.

I passed the time reading her stories. My favorites were the ones written about me.

I don't think I fully realized the meaning of friendship until now. I didn't realize it when I met her and we became best friends, but I realized it the moment she was no longer in my life. I lost the only true light in my life. I've found freedom again back home, but what is freedom if my best friend is caged? What is freedom if it's spent alone? What is happiness if my best friend is still suffering?

I don't know if I'll ever get past this loneliness. Yet, that heaviness in my heart lightens when I think of my future with Ramesh and all the happiness we will bring each other. I can't wait to get to know him and live a life with a man who I know I'll have forever. I wish Mukti could be at my wedding. It won't feel right without her there celebrating with me.

Our friendship got me through each cruel night. She was the reason I kept going. I knew we were struggling together, and hurting together, and surviving together.

I can still feel that half of me missing. Without her, I don't know how to stay strong, and yet all I have to do is remember her warmth, her curiosity and her compassion. And I keep fighting.

She's my sister. No matter how far apart we are from each other, she will always be that.

Forever and always.

I cried for Ro after reading that passage. My cheeks flooded like the city caught in the monsoon. I missed her so much my heart hurt. She appeared in my dreams every night, laughing again. When I woke up I remembered she wasn't happy. I remembered she was still caged, while I was free.

Her words lingered.

What is freedom if my best friend is caged? What is freedom if it's spent alone? What is happiness if my best friend is still suffering?

I went to the computer to check my emails again. I had a message from the Lani Senner Agency member! Noticing the email was sent yesterday, I scurried to John's office.

I opened the door in a rush, forgetting to knock and found him there with another man. They turned to me, surprised by the outburst.

"Oh perfect, just who I needed to talk to!" John exclaimed. "Mukti, this is Aakash. He works for Lani Senner Agency. I agreed to meet with him yesterday after receiving an email from him. He told me you reached out to him for help, and he contacted me right away."

I shook the man's hand awkwardly, still unaccustomed

to this foreign way of greeting, and sat down. They continued their conversation in English as though they had never been interrupted.

"So as I was saying, the Lani Senner Agency has been rescuing girls since 1993 and has had successes and failures. For obvious reasons, it is highly dangerous to raid these brothels, but the legal process is also much simpler due to the obvious legal issues." Then he looked over at me and asked, "Mukti, I was wondering how you found the journal."

"It was very random. I saw a man throwing out a bag of trash when I was on the way back from the center. Then I saw him toss the book in the pile. I found it strange that anyone would throw away a book and it reminded me of *her*, so I waited for him to leave and took it."

"Do you remember where you found it? Would you be able to bring me back there?"

"Yes. It was pretty close to where I'm staying actually. It's by Ajmeri Gate."

"Ah. Yes. That's right on the edge of the red market."

"What's that?"

"It's basically the red-light district for purchasing cheap sex. It's cheap because most of the girls and women there are slaves forced into their work for free."

"Would we be able to go today?" I asked eagerly.

"This is the area where we do most of our work. I'd prefer to go alone, or with another Ajadi member. It's no place for a young girl, and John's presence might draw too much attention. He'll either be seen as a threat or an easy customer for sex."

I dug my nails into my arm. The conversation made my stomach sick. I kept imagining Ro, the most free-spirited girl, broken and forced to sleep with thirty men every day. I couldn't bear it.

The next week kept me as busy as ever. The office had stopped its mission to help organize mine. John went underground into the brothel as a customer. We were able to connect Ruchita's map with the right jamadars. If our plan worked, we would be in and out with no time to spare. The girls had to be evacuated before backup arrived.

As the date approached, my nerves were rattling. And yet something kept me calm. This mission was meant to be.

I found time to read Ruchita's stories. I missed Priya and my family so much. They were back home, and sometimes I felt really alone here. Reading Ro's journal made me feel connected to her. But the pain she described was unbearable. It hurt me to know she had experienced such pain alone.

I wished I could tell her I was coming for her. I wished I'd never left her side. If I hadn't left the village, Ro wouldn't have, either. I abandoned her when she needed me most. That's why she was still suffering.

That night I read the passage about reuniting with her father.

The skies have finally cleared. The sun came out to greet me and so did my father only a few weeks ago. I'm home again, although in a different place. I mean this both literally and figuratively. My father has moved to a new home with a new wife and has decided to keep our old one a secret. I don't like the idea of hiding my past, when all I have ever wanted is to come back to it. But it feels so good to be reunited and free. My skin is fresh and my hair is neat. I feel safe again. But, no matter how far I am away from that horrid place, I can't help but feeling its evils following me. Everywhere I walk I keep looking over my shoulder. I keep a careful eye out, not knowing when evil will find its way back into my life. I pray it doesn't find its way back.

I continued to the next page: a new day.

Apparently I didn't keep a close enough eye out. It wasn't my fault. There is nothing I can do to ward off this evil. It was here when I arrived. I just didn't know it. I met her last week. She came like a snake, slowly slithering around the house with her venom, and when she leaves the room her presence lingers.

I keep my journal with me every day now, no matter where I go. It's because I don't feel safe anymore. I'm not even safe in my own home. I thought I had escaped the evil in my life, but apparently I walked right back into it.

I almost missed the small passage scribbled down at the bottom. I could tell it had been written quickly, as if she were in a panic or danger.

This journal means everything to me. It reminds me of who I am. It reminds me I have an identity, and no one can change me or the words I've written. This is me, and they can't take me away again. I can't let them take me away again.

FLIGHT
(Mukti)

Tonight was the night. The sky grew darker and darker, very slowly I thought. The stars sparkled in the blackness. Smog obscured the moon, but I knew it was still there, protecting us. The city seemed suspiciously silent. Even though the wind was blowing hard, the trees were still. My ears filled with the rushing breeze.

The streets were crowded with lustful men and kinkily dressed women. I stood in the heart of the city, the red market, a place where behind every alley, every club, every shop, and every cage there were smuggled girls trapped against their will. I walked the streets with Aakash in curious horror.

"What are those?" I asked, noticing that the street we were walking on had cage-like cement rooms.

In front of each cage, a girl or woman stood, waiting for men to approach. The steel bars were covered by a thin sheet that served as a curtain. They looked like prison cells.

"They're called pancharis. It's a prostitute's individual room for customers."

I watched a man approach one, bargain with the girl and enter. My jaw dropped in disgust. Everyone in the streets could see him go inside.

Did he feel no shame?

When we returned to the team everyone stood in silence. The only sound that escaped was their exasperated sighs. Our black vans surrounded the shops that bordered the dilapidated brothel a few streets down. Our walky-talkies buzzed. The teams waited inside the vehicles for their cue, but I

270

was too anxious to stay seated. I leaned against the cold door of the truck, drawing pictures in the dirt with my big toe. A black scarf was supposed to protect me from the cold, but the wind found its way in anyway. I shivered in the bitter silence, waiting.

We were fortunate the rain had postponed its showers. Although the sky was dim, the stars provided enough illumination for us to see without a flashlight. I switched my flashlight off and on nervously, off and on, up and down, back and forth. I rubbed my arms, feeling small goosebumps forming from the cold. In the window I saw John with his head against the dashboard, listening on the walkie-talkie, waiting.

Two vans filled with trained men would take care of the jamadars and goondas. The others were empty, waiting for the women and girls soon to be freed.

In place of Raj who broke his leg on short notice, I was put in charge of a small group. I remembered my first case and how terrified I was of failing. But tonight was different. Tonight was personal. Ro and her baby depended on me. How could I live up to that pressure?

John opened his door and stood beside me.

It was time.

The sky had changed to a bluish-grey. The moon played peekaboo between the clouds of smog. Our groups went over the plan one last time. My foot tapped impatiently, waiting for our cue.

I'm coming, Ro.

I prayed under my breath—the same prayer I had prayed for five years in that quarry—for Ro's safety and happiness.

271

Before I finished my prayer, my walkie-talkie buzzed. I was off, speeding through alleyways and entering the eerie brothel. I stepped into the lobby and examined the room. It appeared normal, with a running television and ripped couches. I moved my team up the stairs, trying to ignore the fearful pounding in my chest.

As I entered the hall, the walls seemed to whisper secrets and stories. Bloodstains dotted the clustered floor. Orange bulbs glowed on the ceiling. I walked more slowly the further in we went. I peered in every room. Each had a bed, a cement sink and walls plastered with pornographic photos and provocative women in bikinis. The trashcan was filled with tissues and used condoms. My hands avoided the filthy sheets, covered in stains. Some had cartoon designs, and my heart fell because I knew it was a young girl like Vanhi who probably had lain there.

The first two floors were deserted, but I could feel spirits within the halls, like ghosts, watching us. Icy breezes blew, and my bones rattled in fear. An echo bounced off the wall. It got louder and louder. Gunshots. They faded. I heard my blood pulse in my ears. I hoped it was Lani Agency men firing those guns.

My walkie-talkie buzzed: "Third floor clear."

It was safe to go upstairs. We knew the girls would be hidden in the back and there were only so many places they could be. The man in front of me swung open a door, revealing a horrid sight. Two men, one on the ground and one slouching in a chair, were slumped over dead, blood stains on their chests. In the chair, the man's fingers dangled an inch from the floor, grasping a Cuban cigar. His open mouth drooled blood.

We continued our search. Some girls had already been found. My walkie-talkie buzzed with voices of men announcing their locations.

Again gunshots. The walls resounded with heavy footsteps and my pounding heart. The bulbs above flickered and went out. I tried to turn my flashlight on, but the batteries were out. I felt the walls and listened for sounds of people. A man handed me a flashlight that was working just in time before I ran into a wall.

I turned to find an open door. I shined the flashlight inside to find a room full of floating doll heads in the dark. Their tiny faces peered out in horror. A few girls burst into tears.

My hand pressed against my heart.

I told my group to stop shining the flashlights in their eyes and point them at the door to show the girls where to exit.

"Everything's going to be okay. We're going to help you," I said in broken Hindi.

I reached out to a girl trembling in the corner. She looked up and saw that I was just a girl, too. She let down her guard and climbed into my arms. Slowly, the girls walked into the hall. I scanned the room for Ro, but she was nowhere in sight.

I fought back tears. I missed her so much. I just wanted to hold her again. Where was she?

I whispered to one of the girls, "Do you know Ruchita?"

"Which one?" she asked shyly.

My shoulders slumped. "Never mind."

There came a deathly silence, then echoes of a girl's scream. The doll heads bobbled up and down as we ran through the darkness. Huddled together, they remained silent. I batted my eyelids to hold back tears.

Drew, the woman in charge of communications, spoke urgently through the walkie-talkie. "Mukti, hurry. We need you back here immediately. Where are the girls?"

I felt the pressure push against my outsides. I felt something squeeze my hand and found a little girl clutching it. Her wet eyes looked up at mine, begging me to take the fear away. I picked her up and carried her through the hallways and down the stairs.

"I'm right here, beta. Don't worry. Everything's going to be okay."

All of a sudden his face appeared in my head again. His innocent green eyes pleaded with me. A heavy pang of guilt shuddered through my body. I had failed my first mission. That boy's death was on my hands. I didn't want to fail again. I clutched the girl tightly to my body. I couldn't let another child die.

In a way, the electricity being cut off was helpful because the maliks and goondas protecting the building couldn't see us.

"Mukti, take the group right. There are voices coming in our direction. Hurry!"

Two deep voices shouted across the corridors.

I ordered in a harsh whisper, "Turn off all the flashlights!"

We sprinted down the narrow hall, until a square orange glow caught my eye. A door waited in the distance. I sighed with relief when I saw Drew hold it open for us.

I went down the metal stairs, feeling the urge to escape. The back room smelled like blood. I felt myself getting dizzy spinning down the steps. At the bottom, five or six men met us. The little girl squeezed my hand to comfort me. If she could be strong, I had to be strong, too. Outside the brothel, the armed men led the girls to the vans.

I took a deep breath and thought of Ro. I wondered where she was and what she was thinking. As we walked towards the sound of traffic in the distance, I was digging my nails into my skin to stave off tears. I used to believe that nothing could be worse than the scorching quarry, but I was wrong. This was so much worse. The life that Ruchita lived was so much worse.

I could see the men and women running in panic, gathering the girls and carrying the weak and sick. Everything began to blur. Desperately, I searched for Ruchita, but every face was a stranger's. My chest heaved up and down as I fought back more tears. From the corner of my eye, I saw a small girl running towards us. I stood up ready.

She rambled on about someone, but I couldn't make out her words.

Then the world came into sharp focus when she cried, "Ro! Ro! My—friend—gone—please—find her."

"You know, Ro? Ruchita? My Ro! Where is she?" I screamed. I shook her shoulders trying to get an answer out of her. But I only scared her. She began to cry.

"I'm sorry! I'm sorry! I just really need to find her! I'm Mukti!"

She looked at me with a blank face. "I don't know where she is," she whispered.

A tear fell from my cheek. How did we go through this entire operation and rescue everyone *except* Ro?

"I'm going back in," I said.

Balaji pulled me back. "Mukti, you can't go. It's too dangerous."

This was my mission. He couldn't control me.

"Thanks for your concern, but I'm going in."

The little girl started walking with me, and I realized for the first time who she was.

I knelt and softened my voice, "Is your name Vanhi?"

"You know my name?"

I nodded, knowing I didn't have time to explain. "Vanhi, I need you to stay here for me. I need to make sure you're safe."

She tugged on my pants and pleaded, "Don't leave me. Please."

I saw Balaji talking to the armed guards. They ran back inside. My knees buckled in fear. I hated not being the one in control. I couldn't lose her.

Balaji rubbed my back. "They'll find Ruchita. Mukti, they'll find her."

He sounded so sure, but then a thought hit me: What if she already escaped? I couldn't bear the thought that I'd never see her again.

My eyes were glued to the empty street. The clouds shifted high above us, leaving nothing but a dim haze. I barely blinked. I barely breathed. I couldn't stand waiting. I had to know if she was okay. Vanhi kept tugging on my pants. I brushed through her hair, trying to comfort her. My walkie-talkie squawked, but no one spoke. Everything was silent for fifteen minutes. All I heard was my heart thudding against my chest.

And then it fell. It sunk through my body, all the way to my feet. My knees buckled, unable to support my body. Tears filled my fear-stricken eyes. I watched them carry the limp body towards us. My hand clasped over my mouth. I watched Vanhi collapse next to her frail body. I couldn't move. I couldn't breathe.

I fought back tears, but they erupted. Balaji ran over and hugged me before I collapsed. I burrowed my face in his chest, trying to breathe, trying to wake up.

Wake up, Mukti. It's just a bad dream. Wake up. Please.

I dug my nails into my arms until they bled. Why wasn't I waking up?

I looked over Balaji's shoulder and watched Vanhi. She hugged Ro's body and slapped her face. Her tiny fingers kept trying to open her eyes.

She sobbed into her chest, "Ruchita. Wake up. It's time to go. We're safe now. Ruchita, please. Wake up. Wake up, Ro. This isn't funny. Stop playing around," she pleaded. "Ro! Ro! Please, wake up! Please!"

I closed my eyes and felt the world spin.

I felt a molten anger rage inside me. My other half was gone. Forever. I would never be in her warm embrace again. I would never hear her sweet whispers. I watched her pale, lifeless body, feeling the life slip out of me, too.

She had been my everything—my rock.

I gasped for air, but my lungs were filled with water. My eyes fluttered behind the black whirlpools. The water encircled me, and this time I didn't reach for the surface, because there was no face hovering above the water.

She was gone.

Her freedom child—gone.

This wasn't supposed to be the ending. This couldn't be the end. She was supposed to taste freedom. She was supposed to be a mother. She was supposed to escape and tell her story to the world.

I wanted a happy ending. I needed a happy ending. My father's hazel eyes flashed before me. They pierced my heart. How many lives would I lose? Why did this keep happening? I saw Kushala's burnt face as she cried. Why were we treated like this? What did we do to deserve this?

We were human, too.

Balaji carried me to the van. I still hadn't spoken a word. I had nothing to say. I stared through the smudged glass and saw an opaque world. I searched for the stars and the moon, but they were hidden behind the thick smog. I felt Ruchita's journal in my hands. I stared at its rough cover. Maybe it was my job to tell the world about Ro. My heart shuddered. She was so beautiful—so defiant—so loving. Maybe if the world knew her story they would see us for who we really were. They would see the beauty that lives inside of us, and the beauty that lived inside of her.

I couldn't go to sleep. I paced up and down the hotel room. Balaji had dropped me off hours ago, and the flickering candle was slowly dying.

A soft light peeked through the curtains. The sun was rising, but I didn't watch it because I'd never get to watch it rise with *her* again. I wiped away the imminent tears and looked out my window, as if I saw the world I lived in for the first time.

The mist rolled through the city, fogging up the windows and obscuring all vision. It crept into the streets and shops unnoticed, clogging the city like a storm does to drainpipes. The thick fog prevented anyone from seeing more than the outline of the person in front of them. Able to see only a glimpse of the fabricated reality around them, they remained blinded to a majority of their world. Scared to walk into the unknown, the world stood still in ignorant silence. I inhaled deeply, feeling my rib cage squeeze into my stomach, and released a heavy, slow breath. My breath fogged up the window, and I stared at it for a while, waiting for it to disappear, but it remained. It maintained its awkward shape until my thumb wiped it away. I cleared it just in time to see the kingfisher perched on my building dart off into the open, immaculately blue sky. Its wings danced to a new rhythm, as it twirled three times in the air and soared high above the fog into the distance, never dipping back down into that mist again.

I felt myself leave with that bird.

I would fight for every living slave until I found justice.

I took my flight to freedom, and I never came back.

Epilogue

Shubar and Darshan were probably not charged for their offenses. Even when abusers are convicted of their crimes (infrequent, due to corruption of local government and police), the penalty is minimal (up to $44 and three years in prison). This penalty is almost never enforced on the few dozen who are convicted each year. A slave bringing in $12,900 a year is worth 291 times the penalty risk. This disequilibrium between penalty and profit encourages the business rather than hindering it.

It is even less likely that slaves will report themselves and be freed due to illiteracy, lack of identification, and corruption and discrimination by caste.

Character List/Name Meanings

Mukti

(Name means freedom); 13-year old girl enslaved in a granite quarry in Karnataka, India, born in a small village, Nirega; best friend of Ruchita

Priya

(Name means loved one); Mukti's older sister; *in dedication to my cousins Priya and Alysia*

Sandhya

Mukti's best friend; born into enslavement in a granite quarry

Raj

(Name means king) and Arjun (Name means peacock); Mukti's younger brothers; twins (the Peas); brought to the quarry to help pay for Priya's wedding dowry

Sandhya's Mother

One of the original slaves brought to the granite quarry

Mukti's Father

One of the original slaves brought to the granite quarry who was part of the 1996 chain story

Shubar

Owner of quarry, brother of Darshan

Darshan

Shubar's brother and business partner on the quarry; *in dedication to my Uncle, Darshan Patel*

Premela

Darshan and Shubar's housemaid; lives in the main house; *in dedication to Premela*

Minor Characters:

Jayanti	Darshan's ex-wife; *in dedication to Jayanti*
Sanat	Enslaved on the granite quarry; endowed to Priya
Kushala	(Name means peaceful); friend of Sandhya and Mukti; escaped from quarry and punished by Shubar
Siddarth	Enslaved in the granite quarry; true story of escape and punishment
Tamara	Young girl enslaved in the granite quarry; true story of being sold to dalals to as a punishment to her father, Siddarth
Anita Masi	Mukti's aunt in her village Nirega; *in dedication to Anita Reddy*
Doctor Vrajesh	Gives medical checkups to the slaves in the quarry; *in dedication to my Uncle Vrajesh Patel*
Doctor Parvati	Priya's doctor

* * * * *

John (Jawn)	("Jan" means people); Caucasian man who works at Ajadi, partnering with the government to free slaves
Balaji	Works for Ajadi, helps with translation; *in dedication to friend and translator Balaji*

Shankar	Driver who works for Ajadi; *in dedication to my drivers and friends in Bangalore, Shankar and Michael*
Ajadi	(Means freedom); non-profit organization that works towards eradicated slave labor
Lani Senner Agency	Organization fighting sex slavery in New Dehli; *in dedication to my mother, Mrinalini (Lani) Ingram, and teacher, Mrs. Tami Senner*

Minor Characters:

Natalie and Marshall	John's parents, who dedicated their lives to fighting child slavery around the world; *in dedication to Natalie Marshall*
Tommy	John's little brother, adopted from Thailand after being enslaved; *in dedication to my dad, Tom Ingram*
Aakash	(Name means sky); works for Lani Senner Agency; *in dedication to my brother, Justin Aakash Ingram*
Drew	Communications director for Ajadi; *in dedication to Drew Learner*

* * * * *

Ruchita (Ro)	(Name means young and beautiful); *her nickname is in dedication to Coach Rometra Craig*
Tarun	(Name means youthful); Ruchita's friend on the streets, infamous

285

	pickpocket
Hakesh	Ruchita's father
Daeva	(Name means evil spirit); new wife of Hakesh
Ramesh Ramamurthy	Engaged to Ruchita by arranged marriage
Vanhi	(Name means fire); brought to brothel at age 6
Thalia	Ruchita's friend; sex slave captured at age 7; most beautiful; kept as Malik's personal prostitute
Ayesha	Ruchita's older sister or Adhiya in New Dehli; *in dedication to Ayesha Arora*

Minor Characters:

Srinivas	(Name means abode of wealth); in charge of collecting money from the child labor street performers
Bandhura	(Name means pretty); street prostitute
Gopal	Ruchita's neighbor in the slums
Shivani	Another street performer who didn't have enough coins to meet her day's quota
Mahabala	(Means strength) Malik, brothel owner
Samarya	Sex slave; true story of her arm being broken by a dalal

Facts About Modern-Day Slavery

What is Modern-Day Slavery?

The U.S. Department of State defines modern slavery as "the act of recruiting, harboring, transporting, providing, or obtaining a person for compelled labor or commercial sex acts through the use of force, fraud, or coercion." The most common forms of modern slavery are sex trafficking (including child sex trafficking), forced labor, bonded labor (or debt bondage), domestic servitude, forced child labor, and unlawful recruitment and use of child soldiers.

The issue of modern slavery transcends the physical or monetary restraints that lock people into inhumane conditions. During my research, I learned how issues of poverty, caste, lack of education, and even religion can tear the very fabric of human dignity and identity. In order to find a sustainable solution to slave labor, solutions must address these issues.

Statistics:

There are approximately 21-36 million slaves in the world today and about 14 million of them are in India alone. Approximately 9 million are children.

There are approximately 60,000 in the U.S.

78% are labor victims and 22% are sex slavery victims. 55% are women and girls.

Poverty and Corruption:

In India, approximately 363 million, or 30% of the total population, are living in poverty. To put this into perspective, the number of people in India living on less than $2 per day is more than the entire U.S. population of 322 million. Ninety-three percent of India's population consists of the unorganized labor sector. The majority is engaged in agricultural work. Most do not have access to welfare, and 458 million workers in the unorganized sector do not have social security. The Minimum Wage Act of 1948 routinely goes unenforced.

History:

When the British abolished slavery in its colonies, India was excluded from the agreement, as was the country's debt-bondage issue. The entire system of production depended on slavery, and the British rule depended on the tax revenue coming from India's unpaid forced labor.

Bondage:

What makes bonded labor different from other forms of slavery is the loan. A loan is taken from a laborer often to repay another loan or to meet a financial need for things such as hospital bills, dowry, or education. What makes the loan a bondage is the lack of a better alternative and the inability to repay the loan. Landlords take advantage of the laborers, pressing high interest rates, changing original documents to increase the debt, paying lower wages than the minimum required by law, and charging the laborer for other expenses such as equipment, tools, food, rent and clothes. Even if the laborer knows he or she is being taken advantage of, the individual has no other choice of work, as the landowner owns all the property in the area and the local government usually turns a blind eye or sides with the landowner even in the most abusive cases. Bondage can be an interminable cycle that is passed on to the next generation. This practice originated in ancient Hindu law and makes a son morally (and legally) obligated to clear his father's debt.

Sex slavery:

The number of girls trafficked and forced into sex slavery is appallingly high, and the average lifespan for these girls is less than seven years once they are trafficked. They are beaten, drugged and re-trafficked, and often catch diseases such as HIV.

Sex slavery is one of the most profitable criminal industries in the world, with an estimated 4.5 million victims. Global revenues from slavery come to $150 billion a year, with an annual profit per victim of $29,210. The total amount generated by sex slavery alone (although it comprises only 4% of slavery worldwide) is $99 billion.

In India, sex trafficking has increased as the demand for cheap sex rises and the industry expands its supply to meet the growing demand. In India, prices have decreased more than 50% in the last two decades as a result of increased trafficking in rural India, giving people such as the rickshaw-driver class access to an industry they previously couldn't afford. To maximize the capacity of today's profits, only 0.5% of adult males need to purchase sex on a given day. 6-9% of males worldwide do purchase sex at least once a year.

The global average purchase price of a slave is $1,895, but sex slaves sleep with up to 30 customers a day, usually 6-7 days a week, for an average of 10-20 years, unless they perish before then. Therefore, the cost for a brothel owner (*malak*) to buy a trafficked slave is quickly recouped.

True Stories:
In the summer of 2013, I returned to Karnataka, India on a personal research inquiry for my book. Although I had witnessed child labor and extreme poverty in India, I sought a thorough understanding. With the help of a generous organization, *Jeevika,* I was able to interview more than 65 current and former slaves. I visited common types of modern-day slavery sites, such as silk factories, agriculture farms, and granite quarries. Furious slave masters chased me out of a brick factory. I lived with the Dalit and Muslim communities and heard their heartbreaking stories about unfathomably cruel discrimination.

I have done endless hours of research, on the field and off, through an independent study and by reading countless books, journals, research papers, articles and websites.

Throughout my book, I weaved in the true stories that I learned through my research or heard directly from the current or former slaves. Even though *Freedom Child* is a fictional novel, it is based on realities faced by millions of men, women, and children every day.

The multifaceted nature of human trafficking in India required me to research the economic, social and political aspects of this topic, in addition to the history and evolution of slavery. The history is a critical component, as slavery has been ingrained in the fabric of the Indian economy and social structure since ancient times. During my research, I learned how issues of poverty, caste, lack of education, and even religion can tear the very fabric of human dignity and identity. With such deep roots and intricate causes, there is no straightforward solution and any sustainable solution must address these root issues.

Further Acknowledgements

Through my research I leveraged many books, websites, and articles to enhance my knowledge on root causes and potential solutions. In particular, I used the following sources to validate some of the contentious realities surrounding modern slavery and to help formulate my own personal analysis on the root causes of slavery.

Some notable mentions which have had the most influence on me are *Understanding and Eradicating Bonded Labour in India*, by Jeevika's founder Kiran Kamal Prasad as well as *Bonded Labor: Tackling The System Of Slavery In South Asia* and *Sex Trafficking: Inside the Business Of Modern Slavery* by Harvard Kennedy School's Dr. Siddharth Kara.

Several state and non-profit organizations have created a tremendous amount of research on modern day slavery. I leveraged many of the statistics and trends detailed from these organizations. The *US Department of State Trafficking in Persons Reports – Annual Reports* was introduced to me when I met with them in New Delhi after my field research and interviews in Karnataka. I also referred to the Human Rights Watch organization that publishes an annual *World Report* on human rights. Free the Slaves, the CNN Freedom Project, End Slavery Now, International Justice Mission, and The Hunger Project are other non-profit organizations with tremendous knowledge on this topic. The International Labour Organization, the World Bank, and the International Organization for Migration were also frequent references through my research.

81789720R00173

Made in the USA
San Bernardino, CA
11 July 2018